Tangled Roots

A companion to the Beyond the Eyes trilogy

by Rebekkah Ford

ISBN 13: 978-0-692-26701-1

First Edition October 2014

Dedication

I'd like to dedicate Tangled Roots to my wonderful sister Angel Motter. Thank you so much for your support. It means a lot to me. I love you very much. ((Hugs))

Acknowledgments

I'd like to thank Tarnya Rutheford and Susan Firtik for helping me come up with the title and cover for this book. I gotta say... you two are full of awesome sauce.

Thank you Rosemary Hendry, Debb Lavoie, and Bonnie Tweddle-Schuster for being my beta readers and a huge support of my books. I appreciate it. You girls rock!

Thank you Tarnya Rutheford for your support and help with my street team (Rebekkah Ford's Realm of Fantasy). Did I tell you you're full of awesome sauce? ☺

I'd like to thank my street team for your support. I appreciate it. You're fabulous.

I'd like to give a shout out to my cover artist Stephanie Flint, my editors Chase Nottingham and Christina Pollard Escue. Y'all were a huge help in making Tangled Roots what it is today, and I appreciate you and your dedication.

I'd like to acknowledge my wonderful husband Kevin Ford. You're my best friend, and I can always count on you to make me laugh. I love you more than words can say.

Dad and Mom Wilhelm. Your support means a lot to me. Thank you. I love you.

To my beautiful niece, Ariel Bradford. I'm so proud of you. Love ya!

And finally, I'd like to thank my fans. I appreciate you more than I can say. Y'all rock!

Table of Contents

Note to readers

Tangled Roots can be read as a standalone novel. I wrote it for the fans of the Beyond the Eyes trilogy because a lot of them are fond of Carrie and Tree, who are the two main characters in this tale. Besides, their story adds to the trilogy, where it'll take you deeper into the rabbit hole.

Enjoy! ☺

Tangled Roots

A companion to the Beyond the Eyes trilogy

by Rebekkah Ford

Chapter One

Carrie

I had never given much thought to reincarnation, at least not until the spirit of an ancient witch named Jade made her presence known to me. Somehow, a part of my spirit had reached out to her when I was in a coma, recovering from a car accident. I remembered it as if it happened twenty minutes ago, or so it seemed.

I remembered *all* of it.

Tree had wanted me to tell him every last detail. He wasn't satisfied with the loose interpretation I gave my best friend Paige and her boyfriend Nathan. It wasn't like I didn't want to divulge my fantastical experience in another realm. I did and still planned to do so, but they had too much on their plates right now. Actually, Paige had many crosses to bear, and I would not load another one on her, at least not until she could relax a bit. Maybe take a short sabbatical with Nathan, away from all this strife concerning the dark spirits. With my incessant urging, Paige finally gave into my pleas to do just that. Of course she waited until I was out of the hospital for a few weeks, and being the most awesome best friend ever, she threw a surprise welcome home party for me.

"Don't worry," she had said, slinging her arm around my

shoulders as I stood in my living room in amazement, looking at the black and red glittery WELCOME HOME banner placed on the wall above the bar that divided the kitchen from the living room. She even made a red velvet cake for me. "There are no clowns here," she finished saying, bumping my hip with hers. I laughed. She knew I hated clowns, and her little remark warmed my heart.

Now, she and Nathan were in England visiting Nathan's friend Pip, and I missed her terribly. They were going to be gone from Astoria, Oregon for the whole month of November. A whole frickin' month. We'd never been away from each other that long, and it felt like a part of me was missing.

"Describe Jade to me," Tree said, putting a filter in his brown and white 1968 International Scout. The oil he drained mingled with the dirty, gassy smells in his dad's garage. I was used to it, and oddly enough, it gave me comfort.

I picked the socket wrench off the floor. The heavy metal felt cool in my hand as I thumped it against my palm, imagining her in my mind. "She was beautiful," I said. "Her black skin made her green eyes pop. They were startling in the sense that when you gazed into them, you felt like you were standing on a plateau, looking through a lens with restrained knowledge, so eager to be released."

Tree rolled out from under the engine on the creeper. His long legs seemed to stretch forever. Rubbing his forehead with the edge of his thumb, he looked at me. "Nathan said the same thing, except his description of her paled in comparison to yours. Maybe you should consider being a writer."

"Whatever." I snorted. "Have you forgotten... the many book reports I had Paige do for me?"

He picked up a rag and threw it at me. "No, but it seems since you woke up from your coma, you can perceive and focus on things a lot clearer than before."

I snatched the cloth before it touched my chest. It was damp and grimy from oil. Gross. I tossed it in a bucket behind me and placed the wrench in the tool box against the wall. "Maybe so." I shrugged, not really knowing how to respond to his observation.

"What else do you remember about her?" he asked, prompting me to continue as he proceeded to add fresh oil to his Scout.

I handed him the bottles as I continued, "There was fluidity to her graceful movements, like a ballet dancer telling a story through animated gestures."

"Those words are what I'm talking about," Tree said, glancing over his shoulder at me.

"What?"

"Your descriptions. I'm starting to think you came back with some heightened abilities, or something along those lines."

"I don't know," I answered, waving it off because I didn't want to go there at the moment. "But let me continue. I don't want to lose my train of thought." I slapped another container in his palm and screwed the top off for him.

"Go on, then." He turned back to what he was doing.

"Okay, well, I remember her dark, purple robes billowing behind her as she approached me in the realm of rehabilitation, where I was sent by Paige's parents to recover from my accident."

"What was it like?"

"We were in a vast meadow surrounded by enormous mountains forming a barrier around us. The mountains were covered in lush, thick emerald green grass and tall trees. The waterfalls cascading from them had prisms of colors dancing along the front. I remember becoming immediately enchanted by the beauty of it all," I said. "I could hear a soft melody playing—part instrumental and part humming. It sounded like a peaceful lullaby." I closed my eyes and softly hummed the song. Of course, my rendition sucked. Regardless, though, I heard the music in my head and could easily fall under its spell.

Something that sounded like a plastic bottle hit the floor.

I opened my eyes to Tree staring at me in awe. "It's a lullaby," he said. "I've heard the tune before."

I furrowed my brows. "Where?"

"After Paige did her dream walking thing to save you, she hummed it for me."

"She must have heard the melody when I crossed over to the other realm," I mused.

"She did," Tree said.

"How do you know it's a lullaby?"

"I don't know." He touched his black knit beanie hat and rubbed the material against his forehead. "Ever since Michael told me I was on the path to becoming a light walker, pieces of knowledge from different realms have been filtering into my conscious mind. It's crazy."

I found it both interesting and disconcerting that Tree's soul was striving to become a light walker, or guardian angel in human terms. From what I understood, his spirit had to go through a shit load of lives in order to become one. Michael told him, in order to reach a deep understanding about things, Tree had to experience every aspect of it. Once he arrived at the apex of his training, he'd be able to move onto the next level in the spiritual realm where he'd be allowed access into Nirvana. I of course was exempt from it, which I totally understood, but what concerned me was what would happen to us? It depressed me to even acknowledge those cold hard facts, so rarely did I allow those thoughts take form in my mind.

"You're right. The melody is a lullaby," I confirmed, sidestepping his last comment. I wasn't ready to dip my toes into the pool of knowledge seeping through the cracks of his subconscious mind. Not yet. "The music lulls the spirit to a restful state. Most spirits who enter this realm go there to be cleansed, to sleep, then reawakened and counseled," I said. I could almost smell the pine from the thick forest there.

Tree screwed his face in concentration, his brown eyes staring past me at nothing in particular. "I think I know the answer to this question, but I'm going to ask it anyway. How does a spirit get cleansed? How does the process work?"

"They enter from the northern portal, then they go straight to the west, which represents water, death, and initiation. From there, they go through a waterfall and to the cleansing chamber."

"What's the cleansing chamber like?"

"It's like a glass coffin set into the wall of the mountain," I replied.

"What happens when the spirit enters the chamber? What does it do?"

I rubbed my nose and pushed my finger onto the side of it, closing my eyes, trying to figure out the best way to tell him. Moving my hand away from my face, I sighed and looked at him. "I'll try to explain how it works the best I can." I took a deep breath. I didn't know if I could, or if he'd grasp the whole concept.

"Go on," he said. He knew full well that I tended to stall when I was unsure or nervous about something.

"Okay." I took another deep breath. "When a spirit steps inside the chamber, it's like its essence explodes. You see, we're an energy force and each experience we have throughout our existence becomes a part of it—positive and negative. So the energy disperses, and a fine mist fills the chamber, soothing all parts of the spirit from the life it just led. After the spirit is rested, it enters another realm, within the first to converse with its guides."

"I have no recollection of such a place," Tree said. "I thought maybe I would, but I don't. Maybe I'd never been there before."

"I'm sure you have," I said, hearing the confidence in my voice.

He made a face. "Why would you think so?"

I rolled my eyes. "Duh. You've been through countless lives, both good and bad. I have no doubt that at some point, you had to be rehabilitated."

"Good point." He grabbed my wrist and pulled me into his warm embrace. "So tell me more, or should I tickle it out of you?" He wiggled his fingers against my side, causing me to squeal and squirm against him.

I giggled and pushed his hand off me. "I'll tell you. I'll tell you," I gasped. "But you need to take a shower first." I pulled away, causing him to drop his arms, and I pinched my nose to emphasize my statement. "You smell greasy and oily." My words came out all nasally.

He stood straighter and knocked his fist against his chest. "I smell manly. Ya know why?" His lips twitched, as if he were holding back a smile.

"Why?"

"Because I do manly jobs." He raised his grimy hands, palms facing me. They were huge and could totally cover my face and part of my head. "See how rough and calloused they are?"

"Yes," I answered. "I also see black goo under your fingernails."

"These hands are creating our future," he said, ignoring my last response, "in a dying vocation due to the lack of interest our generation has for it. They'd rather take desk jobs, working on computers than industrial work—the very jobs that built our nation, such as a mechanic"—he pointed to himself and grinned—"a machinist, a painter, etcetera, etcetera. The manly jobs are a dying breed. What's going to happen to our country when these trades expire with the people who once made a living building the world we live in today?"

I chewed on my bottom lip. "I've never thought about that before." What would happen to our country if we no longer had people help maintain and build its infrastructures? If Tree was right, our future looked rather bleak.

"Yup. So this wonderful aroma you're smelling off me is the scent created from the backbones of people such as myself, so society can step away from their primitive conditions to a comfortable one."

"Okay, you're right, but now I'm depressed." I frowned.

"Don't be," he said, picking the empty plastic containers off the floor. "It is what it is. If I didn't have hope for the future, I wouldn't be helping Paige and Nathan." He chucked the bottles in a large trash can. They thunked against each other, startling me. "Bael is the oldest dark spirit of them all. If he had his way, we'd be far less populated and living like we did hundreds and hundreds of years ago."

"We are the Devil's third... well, actually fourth, counting Nathan of course," I said, feeling my mood brightening. "With us against Bael, he'll never get what he's after."

"Precisely, which is why I need you to tell me everything you know, so we can figure out a way to tap into the part of your soul that was once a witch in a previous life. We need to build a strong force between the four of us, then find those artifacts when Paige and Nathan return."

I bit my lip. "I don't know how we're going to accomplish it all." I stared at my black Doc Marten boots, feeling hopeless again.

"Hey." Tree lifted my chin so I had to look at him, concern filling his brown eyes. "We will prevail. It won't be easy, but something worth having never is."

"I suppose," I mumbled, shrugging.

"C'mon." He took my hand and intertwined our fingers. "I'll go take a shower while you watch reruns of *Buffy the Vampire Slayer*, then we'll talk more about this."

"I love Buffy," I said as we walked toward the garage door, stepping over the puddles of grease. "She reminds me of Paige."

"So then you would be Willow, right?" Tree pushed the button on the wall. The garage door clunked and rattled as it slowly lifted.

I smiled. "Yeah, and you would be Spike because he's cool and dresses like a punk rocker."

Tree laughed and wrinkled his nose. "But Spike was in love with Buffy, and Paige is like a sister to me. I've never had those types of feelings for her, it would be like incest." He shook his head as if he were trying to dislodge a horrible image from his mind. "I don't even want to think about it."

We stepped out into the cool night. The skeletal oaks in Tree's yard looked black and haunting against the bright moon. He went back inside the garage to push the button again. While I waited, someone riding a bicycle in our direction caught my attention. I absently wondered if it was a neighborhood kid going home for the night. Tree darted out of the garage as the door descended with a weird groaning noise.

"Lucky for me you only have feelings for yours truly." I hooked my arm through his and hugged his bicep.

"I've always loved you," he said. He made a move like he was going to kiss me, but something caught his eye—the bicycle rider. "Who is that?"

"I don't know." I could see now it was a boy around the age of twelve. If he were my child, he wouldn't be out here at night by himself. What was wrong with his parents? "I thought maybe he was one of your neighbors."

"I've never seen him before."

The boy turned off the street in front of Tree's house, onto his driveway. "Excuse me," he said, pedaling to us. His brown hair was disheveled, and I quickly made the assessment he styled it that way on purpose. He had a BMX bike, Vans skater shoes, and a vintage Suicidal Tendencies T-shirt over a long sleeve thermal shirt. If anything this kid had good taste, and I found myself at ease around him. "Are you Carrie Jacobson?" he asked.

"Yes, I am. Why?" *How in the hell did he know me?*

He reached into his pocket and pulled out a folded piece of paper. "I'm supposed to give this to you." He handed it to me.

"Who is it from?" Tree asked.

"My great grandmother," he replied. "My name is Rex."

"Why would your grandmother give me a note?" I asked, eager to open it, but something inside me told me to wait.

"You're a witch aren't cha?" Rex asked.

I shoved the letter in my cargo pants pocket. "Maybe... I don't know. Why?"

He smiled, the splatter of freckles bunching on his round face. "Read it, and I'll see ya soon." He turned his bike around and left the way he came. We watched in stunned silence as he turned the corner at the end of the street and disappeared from our sight.

Chapter Two

Carrie

The letter was written in wavy chicken-scratch. I had no doubt in my mind that an elderly person wrote this. The boy... Rex? He was probably telling the truth. His grandmother must have written it.

"Can you read the note to me again?" Tree asked, grabbing a pair of black jeans out of his dresser. He was wearing Spider Man boxers, which I found adorable on him, and I couldn't help but admire his tall, muscular frame and taut stomach. I had the sudden urge to push him on his bed and squirt a trail of Hershey syrup down his chest, then slowly lick it off him.

Focus, Carrie. This letter is important.

I blinked at my own mental prodding and shifted my gaze at the paper I held. "Dear Ms. Carrie Jacobson," I began. "My name is Abigail Lockwood. I regret to contact you through impersonal means, but due to the nature of the situation at hand, there were no other options. I will get to the point. Jade contacted me. I'm sure you know whom I'm speaking of, yes? Because I have one foot in this world and one in the next, the line of communication was open to her through me. Not to mention, I was once a practicing witch. Jade and I had a lengthy conversation about you, and she recruited me into helping reawaken your magical abilities. There is much for me to share with you besides magic. My great grandson Rex is a special fellow. He will contact you sometime tomorrow, to bring you to where I rest my head at night. Sincerely, Abigail." I handed the note to Tree. "How did Rex know where I was?" I asked when it suddenly hit me that he showed up here and not my house.

"She did say he was special," Tree answered. "Maybe he's a witch as well and did a locator spell on you."

"Yeah, maybe." I shrugged, then grabbed the kangaroo pocket on his Sex Pistols sweatshirt and yanked him to me. He sat, appearing deep in thought. "What are you thinking?"

"I think this is genuine," he said, shaking the paper before folding it. He gave it back to me. "But you're not going without me."

"I wouldn't want to anyway," I admitted. My mind spun as Abigail's words finally sunk in. She was going to help me become the witch I once was, but she was obviously old. How would she possibly be able too? She probably went to bed at seven o'clock and drank Ensure.

"What?" Tree asked, eyeing me funny. "Why do you suddenly look disappointed?"

"She's old," is all I said.

"What does that have to do with anything? Yoda was an old ass dude, yet he taught Luke how to become a Jedi."

I laughed and shoved his shoulder. "You're such a dork. This isn't *Star Wars*, nerd."

"Does it matter?" He gave me his signature goofy grin, bringing a smile to my face. "The same principal still applies."

"I suppose." He might have a point, but I couldn't help the image of a prune-faced woman who smelled like Vicks vapor rub floating in my mind.

"So tomorrow we'll hangout at your house and wait for Rex." Tree stood, took my hand and pulled me to my feet. He bent his head and placed his soft lips on mine. He was too tall for me to lace my arms around his shoulders, so I lowered myself on his bed. He followed, bracing himself above me as our kiss deepened, tongues connecting. Parts of my body heated. I wrapped my legs around his waist and moaned as I dug my nails into his back. "Carrie," he whispered in my mouth.

"Wh-what?" I murmured when I felt him hesitate. Why was he stopping? His parents were in Vegas, so what was the problem?

"Your phone is vibrating in your pocket."

I stopped moving, then felt it.

Shit.

Tree rolled on his side, and I pulled my cell out of my pocket. The caller was my mom.

"Hi, Mom."

"Carrie, dear. How are you feeling?"

I flopped face-up next to Tree and wiggled my tongue at him. He made a move to pinch it, but his finger and thumb were met with my lips instead. I opened my mouth in a silent laugh and pointed at him. "I'm fine," I said, biting back my giggles.

"I think you should come home and relax for the rest of the evening."

"I'm relaxing here at Tree's house."

"Carrie," she said, her voice dropping to a stern tone, "do you remember what the doctor said before he released you from the hospital?"

Of course I remembered, and she knew I did but wanted me to say it out loud. I glanced at Tree. He was looking at me, the space between his brows wrinkled. I never told him this piece of information because I thought it wasn't a big deal. Now, I was in the hot seat, and the way Mom was acting, regret bloomed inside me. Maybe I should have mentioned it to him.

I sighed. "Yes. He said I needed to take it easy for the next two months."

"Why?" she prompted.

"Because if I don't, my body will wear down to the point of exhaustion."

"What else?"

"No strenuous activities... mentally or physically, and I need to avoid another jolt or blow to my head."

"Precisely," she said, sounding pleased. "So I expect you home shortly."

"But, Mom, the doctors and medical staff at the hospital were blown away by my fast recovery. Some even said it was a miracle," I argued.

Tree stood and motioned for me to stand. I didn't.

"It was," she said. "But we don't want to test fate, so I expect you home shortly. I'll make you some homemade hot chocolate, and we can watch a movie."

There was no reasoning with her. I had no choice but to comply. "Fine. I'll be home soon." I stood and followed Tree down the hall to his living room.

"Good girl," she replied. "I love you."

"Love you, too, Mom." I cut the connection and with a scowl on my face, I shoved my phone in my pocket. "This is ridiculous."

"Why didn't you tell me?" Tree asked, slipping a black beanie hat over his head.

I watched him and found myself still trying to get used to him not having a Mohawk. Every time I thought about Aosoth shaving his head and what her minions had done to him, my blood boiled with anger, heating my skin. I imagined it jacked up my blood pressure, so I replaced those thoughts with what happened to her and Roeick in the cave in Africa. They got what they deserved.

"I didn't think it was very important," I said, shrugging into my jacket.

"That's a lame ass excuse, and you know it." Tree already had his trench coat on and keys in hand.

"Are you anxious to get rid of me?" I glanced around his living room which was a homey, comfortable setting. The L-shaped brown couch and matching recliner looked inviting in front of the big screen TV. The coffee table was an old shipping trunk with an array of magazines scattered across it. I tilted my head to see which ones: *Hot Rod* magazine, *People*, *Guitar*, and two others I couldn't make out. More than likely they were comic books.

"Don't be a shit and change the subject," he replied.

I followed him outside into the brisk night. The temperature was dropping, and I hugged my jacket closer for warmth. "No, seriously. I didn't think it was a big deal." I got in step with Tree as we cut across his driveway to his mom's red Kia.

He pressed the button to unlock the doors and moved to the driver's side. I hopped in and inhaled the new car smell still present. The leather seats creaked beneath us. I was staring out the passenger's window while I waited for his reply when I thought I saw a shadow behind the large oak. I narrowed my eyes, straining them to see what it was. An owl hooted, and I looked up. High above on a bare branch I saw the bird's large silhouette against the bright, yellow moon that was almost full. I did a mental shrug. The shadow was probably him or nothing at all.

"Okay, well it is to me." He started the engine and backed out of the driveway. "Maybe you shouldn't see Abigail tomorrow," he said.

"Why? Because you think it might be too much for my fragile"—I did air quotes—"state to see what she has to say or if she can help me reconnect with my magical side?"

"I don't have to give you the answer. You already know it," he simply stated.

I lifted my chin. "Well, I'm going."

Tree braked at a four-way stop sign and met my gaze. "I have no right to tell you what to do. You are your own person. If this is what you want, so be it. I'm going with you, though, and if in any way I see it's taking a toll on you, we're leaving... even if I have to pick you up and haul your ass out of there."

"Fair enough." An image of him slinging me over his broad shoulders danced through my mind. He was built like a bouncer, and I knew full well he would have no problem following through with his promise. I chewed on my thumbnail while my mind wandered on what Abigail was like, what she had to offer, and what did she mean when she said Rex was special? I wished Paige were here so I could talk to her about it and invite her to come along. I contemplated calling her, but quickly decided against the idea. She needed a break. She'd been through a lot lately and needed a reprieve from it all. I could deal with this on my own, and oddly enough, I wasn't afraid. Nervous maybe—but not scared.

"Do you want me to stop for some food you can take home with you? I'm sure you're hungry."

"No, but thanks for offering. I'm sure my mom made something."

"You need to learn how to cook like your mom." Tree flashed me a silly grin.

"I wasn't blessed with culinary skills," I admitted. "But I can make a mean grilled cheese sandwich." I flashed him a big toothy grin and batted my eyelashes.

He laughed. "I predict, then, our future together will be filled with lots of takeout food and handouts from our mothers."

"Fine with me," I said as he pulled into my driveway.

"Call me tomorrow when you wake up." Tree leaned over the

console. His warm lips touched mine. There was nothing sexy about the kiss. It was too quick and made me wonder if he was going to treat me like a china doll until I got a clean bill of health.

I sighed, turned away from him, and opened the door. The light to the front porch flicked on. Mom must have heard us pull up. I swear, if she and Tree continued to coddle me I was going to scream. "See ya later."

"Hey." His hand rested on my arm. "What's wrong?"

I paused and faced him. "Don't baby me. Stop it. Okay?"

The corner of his mouth tilted downward. "I almost lost you, Carrie. Please don't hold it against me for taking extra precautions while your body is still healing from the trauma it sustained." He took my hand and kissed it. "I love you and would be devastated if our carelessness jeopardized your life."

My heart squeezed. I could see his point. If I were in his shoes, I'd be the same way. I imagined it was horrible for him when I was in a coma with the possibility of dying. I made a mental note to remind myself of those things when he or Mom started driving me bat shit.

"I love you, too," I said.

"Are we cool?"

His hand was still holding mine. I raised it to my mouth and bit his knuckle. "Yup. It's all good."

"I'll see ya tomorrow, then?"

I opened the door and stepped out. A thick smell of rain hung low in the air. I leaned in. "Sure thing, chicken wing." I winked and closed the door. Turning on my heel, I headed to my front door when an owl hooted above. I looked up and squinted at the tall elms next to my house. I couldn't locate him but had a strange feeling he was watching me.

Could it be the same owl I saw at Tree's house?

Hey, maybe he was from Hogwarts and was here to deliver me a note. I was a witch... well, used to be. I smiled at the pleasant thought. If only it were true and a world like the one J.K. Rowling created existed.

Tree tooted the horn, causing me to glance over my shoulder. He waved goodbye as he pulled out of the driveway. I returned his gesture, then escaped into the warm confines of my house, wondering what tomorrow would bring and if I actually had magical powers.

Chapter Three

Tree

As I drove home, I was completely on edge. Carrie was fine, I told myself. I had to trust in her knowing her body better than anyone else. She wouldn't risk her life to satisfy her curiosities. Besides, the powers that be—whomever they were—wouldn't have gone to all this trouble to keep her alive, only to snuff it out shortly after. But regardless of those facts, doubt and the fear of losing her twisted my stomach. I turned on the radio to calm my nerves. "Sober" by Tool was playing. I cranked it up and sang at the top of my lungs, loving the guitar riffs—so powerful and dark. Maybe someday I could play as well. I haven't fired up my Jackson in a while now. I then remembered I had broken a string the last time I played and never replaced it. Why hadn't I? I had a whole pack lying on my amp. I tried to think back, but then got carried away with the music playing and fell into its rich, haunting melodies. I continued to belt out the words, tapping my thumb against the steering wheel. I could feel the shroud of uncertainty and anxiety lifting as I rocked my upper body to the beat. The golden hue from the streetlamps paved my way down quiet neighborhoods and the vacant back roads I took home.

The song ended when I reached my house. With my spirits lifted,

I exited the Kia and crossed the driveway, spinning the ring of the car keys around my finger. Movement in my periphery vision halted me in my tracks. The dull light from the lamppost revealed a huge dog standing in the yard across from me; a German shorthaired pointer. His coat glistened, as if there were tiny crystals embedded in his fur. He was closely watching me. He must have weighed damn near one hundred and twenty pounds. He lowered his head and tilted it to the right, then to the left, like he was trying to figure me out or didn't know what to think of me. I thought of Paige, who could communicate with animals. If she were here, she would be able to tell me what this pooch was thinking. I decided to engage him—or at least try.

I took slow, deliberate steps, hunching my back so I didn't appear threatening. An owl hooted behind me, but I ignored it. "Are you hungry?" I asked in a soft, even voice.

The canine's gaze darted upward, past me. A blast of flapping wings and hooting came at me at a whopping speed. I ducked, and then realized the large owl wasn't after me. It flew in circles above the dog, which barked at it a couple times. The canine gave me one last glance before he trotted off, disappearing out of sight.

"Bizarre," I said to myself, rubbing the knitted material of my beanie against my forehead. *What the hell was that all about?*

I stood, staring after them, wondering. As far as I knew, dark spirits could only dwell in soulless humans and humans with a soul, if they were invited in. So scratch off the idea of them possessing animals. I glanced around the yard, searching for anything out of the ordinary, wishing I had the ability to detect a dark spirit when it was around like the immortals could. I narrowed my eyes at the bare trees in my yard and around my house.

Nothing.

Something wet hit the back of my hand. I looked up and was tagged in the eye. A steady rain began to fall, causing me to dart beneath the roof of my porch. I made a move to unlock the door, and then paused. My back stiffened. Someone was out there watching me. I didn't know how I knew—I just did. I *felt* it. The hair stood up on the back of my neck. Turning around, I mentally prepared myself for a possible fight, thankful for the hand-to-hand combat techniques Nathan trained me in. I also had the knife he gave me and as an added source of protection, pepper spray. Through the sheet of rain, a male figure emerged to the left side of my yard from behind a large oak. The same place the owl was. The dude walked toward me in slow, confident steps. Water bounced off the umbrella he held to shield himself from the onslaught of rain. As he got closer, I had no doubt in my mind who it was.

Ayperos.

He had a penchant for a certain type of human to possess. He preferred the long, dark-haired type. The kind you would see on the cover of a cheesy romance novel. I almost had to laugh at how lame he was. Did chicks really dig those types of men? Go figure.

"Jack," he said, stopping a few feet away from me. His lips formed a thin smile.

The asshole didn't like me, but the feeling was mutual. So I was curious why he decided to grace me with his annoying presence.

"What brings you here, Ayperos?" I took my hand out of my pocket and relaxed a little. His demeanor was nonthreatening as he stood in an easygoing manner.

"I see you had company," he said, pointing in the direction the animals had gone. "They have their eyes on you and Carrie."

"What the hell are you talking about?" He said less than twenty words, and he was already getting on my last frickin' nerve. Evasive shit didn't fly with me. I crossed my arms over my chest, waiting for his reply.

He brushed his black duster jacket like he was wiping away a piece of food. "I heard you're on the path to becoming a"—he looked at me and made a face—"light walker."

"So it seems," I said with a shrug, remembering when Michael shared the important bit of information telling me I was well on my way to becoming an angelic being, more or less. Since then, it was like a crevice had widened within my soul, and I'd been more attuned to things. I'd fallen into the deep abyss and was going where no man had gone before... wait. Where had I heard that line? *Star Trek*. Except it was: boldly go where no man has gone before. I laughed at myself.

"Something funny?"

"I find it comical you abhor the very beings who would help you without question. In fact, it might be me saving your eternal soul," I replied, not willing to share my personal joke.

He snorted. "I don't deal with traitors, so get that ridiculous nonsense out of your pea brain."

I held my hands out, palms facing skyward. "Just saying."

"I'm here on direct orders," he said, changing the subject.

"How is Bael by the way? He wasn't too thrilled when Michael broke the blood oath Anwar had performed with him, or the fact that I'm part of the Devil's third," I said with an edge of sarcasm. I was getting under his skin, I could tell by the way he clenched his jaw and flexed its muscles. Annoying him gave me a sense of satisfaction.

"He's superb," he responded between a perfect set of teeth.

"Awesome," I said. "Please do tell him there's not a chance in hell we'll help him find the Arc of the Covenant, Aaron's rod, or any other magical tools the light walkers created and bestowed upon humanity."

"You have a lot to learn, boy."

"Maybe so, but it is what it is," I said nonchalantly. "So are you going to enlighten me on why you came to my house and graced me with your presence?"

"If I had it my way, I wouldn't be here," he mumbled.

"But you're Bael's sock-puppet, so go on."

His lips tightened in a straight line, showing again how much he despised being here. "I believe in Bael's cause and what he stands for. Enough said," he spat.

"I'm hungry, so get to the point of your visit." I motioned for him to continue.

"As I told you earlier... you, Carrie, and Paige are being watched by entities other than the dark spirits."

A sudden chill went up my spine, but I hid it by scratching the back of my neck and eyeing him cautiously. "What do you mean?"

"You'll find out shortly," he said covertly. "I'm only here to warn you."

"Yeah, okay." He was a monkey spank and was probably making this shit up, though a haunting feeling in my gut said otherwise.

He smiled coolly, his hard, dark eyes on my face. "I couldn't care less about you, but Paige and Carrie I'm quite fond of. However, being that you're a sick joke played on us by forces deemed higher than us, we have no choice but to include you into the scope of Bael's wondrous plan and the reason why I'm here." He paused and slightly turned, peering through the rain. In the distance, two yellow lights appeared. Headlights. "I believe my party is here to whisk me away where a steady flow of liquor will remove the awful taste in my mouth, and a bed full of gorgeous women will appease every desire this body craves."

"You're done?" I asked, perturbed. "You come here warning me about some dangerous shit or whatever, yet you're being vague about it. What kind of bullshit are you shoveling?" As the vehicle approached, I realized it was a limo. Even with the windows rolled up, I could hear jazz music blaring from inside. I watched as it pulled into my driveway, and then backed out onto the street, facing the way it came. You got to be kidding me.

"What did you say just moments ago... 'It is what it is'?" He met my gaze and continued, his features softening, "We know about Abigail and encourage Carrie to seek guidance from her. She will tell you and Carrie what you two need to know. Pass it on to Paige. Like Bael, we're well aware she's on sabbatical, but she needs to know what you will soon discover." He turned and swaggered to his entourage. When he reached the door, it flew open. A hot blonde with humongous tits pouring out of a low cut red dress bent over the white leather seat. She waved him in. He closed his umbrella, and as he put a foot in the limo, the chick threw her arms around his shoulders and pulled him all the way inside. The door closed, and the limo eased down the street. I watched until it turned the corner, disappearing from sight.

Ass wipe!

Images of what his night would entail flowed through my head like a fountain of rich chocolate. A part of me thought, lucky bastard, but then Carrie entered my mind. I wouldn't trade her for anything, but I couldn't stop the desire to know what it would be like to have two hot chicks in bed with me. I went inside, replacing those racy thoughts with finding something to eat instead. Turning on lights, I put my coat away in the hall closet and went into the kitchen. I opened the refrigerator and grabbed the whole milk instead of the skim. My mom was on a health food diet kick, even though she didn't need it. To me skim was watered down milk. Not appealing in the least little bit. I opened the cupboard and snatched the box of Crunch Berries. After I got a bowl and spoon and poured my cereal and milk, I went into the living room and flopped on the couch. Sid hopped on the other side and proceeded to meow at me.

"Hey, fat boy," I said, reaching out and petting his orange, striped head. I took a bite, savoring the crunchy, buttery, berry taste. Sid head-butted my hand and arm, urging me to continue giving him some acknowledgments. I scratched him behind his ears, and then gently nudged him off the couch. "Don't worry, buddy," I said when his large, green eyes looked up at me, and he released a kitty-like meow. "I'll save you some milk." He watched me as I ate, then finally gave up and laid down. Besides the crunching noises I made, the house was frozen in silence—or so it seemed.

All kinds of thoughts flooded my head.

I thought and thought.

But my mind was utter chaos.

A clustered fuck.

After I finished the cereal and gave Sid the milk, I returned to the couch and sat. I was determined to still my brain so I could focus on recent events. Apparently, the dark spirits were watching us. Ayperos knew about Paige leaving and about Abigail. It didn't surprise me really. Bael needed us. Of course he'd have us under surveillance. But what the hell was Ayperos talking about when he said we were being watched by entities other than them? And what did the dog and owl have to do with it? The more I spun my wheels, the more confused I became. My only saving grace was an elderly lady whom we never met before. I leaned back and closed my eyes.

Other entities?

Ever since the day Paige turned immortal, my life hadn't been the same. Dark spirits dwelled in soulless humans, magic existed, light walkers were real, or angels as humans like myself had known them to be, and immortality was a fact—well, in a sense. The immortals could die if they were bled out or their heads were severed from their bodies, so I guess they weren't actually immortal, right? But in a loose interpretation, they were. Oh, and Bigfoot. Yes, the damn yeti was true. So it stood to reason there were other beings we weren't aware of. I bet even Nathan wasn't educated in what else could be skulking in the shadows of our world. He was too busy doing what he did best since the 1800s—tracking dark spirits. Those were the last thoughts I could remember.

I must have crashed, because the next thing I knew, I was dreaming, or maybe I was in between sleep and awake. I felt weightless, unbounded by flesh and bones. There was nothing around me, only blackness.

Then, a female voice spoke in a breathy, melodious tone. "Jack, the time will come when your connection to the light walkers who were exiled from Nirvana will grow. The process has already begun, but first you must assist Carrie. Use your observation like a whetstone to sharpen your intuition. You're going to need it more and more each day, and in the end, it'll help you reach your goals."

I jerked into a sitting position and cried out. Dropping my head in my hands, I rubbed my throbbing temples. Groaning, I imagined my brain exploding inside my skull. Within a minute or two, the pain lifted. I breathed a sigh of relief. Whomever the woman was, she had to be a light walker, because the same thing happened when Michael made his presence known to me. God, I hoped I wasn't cursed with these debilitating headaches every time a higher being wanted to connect with me.

I went into the kitchen and poured myself a glass of chocolate milk. The clock on the microwave said 3:17 in the morning. I gulped down the milk, my mind too fuzzy to ponder what was said to me. Exhaustion turned my bone marrow to lead. I needed to sleep. I placed the glass inside the sink, turned off all the lights, and made it to my bedroom at the end of the hall. I kicked off my shoes, took my jeans and sweatshirt off, and flopped on my bed. The last thing I could remember was a dog howling in the distance.

Chapter Four

Carrie

My muscles were stiff. How long had I slept? I glanced at the alarm clock on my dresser. 10:42 a.m.

Twelve frickin' hours.

Holy, shit!

I guess I must have needed it, but damn. I hated sleeping this long when I had no idea when Rex would show up to tell us where Abigail lived. I pushed the covers off and stepped out of bed. My room was bathed in a dull, gray light. It seemed like evening instead of morning. I peeked through my blinds. The sky was the color of lead with white wispy clouds spreading across it like splayed fingers. The grass in our yard was turning brown; a quiet reminder winter would soon be upon us. I stepped away and hugged myself. The idea of it being cold outside caused a chill in my bones. I shivered and pulled a black hoodie over my Rugrats T-shirt and headed to the kitchen. I had the house to myself. Thank God. My mom was great, but her constant hen pecking and worrying was getting on my last nerve. Dad was less obtrusive. He knew when to back off. I imagined right now he was speaking to a client about a possible loan. He was a financial officer at our local bank.

"Hi, Odell." My old ass basset hound was coming from the living room. When he reached my feet, he shook his body, causing the dog tags around his neck to make a loud, rattling sound. I knelt to pet him and stared into his droopy, brown eyes. "I love you." Hugging him, I kissed his head and stood. "Do you want a snack?" I opened a cupboard door where we kept his treats and shook the box of miniature bones for added measure. Wagging his tail, he looked at me and woofed. He was so damn cute. "Okay, here you go," I said, laughing, handing him a biscuit. He gladly took it, making quick crunching noises as he gobbled it. "You should chew more slowly," I advised him, giving him another one, then focused my attention on making some coffee. I thought about calling Tree or texting him, but decided to wait until I had some caffeine in my system. Odell barked several times behind me, interrupting my thoughts. "You're not getting any more snacks," I told him, thinking food was what he wanted. But when a string of high-pitched whimpers followed, I turned to look at him. He stood in front of the sliding glass window. His head and upper body were covered by the curtains, but his backside was moving back and forth, his nails clicking on the linoleum. "What is it boy?"

More whimpers.

I peeked above him between the two curtains. An enormous liver-colored dog stood in my backyard staring right at us. He must have weighed over a hundred pounds. He didn't appear threatening though, and I had a fleeting thought he must be hungry, and I should feed him, but something in his whiskey colored eyes kept me frozen in my spot. A flicker of some kind of emotion passed through them.

Longing?

Helplessness?

My throat tightened when seized by an overwhelming heart-wrenching sadness. Without processing what I was doing, I pushed Odell back with my foot and made a move to go outside, but then stopped when the dog turned and ran.

The theme song to *Buffy the Vampire Slayer* played in the background, jolting me into action. I sprinted to my room and snatched my phone off my dresser. It was Tree. "Hey, babe," I said, my voice sounding scratchy from sudden dryness.

"What's wrong?"

"How do you know there's something wrong?"

"Is there?"

"Well, something really weird just happened."

"Does it involve an owl and a dog?"

Chills broke across my body. Sitting on the edge of my bed, I squeaked, "How did you know?" I forgot about the owl last night until he mentioned it.

"Tell me what happened first." He sounded concerned, which stirred a haunting, hollow feeling in my gut.

Taking a deep breath, I relayed everything. When I finished, he told me what happened last night after he dropped me off, including Ayperos' visit.

"Other entities?" I echoed. "Do you think Paige accidently opened dimensional doorways when she cast that spell to help me?" I hoped not, but we had to consider all possibilities at this point.

"I don't know," he answered.

I released a rush of air from my lungs, not realizing I was holding it. "How are we going to know?"

"I believe Abigail will tell us when we see her today."

"Because Ayperos mentioned Abigail to you last night?"

"No," he answered. "It's a hunch I have from the note Rex gave you from her."

"Okay." I didn't know what to think at this point and wished Paige and Nathan were here. Nathan would know what to do.

"I'm going to leave in five minutes. I'll be at your house shortly."

"I just woke up," I said without thought. I hadn't even had my coffee or breakfast, I reminded myself.

"Have you eaten yet?" he asked as if he read my thoughts.

"No."

"I'll pick up some breakfast bagels on my way."

"You rock," I said, perking right up. I loved those. Tree knew how to please me in more ways than one.

He laughed. "I do my best... I love you."

"I love you, too. See you in a few."

After we said goodbye, I got dressed, choosing to wear jeans, a plain white T-shirt, and a black pullover hoodie with a shamrock on it and the words *Magically Delicious* across it in an arch. My hair was a disaster. I brushed it while the flatiron heated and frowned in the mirror at the small semi-bald spot on my head. While I was in a coma, the doctor had to shave a spot on my head, so he could stick some kind of drain tube in my skull to remove the cerebrospinal fluid. It wasn't attractive. At all. I didn't like it one bit. And because I had dark hair, it seemed to stand out. However, I reminded myself, Dr. Sweeney did help save my life. I patted the missing notch of hair and decided not to let it bother me. I straightened my shoulder length tresses, loving the dark red tips, and then applied some makeup. As I headed out of the room, a friendly, familiar knock came from the front door. "Hey, you," I said, opening it to Tree's smiling face. I noticed a white sack in his hand and could smell fresh bread and bacon.

"Hi." He bent his head down while I stood on tiptoe to kiss him. It was short and sweet, but I felt a longing from him by the way his lips lingered on mine, as if he wanted to hold me inside him. Damn, the feeling was mutual. I took a step back, not wanting to press my luck. At least he didn't hesitate like he had last night. "I just made coffee. Want some?"

"I already had two cups... but what the hell. I'll get jacked up on caffeine. Only don't expect me to get all hyper and talk a million miles an hour like Paige."

Laughing, I took the bag from him and headed to the kitchen. "She's so funny when she gets that way." I set our food on the table and poured coffee into two mugs.

"She's a riot," he said, taking a seat at the table. "I hope she and Nathan are having a good time."

"I'm sure they are." I sat beside him and unwrapped my sandwich. "I don't want them to know what's happening right now, so let's wait until they get home."

He looked at me above the rim of his mug. "I agree, and to be honest, I have no idea what we're getting into."

"Same here." I took a huge bite out of my bagel. The soft, cheesy bread complimented the bacon and egg wonderfully. "Mmmmm. Yummy. Thank you," I said between bites.

"You're most welcome." He bit into his and gave me a sidelong glance. "I know how to please my girl."

"In more ways than one," I replied, waggling my eyebrows.

"Good to know." He smiled, and then nodded toward the microwave. "Did you see the sticky note?"

I looked behind me. "No." I rose to see what it said. "Mom." I glanced over my shoulder at him and made a face, then read the note out loud: "Good morning, sunshine. I'll be working late tonight. I forgot to tell you, I'm rearranging the store. Your father is going to help me when he gets off of work, then he's taking me out for dinner. It's our twentieth anniversary." *Shit. I forgot. Damn.*

"You totally spaced it," Tree said in a sing song voice.

I ignored him and kept reading, "If it slipped your mind, don't feel bad. You've been through quite an ordeal. We understand. Whatever you decide to do today, please take it easy and don't overdo things. Love you, sweetheart. Mom."

"You should buy her flowers," Tree suggested.

"Great idea," I said, rushing to my room to get my black and pink rhinestone skull and crossbones purse. When I reentered the kitchen, Tree had the phonebook out and opened to the yellow pages. "Which one should I call?" There were two pages filled with different types of flower shops. I'd never ordered a bouquet before and hadn't the foggiest idea how.

"Order from Full Bloom." He pointed to an ad with a picture of a floral arrangement and a list of things provided. "They also deliver candy and balloons."

"Perfect." I pulled my credit card out and keyed the phone number. A pleasant voice answered. I told her what I wanted, throwing in a box of chocolates and a Happy Anniversary balloon, then gave her my mom's name and the name of her antique store. After I rattled off my credit card information, I told the nice lady thank you and ended the call. The slimy, guilty feeing I felt mere moments ago vanished. I then imagined Mom's smiling face when she'd receive the delivery, and my heart warmed.

"Now you have a clear conscience," Tree said.

Nodding, I went to hug him, but then several small knocks came from the front door, halting me. "Rex?" I guessed.

Tree stepped past me. "There's only one way to find out." He reached behind him and took my hand.

"What if it's not?" I suddenly felt nervous, thinking maybe it was a dark spirit or something equally as sinister.

Tree pushed aside the curtains covering the front window to look. "It's Rex."

Sighing with relief, I opened the door. "Rex."

"The one and only," he said, his grin revealing a crooked eyetooth.

"Hey, Rex," Tree said, inviting him in and closing the door.

"Why are you wearing the same clothes?" I asked, wondering what sort of parental supervision he had.

"I'm eccentric," he answered. "Like that one dude with the wild hair... Einstein?"

"Did you have breakfast?" I asked.

"Yeah, I ate already." He rolled his eyes like all children did when their mothers were being annoying. I then realized I was causing him to file me in that category. I decided to back off. "Grams made me toad in the hole."

My hand flitted to my chest. "What?" The horror was evident in my voice. I envisioned a batty witch with a jar full of toads, used to create some sort of weird ass recipe for longevity or some shit like that. I then realized my overactive imagination was conjuring up those disturbing images, so I asked, "What is it?"

"Toad in the hole," Tree said, "is a piece of toasted bread with an egg in the center. However, in England it's sausage cooked in Yorkshire pudding."

"Oh," I said. "Well, it sounds good."

Rex pointed at me, cracking up. "You actually thought I ate an amphibian. That's hilarious... Grams may have some toys in the attic, but she still has most of her wits."

"Toys in the attic. What do you mean?" Tree was testing him. I could tell by his raised eyebrow and the tilt in his mouth.

Rex made a swirling gesture next to his ear. "A little mad."

I gave Tree a look. His expression was equal parts amusement and curiosity. Doubt sprouted skeptical thoughts in my head, each one tagged with whether Abigail could truly help me or not. She was old, a bit looney, and had her great grandson be her messenger boy. What in the world was I getting myself into? I chewed on my fingernail, torn on what to do. Ayperos told Tree that he and Bael encouraged this meeting with Abigail. Why? And he basically told Tree they were keeping an eye on us. He also warned of other entities. This dark world

I was now entangled in seemed to get deeper and more complicated by the day.

"Where does Grams live?" Tree asked.

"Fifty minutes or so from here by car," Rex replied. "We'll be taking East Columbia River Highway."

"You rode your bike all the way here from there?" Shock over a boy coming so far by bicycle caused the words to spill out of my mouth. "Where's your mother or father?"

"Do you really want me to answer your questions?" Rex asked in a slow, dramatic voice, eyebrows raised.

"Yes," Tree and I said in unison.

He shook his head. "Grams isn't going to be pleased about this."

"Why?" I asked.

"She's not one to allow the side show steal from the main event," he answered.

Tree pointed at him. "You're pretty smart, kid. I take it you're the side show?"

"Your grandmother did mention in her letter you were special," I said, curiously eyeing the boy in a hesitant manner. I wasn't too sure about the situation. What if he had a bizarre supernatural ability, like create fire with a certain look in his amber eyes? I folded my arms across my chest, watching him closely.

Rex grimaced. "I hate when she refers to me as *special*. It makes me feel... what does society call it now to be politically correct and not offensive? Because I would say a drooler riding the short bus."

Tree laughed.

"Mentally challenged would be the correct term," I offered.

Rex shrugged. "Okay, let's go with that then."

"Anyway," I said, growing impatient. "Are you going to answer my two questions or not?"

"I'm a ghost," he blurted. "And my parents are living their lives in

Washington."

"Yeah, right." I rolled my eyes. Who was this twelve-year-old kidding? Paige had conjured spirits before, and they couldn't stay for long periods of time. Rex's form was also solid, and when he touched an object, his hand didn't go through it. I was beginning to think Tree and I were being played. This had to be a sick joke Ayperos and the other dark spirits cooked up, just to fuck with us. "We've seen spectral beings before, and it's obvious you're not one."

"She's right and..." Tree began to say, then stopped. His body stiffened when he locked eyes with Rex. Strange words flowed from Tree's mouth in a language I didn't recognize, but it was apparent he understood each one. There was an intense expression on his face.

Rex shook his head. His lips moved, but no words escaped them.

Their interaction went on for a few minutes, and I was at a loss for what to do. I thought about clapping my hands and breaking them from the trance-like state they appeared to be in, but I decided not to. For some reason, this needed to take place. Like I thought earlier, things seemed to get more complicated by the day.

Tree blinked and looked at me, stupefied. "What time is it?"

I sent him a weird look. Why didn't he check his watch? But instead I glanced at mine. "Ten minutes until noon, why?"

"Really?" He gaped at me.

My gaze shifted from Tree to Rex, who stood with an unreadable expression, then back to Tree again. "Yeah."

Tree rubbed his forehead. "Wow. That was... wild."

"I told you," Rex said.

"Okay, one of you needs to fill me in on what just happened," I said, feeling left out and a bit perturbed.

"Rex is telling the truth," Tree said, turning to me.

"What?" I snorted. I didn't know what kind of hocus pocus shit took place, but it was going to take more than a lame ass explanation to convince me Rex was a ghost. Normally, it wouldn't; however, with everything my friends and I have been through with the dark spirits, I knew how clever they could be—randomly throwing smoke and mirrors to hide their deceit.

"She's not buying it," Tree said to Rex. "You need to show her."

A mischievous grin formed on Rex's face, and he vanished.

My heart jumped in my throat. Turning in quick circles, I discovered he was gone. "Where did he go?"

"I'm here," his disembodied voice said, snickering, clearly enjoying his demonstration.

He popped right in front of me, causing me to shriek and stumble into Tree. Tree wrapped his arms around me from behind, caging me to his body. I took comfort in his warmth and strong physique.

"I don't understand," I said. My mind kept wheeling backward to the other spirits I'd seen and were told about by Paige. How come they were only given a handful of minutes to visit here, but Rex's time seemed unlimited? It didn't seem fair.

Tree tightened his arms around me and kissed my cheek. "Why don't you go get your purse and keys? We need to go to Abigail's house," he whispered next to my ear, his hot breath brushing against my skin.

I lifted my shoulder next to my earlobe and cringed. "You're tickling my ear." I giggled. His embrace loosened enough for me to turn and face him. Bewilderment pooled in his deep, brown eyes, and there was a distant edge to them. It was as if his orbs were a reflection of a gateway to another world. He closed his eyes for a brief moment, and when he looked at me again, they were replaced with love. Anxious to find out what was going on and to meet Abigail, I hopped on my tiptoes, pecked Tree on the lips, and said, "I'll be right back." I left the living room in a rush, wondering what I'd be doing this time tomorrow and what new things I'd know.

Chapter Five

Tree

C arrie darted out of the room to collect her stuff, which gave me a few moments to process what recently went down. When she told me the time, I about fell over, because I thought for sure I'd been gone for hours.

Somehow I was wrenched from our world and catapulted into another plane of existence. It had to have been the etheric plane; the one closest to earth. Paige's grandmother Kora had mentioned it when we last saw her. It was a dim and misty region. My mind wheeled backward, replaying the event as if I were reliving the experience all over again.

Rex and I were standing in an open field beneath a vast purplish, gray sky. It felt like we were in a bubble, and when my thoughts made the comparison to a snow globe—replacing the white flakey stuff with fog—the information fell into my head, like a rush of water filling a dry well. We were entombed inside some force field, shielded from prying eyes and intrusive thoughts. My lips began to form around strange words instantly familiar to me. They sounded odd but comforting to my ears. I knew without a doubt the language was of the light walkers. I spoke to Rex, but he couldn't understand me, so I reverted to the elementary tongue humans used to communicate. I told him he should move on. There were others looking forward to seeing him. He shook his head no. Then, I had the sudden realization we weren't alone. I felt another presence with us, and when I acknowledged it through thought alone, a man manifested before our eyes.

Gabriel.

Whispers of his name whooshed around me in a collective symphony of feminine astonishment and wonder.

Gabriel.

In the cave in Africa, Michael had told me there were others like himself whom had fallen from grace due to their love for humanity. Through free will, they rebelled against the universal creed. They fashioned tools in their sacred realm, then sent them to earth so humans could protect themselves from malevolent beings who dwelled among them. Michael received his ring back from King Solomon. He destroyed it and in return, he regained access to Nirvana. He'd been redeemed. His brothers, on the other hand, had chosen to remain in their standing, and I had access to them as an apprentice light walker. It was up to me to convince them to do the right thing. It was up to me, Carrie, and Paige to find those tools before they fell into the wrong hands. Bael's. Nathan had some part in this, but I had no knowledge of what it was.

"Jack," Gabriel said with a friendly smile. There was a happy glint in his sandstone eyes which sparked something in me to compare him to Michael.

He was almost the complete opposite of Michael in looks and demeanor, I realized. Gabriel had black hair curling next to his ears, whereas Michael's was pale and straight. Gabriel's height mirrored Michael's though. In fact, he stood an inch taller than me, and I was six-five. He had a muscular frame like his brother's, but those were the only two things they seemed to share. When I met Michael, he was serious and determined to right his wrongs. Gabriel, I had a feeling, was the complete opposite.

"Gabriel," I said with a nod.

Gabriel turned to Rex and moved his hand in a circle in front of him. He then curled his fingers into a fist and flung them out, splaying them, palm facing Rex. Rex scowled and disappeared. "He doesn't need to hear our conversation," Gabriel told me.

"Where are we?" I asked, watching fog swirl around the field. I stared off into the distance. Shadowy figures peeled from the ground. They sat up, looked around, and stood. It was one of the creepiest and most wicked things I'd ever seen.

"We are on one of the lowest astral sub-planes, next to the astral cemetery," he told me. "Danger lurks here, but you're under protection, so fear not my friend."

"I take it dark spirits can roam in this realm?" I didn't know why I asked. I already knew the answer. It was obvious. I think my nerves were running my mouth. I needed to chill out and relax, I mentally told myself.

"Yes," Gabriel replied. "It's a recruiting station."

Holy hell. I'd never even thought of such a thing and was taken aback learning malevolent beings had a place to approach souls and peddle their way of existence. I imagined, though, this only occurred to certain ones, such as people who lived a hard and negative life on earth or who already had carried out evil deeds.

"Why am I here?" I asked, watching these entities mill about in what seemed like a dazed and confused state. I tore my gaze away and forced myself to focus on Gabriel.

"I wanted to connect with you." He placed his hand on my shoulder and squeezed like a buddy would do to punctuate his sincerity. "Thanks to my brother, your awareness in the path you have chosen has uncorked the Genie's bottle within a deep part of your soul.

If you continue to stimulate it, fragments of the knowledge you've already gained will affect your senses. I for one," he said, touching his chest, "am all for it."

"Why?"

"Anyone who is willing to protect humanity against dark forces, such as the immortals, I hold in high regard. You not only are best friends with three of them but have volunteered to take up arms against malignant beings by their side, even though you are mortal." A proud expression formed on his face and respect sparkled in his eyes.

I shrugged. "That's how I roll."

"It's who you are," Gabriel said. "You're a lot like me and my brothers."

"You mean the ones who rebelled by making magical tools in a higher realm and then bringing them here to earth?" I kept my voice steady and conversational. I didn't want him to think I was passing judgment on him. I wasn't. I understood why they took drastic measures to give humanity a chance to protect itself, and frankly, I was on the fence about it. Would I have done the same thing?

"Yes. You remind me of myself long ago when I was a fledgling such as yourself. As you know," he paused, and then went on, "it's a requirement for a soul to go through countless life cycles in order to become a light walker. By doing so, our experiences gives us the knowledge, compassion, and love we need to aid others. Humanity stole my heart when I became one of them, and it appears to me they captured yours, as well."

"Maybe," I admitted. "But I don't know."

"You are a fledgling," he said with a warm smile. "Regardless, I see a potential in you I've never encountered before. I find it remarkable."

"Um... thanks," I said, not knowing how to respond to a compliment given by a highly evolved being. I wasn't sure if it was well deserved or not. In all my life, I'd never set out to be the perfect example of how one should carry out his existence. To be honest, I didn't think I was. I had a low tolerance for injustice and rude, ignorant behavior. Liars were another pet peeve. Come to think of it, I had quite a long list of things to set me off and would probably dock points off Gabriel's impression of me. So, no, thinking about it, I had to disagree with his statement.

"I can see by the frown on your face that you hold reservations against my opinion of you." Gabriel stood in a relaxed manner, showing no signs of offense to my objection. I got the feeling he was one to appreciate independent thought, and I found myself liking him more and more as our conversation progressed.

"I do," I admitted offhandedly, wanting to change the subject. "But if you don't mind, I would like to ask you a question."

"Of course."

"Actually," I said, shifting my weight from the sudden rush of anxiety I felt, "I have more than one."

Gabriel touched my arm and gave it several comforting pats. "There is no need to be nervous. You can ask me anything, and I will give you an honest answer."

When he pulled his hand away, I fired off the first question. "Why won't you fight off the dark spirits like the immortals do?"

Now it was Gabriel's turn to frown. "I am incapable to do so... earth is part of my brother's domain."

"Bael?"

"Correct. But there are universal holes in your world which overshadow his abilities."

"What do you mean?" Universal holes? An image of the moon's surface popped in my mind.

"Doorways to different dimensions." He rubbed the edge of his chin in thought. "Oh, yes," he added, "magic and free will... I need to toss those two onto this playing field."

Paige entered my thoughts. She was a skeleton key with abilities to open the doors to the realms closest to ours. She also had some magical abilities we were still unsure of. Then there was my Carrie, who was once a witch in a previous life. We were the Devil's third. Bael needed us to help him gain full control over our world; to make it his own. Soon, all three of us, and Nathan, will regroup to decide the best course of action to take.

"The tools," I blurted. We had to find each one before it fell into the wrong hands and then try to convince the light walker who created the object to destroy it.

"I have no idea where they are," Gabriel said. "I may be a divine being, but I do not have the power to see all things or the ability to roam freely in your world."

"How come?"

"The vibrational energy is too slow and dense for my much higher level. It's why I can only connect when certain circumstances arises and for a short period of time. Also, due to my rebellious act, I am denied access to bringing new magical objects into other realms. Summerland is my home."

"Since I'm a light walker in training, and I'm still human, I can connect with you and others like yourself, right?"

"If your energy is in accordance with ours at the time, it can create a direct line of communication with us. Unknowingly, you connected with Michael in the cave in Africa. It alarmed him, and he latched onto it with great force. He'd been waiting for that very opportune moment for thousands of years."

"What about now?" I was about to clarify my statement, but he was quick, over-stepping my opportunity to do so. I had to give him brownie points for his sharp mind.

"Rex's spiritual presence and your desire to understand your present situation activated a universal thread of communication to us light walkers residing in Summerland. I was the one who decided to come forth, because I wanted to visit with you."

"Michael told me about Raphael, who created the Arc of the Covenant. He said Raphael and the rest of his brothers showed no interest in destroying the tools they made." Something caught the edge of my vision. I glanced and saw a female dressed in a bathrobe meandering toward us. There was a glazed look in her dark eyes. She appeared lost. I wanted to reach out and help her. I stretched my hand, and it hit a solid, invisible barrier.

"You're not in a position to assist her at the moment," Gabriel said, pulling my attention back to him. "My reply to your comment is this: Michael is correct. Raphael and the others choose to stand by their decision."

"And you?"

"I have no regret in my reasons behind my actions. I stand by them to this day. However, I didn't realize how frail a human's will to do what is righteous is. It's weak. Most would use the power for their own selfish needs and agendas, instead of as a tool to thwart evil. Therefore, once the item I created is found, I will follow in Michael's footsteps and destroy it."

"What did you make, and how do I consciously connect with you?"

"I made a vest that protects the wearer from dying in battle or from any mishaps. In regards to you connecting with us, it'll take practice for you to do so. Then, it's a matter of if we will answer your call. I, of course, will."

I blinked, thinking how badass that would be to have an article of clothing infused with magic. If I had it, I'd be like a superhero. I wouldn't be able to fly like Superman, but I certainly would be a force to be reckoned with in combat. I wanted the vest and opened my mouth to try and convince Gabriel its power wouldn't taint me, but my eyes began to burn. I closed them, and when I opened them, I was back in Carrie's living room.

The more I thought about the vest, the more I wanted to know about it. What was the material made of? What happened to the person who owned it last?

"I'm ready," Carrie said, practically bouncing into the room. She stopped next to me and looked around. "Where's Rex?"

"Behind you," Rex answered. He was sitting on the bar dividing the living room from the kitchen and had a huge grin on his face. "Now you know the truth about me, why hide it?"

"Well, we don't know *everything* about you," Carrie said, rolling her eyes, pretending to be annoyed. "Jeesh."

"Grams will fill you in on the rest," he said, his expression still bright and cheery. "Let's go." He vanished.

Carrie turned in circles. "Where is he?"

"I'm guessing he's waiting for us in the Scout," I said, heading for the front door. Carrie followed me outside. There was a nip in the cool air, and the sky was a gunmetal gray with a few heavy clouds scattered across it. Rex was sitting in the driver's seat waving at us. I nodded toward him. "There he is." I shook my head and pointed to the backseat. He made a funny face, saluted me, and disappeared, only to reappear in the back.

Carrie giggled. "He's silly. I'm starting to really like him."

"He is a likeable person," I agreed.

Carrie turned to face me, catching me off guard. She placed her hand on my chest. "Are you going to tell me what happened to you when you were in that trance-like state and talking all weird?"

"I will," I promised, keeping my voice low, shooting glances over her shoulder to make sure Rex was still there. He was. It looked like he had one of my comic books. He was casually sitting with his foot resting against the driver's backseat. "But I have to wait until we're alone."

"Why?"

"Because Gabriel didn't want Rex to know what he told me."

"Gabriel?" She stared past me in thought, and then her gaze swept across my face. I watched the change in her eyes go from a blank slate to a spark of excitement. She gasped and took hold of my arm, pulling me down. Throwing her arms around my shoulders, she whispered. "The light walker who rebelled?"

"Yes," I whispered back. "I'll tell you more about it at a better time."

Carrie pulled away and shoved my shoulder back. "Not fair, punk ass. It seems like I'm always left out." She crossed her arms and pretended to pout.

Her facade quickly failed when I bent toward her with my hands out. She broke into a smile, and I swept her into my arms, threw her over my shoulder, and tickled her. She screeched in laughter.

"Punk ass, huh?" I said, holding her legs down as she continued to squirm against my back.

"You are," she said between giggles, "even... even though I understand why."

"You're a fart knocker," I countered.

"I am not," Carrie said. She had hold of my coat and was working to push it up, along with my sweatshirt. Cool air smacked the small of my back. "You're the farter in the relationship. In fact, boys do that more than girls."

I bounced on my feet, jiggling her. "That's why we're not full of gaseous air like females, who releases it out of their mouth instead. Haven't you heard of diarrhea of the mouth?"

Carrie guffawed. "You're disgusting... I'll show you."

Her cold fingers snaked down my jeans. I bent forward to flip her off me and felt material go up my ass crack. An owl hooted in a nearby tree, but I was too preoccupied to look.

"Wedgie," she called out, releasing my boxer shorts. I set her on her feet, and she ran to the Scout. She hopped in, said something to Rex, and their mouths fell open in what I suspect was laughter.

I pointed at them, biting back a smile. "Paybacks are a bit—" Out the corner of my eye I saw the dog from last night trotting from behind the house. He sat in the yard beside the garage and stared at me with intense golden eyes.

"Drenth!" Rex yelled. The dog's gaze snapped on the vehicle where Rex was sitting, but Rex had vanished. "Time to bail," he said next to me, startling me.

"Don't do that," I told him between clenched teeth, noticing the anxious look on his face.

"C'mon. They're bad news," he urged, then disappeared.

I rushed to my Scout and saw Rex reappear in the backseat, waving me on. Carrie had a confused, bewildered look on her face, not understanding the circumstances, I presumed. The dog whined several times. The sound wrenched my heart until it dropped into a low, feral growl. I glanced over my shoulder. He was crouched, poised to attack, his top lip curling over long sharp teeth. Cujo immediately entered my mind. Carrie screamed for me to hurry. I hopped in and closed the door. A loud thud caused me to look out the window. Nothing was there. Carrie's high-pitched scream tore my attention. The canine was peering in the passenger's window at her. She fell silent and stared into his face.

"Let's go. Let's go," Rex chanted.

I stuck the key in the ignition and backed out of the driveway onto the asphalt. "What the hell is a drenth?" I asked, turning off Carrie's street, heading toward Highway 30.

"Grams will tell you," Rex said.

"Screw that." Carrie turned to him. "We want to know now, and I want to know why they seem familiar to me."

Rex shook his head and sighed. "I'm sure I'm already in loads of trouble for telling you I'm a ghost."

"So what difference would it make if you told us or not?" I asked.

Rex shrugged. "Not much, I suppose."

"Well, then, spit it out," Carrie said.

"Fine." Rex sighed again. "But I'm not going to go into too much detail. Grams can fill you in."

"We're listening," I replied as my mind attempted to churn out all kinds of ideas of what they were. I thought being an apprentice light walker, I might know or have some sort of memory, but nothing struck a chord within the recesses of my soul.

"I understand," Carrie told him. "But please tell us at least what they are and why all of a sudden they're bothering us."

Rex opened his mouth, spilling words to shift my world even further out of place.

Chapter Six

Carrie

I had no idea what Rex was going to tell us about these drenths. What the hell were they?

The name alone made them seem dark and slimy, like creatures living in the sewers beneath New York City. Creatures who sure seemed interested in Tree and me. But why now? I suddenly had a deeper understanding of what Paige went through. If it wasn't one thing it was another. Would the drama ever end? The dark supernatural world was bottomless. I found myself questioning if I had any regrets in wanting to take part in it. No, I quickly decided, there were no regrets. I would fight to the death to do what was right.

Tree's hand kept squeezing the steering wheel, his thumb pressing into it. His shoulders were bunched next to his ears. Things weighed heavy on his mind. I met Tree when we were in kindergarten, so I could pick out the signs to tell how he was feeling. He kept glancing in the rearview mirror at Rex, who said he'd be in loads of trouble, but we needed to know, and I had no patience to wait for Abigail to tell us. The drive to her house would probably take a good half hour or so. There was no way I was going to sit and wonder what those whatever, whatever's, were. Thank God Rex caved and would at least tell us something about them.

"These drenths," he began as I stared at him, my mind still trying to convince itself Rex was a ghost. He looked as real to me as anyone else. How could he be dead? "These drenths," he repeated, "were witches who were part of a coven back in the 1600s. With the help from their high priestess, they aligned themselves with darkness, seeking powers to gain whatever their hearts desired. They were the ones who sparked the inquisition and caused innocent people to die."

My heart dropped. "Omigod." My stomach churned and a slight nauseous feeling settled in. "Was it in Massachusetts?" I knew about the Salem witch trials, but then again, I think everyone knew about them. You'd have to be living under a rock your whole life to not know.

He shook his head. "No, it was in Bamberg, Germany. They happened earlier, and a lot more people died."

"What happened?" Tree asked, slowing behind a brown Dodge pickup.

We were in lunch hour traffic in downtown Astoria. Tree could have taken a better, less congested route, but I figured out of habit and routine he took this one. I tore my gaze away from the vehicles pulling out of the driveways in front of the cafés and focused on Rex.

"When the accusations of witchcraft proliferated, and a *witch house*, as they called it, was built, complete with a torture chamber adorned with biblical text, their high priestess cast a spell on her coven." Rex frowned and continued with an exhaustive sigh. "They were cursed into the form of a dog, so they could escape the horrors. They would stay in that form until their leader came back for them and break the spell."

"What happened to her?" I asked, chewing on my nails.

"Her boyfriend, knowing the prince bishop was coming for her, took matters into his own hands," Rex said and fell silent.

"What did he do?" Tree pressed.

"He killed her," Rex answered.

My mouth fell open. "Are you serious?" At first I couldn't understand why her lover would end her life, but then I thought about all the horrific torture devices used on suspected witches. They probably discussed her demise, and she wanted him to do it to spare her the agony of being punished for what she was.

Rex nodded. "I'm not going to tell you anymore about it. Grams will fill you in soon enough."

We were now driving on the East Columbia Highway. I loved this scenic route, surrounded by thick forest, towering cliffs, and a large body of river in between. Years ago, I had hiked the trails along this byway with Tree, Paige, and Brayden. We were met with sweeping panoramic views that literally took our breath away and discovered a few waterfalls hidden off the beaten path. I leaned my head against the seat and stared out the window while Rex gave Tree further directions to Abigail's house. Although the vegetation had lost its rich green colors to a dull brown due to the approaching winter, the marvelous views held a wondrous, magical tale yet spoken. It seemed fitting to the predicament I was in. Soon I'd discover more about myself, more about the sleeping part of my soul that held a story of a fertile life as a witch. Abigail was supposed to reawaken it. I still wasn't a hundred percent sure about this whole thing. But as we neared our destination, my heart raced at the sudden excitement bubbling inside me.

"Turn there." Rex pointed to a narrow side road lined with Douglas firs. "It's not far from here."

"Is Abigail your mom's mother?" I asked, trying to distract myself to calm my nerves.

"No. She's my mom's grandmother," he answered. "My mom was an only child," he added.

"Like me and Paige," I said, voicing my thoughts out loud. "Do they talk at all?"

Rex's expression fell into a somber one. I immediately felt bad for bringing it up and opened my mouth to say so, but he spoke before I could get the words out. "No. Mom thinks Grams is loony bins and quit speaking to her altogether after my death. The last straw was when Grams tried to comfort Mom by telling her I was more alive than ever, and she could see and speak to me."

"When did you die?" Tree asked, slowing for a couple does that were crossing the road in front of us.

The corner of Rex's mouth turned up. "1984."

I whipped around to look at him. "Huh? Are you serious?"

"That explains the clothes and his intelligence," Tree mused.

"I'm totally serious," Rex replied and laughed. "I'm as old as your parents or maybe even older. If I were still human, I mean." He paused and scooted forward on his seat so he was leaning between ours. "Turn right here." He gestured to an even narrower road squeezed in the middle of heavy forest. "Grams' house is up ahead." He gave me a sidelong glance. "You're going to love this."

Love what?

But then I saw it, and omigod, I was in love. "Wow," is all I could say.

Abigail had a storybook house. The two pitched roofs were pointed like witches' hats with cedar shakes that appeared thatched. The heavy rolled eaves and leaded shuttered windows set in a half-timbering frame added to its character. Part of the stucco yellowed wall sloped on one side. I wondered what room encompassed that side of the house.

"I knew you would appreciate it," Rex said, pleased he was right.

"Once upon a time ago," Tree said, marveling at Abigail's charming cottage as he drove between a rustic picket fence made of warped wooden pickets, "Carrie was into fairytales, Disney cartoons, and dreamed of being a princess." There was warmth and adoration in his tone that melted my heart. The memories we shared were priceless, and I wouldn't have had it any other way.

"Tree has a good memory," I said, winking at him. I looked at Rex, my nerves reigniting at meeting Abigail and the precarious situation we were in. Doubts about myself plucked at the back of my brain. "Please don't disappear on us."

He made a gesture of crossing his heart. "I won't." He opened the door and hopped out, which still had me befuddled on how he could do that. "C'mon. Grams is waiting for you."

Tree took my hand and squeezed it. "I'm in this with you, so don't worry." He paused, then a resolute tone entered his voice. "But if your health starts to get effected by whatever it is you do, I'm dragging your ass home. End of story."

"Okay," I said, squeezing his hand back. "I promise I'll try and be aware of my limitations." I wanted to say I was fine, but then it would open a heated debate, so I exited the Scout instead.

Abigail's property was surrounded by bizarre, gnarled, twisted trees. The whole setting reminded me of a Tim Burton movie. I couldn't help but grin at the sudden elation I felt being here.

We followed Rex along a misshaped cobbled-stone path curving in different directions to a round, wooden door. Parts of the horizontal grain were deep and blackened with age. Tree and I exchanged a surprised look when we noticed an owl carved in beautiful detail toward the top, like he was a sentinel or something. It made me wonder about the owl we encountered yesterday, and I was sure Tree was pondering the same thing. I took his hand in mine, my heart pounding against my rib cage. Doubt raced through my mind again, like what if I won't be able to reconnect with the witch's part of my soul? What if I remained the useless one in our group? I'd never told anyone this, not even Tree, but after Paige told us she was immortal, and a whole new dark, underbelly world opened up to us, I'd been feeling like the sterile one in the group. What good was I compared to Paige, Nathan, and Tree? I had no skills to offer. Nothing. So as Rex opened the door, I silently prayed Abigail could help me, and I'd be one badass chick alongside Paige, able to hold my own.

"Grams," Rex called out, stepping inside.

We entered into a spacious room with heavy, exposed wooden beams and worn timber floors. A round crimson rug covered the middle of the room. The red material faded into a cream shade with a picture of a maiden kneeling in a garden. A shiny, dark oak staircase poked out in the far left corner across from us. In between the spiral rungs were square intricate pictures carved out of the wood, like the owl on top of the front door. I squinted to make out the scenes, but it was all blurry. I did an internal sigh. I seriously needed glasses.

"I'm in the potions room," a small, crackly voice answered.

"Okay, Grams." Rex's gaze darted around us. He smiled. "Wicked place, huh?"

"This house is brimming with magical energy," Tree replied, taking in the distressed yellowish walls and all the dark wood trim.

There were three doorways, evenly spaced apart on our right. All of them were oddly shaped. The one in the middle was in the shape of a keyhole. To our left was a round archway that opened into a small sitting room filled with beautiful Victorian antique furniture. Oak French doors adorned the back wall.

I breathed in the scent of lavender, feeling the tightness in my muscles loosen. "How do you know?" I asked, slowly breathing out.

Tree shrugged. "I can feel it."

I can't feel anything mystical.

I couldn't help but perceive myself as more and more useless. A piece of my hope crumbled and self-doubt clawed at my insides. Our visit was probably a waste of time, but it was too late to turn back.

Besides, my curiosity outranked my sudden desire to crawl in a hole and disappear in the land of uselessness.

"This way," Rex said.

We followed him to the keyhole door. When we walked in, the first thing I noticed was the round stone fireplace that narrowed and stretched up the wall. In the center was a cast iron cauldron. There were charming nooks and crannies in this large room, and the surfaces melted into one another along the curved walls. A glass apothecary, filled with tiny bottles, lined one of the walls. All those features immediately caught my eyes, and a sense of familiarity engulfed me. The piece of hope I lost mere seconds ago reattached itself. Crossing my fingers behind my back, I prayed déjà vu was a positive sign.

"Welcome," the same voice I heard earlier said behind a wingback chair on the far side of the room. Abigail stepped out from behind it brandishing a tiny ball between her thumb and forefinger. She held it up so we could see it and smiled. "I lost my marble." She kissed it, then pulled out a leather pouch from the deep pocket of her dark purple robe. She deposited the glass ball in it and stuck the bag back in its place.

I sent Tree a doubtful look. Abigail was old. I mean, really old. And she was little, like elf size. Hell, she even looked like one with her round, wrinkled face and long, thin nose. She must have been only four-foot-eight, if that. She had a hump near her shoulder blades causing her upper body to hunch like a question mark.

Tree leaned next to my ear and whispered, "Yoda."

I sharply looked at him, and he smiled. He had an amused, easygoing expression on his face. He didn't have to signal to me his thoughts on the matter. I knew what they were just by looking at him. He wanted us to give Abigail a chance to help me and see what she could do. If it was all bogus, we'd bail.

"Hi, I'm Carrie," I said, extending my hand.

Abigail shuffled toward me. "Yes, I know, dear." Her frail hand slipped into mine. A tingling sensation swirled around my palm. "You feel it, don't you?"

I tore my gaze off our hands still locked together to her peering, milky light blue eyes. Cataracts. It was a wonder she could even see. But there was a joyful glint in them that was contagious, cancelling out her aging flaws. A light-hearted happiness swooped inside me, followed by a sense of kinship.

I couldn't help but smile. "I do. What is it?"

Abigail released her grip and turned away. Slowly she moved toward the wingback chair. "Why don't we sit and visit for a while, and I'll do my best to satisfy your curiosities."

Rex, who was standing off to the side in observation, disappeared, only to reappear on the couch next to the chair. He patted the seat next to him, waving us to sit.

I took the spot next to him with Tree on the other side of me. Tree slung his arm over my shoulders, and I leaned into him for comfort and much needed support.

"Oh, fiddle sticks," Abigail said, right when she was about to sit. "Where are my manners?" She waved her hand over the rustic coffee table in front of us and said some weird ass mumbo jumbo shit. A tea set and a stack of small, round plates and forks appeared along with a square cake covered in what looked like cream cheese icing. "I hope you like tea and spice cake."

"Um, I love it," I answered, staring at her dumbstruck. "How did you do that?"

"This is an enchanted house and the only place I can do magic in," she replied. I could hear the sadness in her tone and wondered why her abilities were on house arrest. "When I die, the glamour will as well." She made an inviting, sweeping gesture with her hand. "Please help yourself. Don't be shy."

Rex, Tree, and I dug into the scrumptious snack. I added some cream (omg, it was real cream) and sugar to my tea, and it tasted awesome.

"The reason your palm was prickling," Abigail said to me while she settled herself into the chair, adjusting her robe around her legs, "is because we're witches. People with paranormal abilities are able to detect one another, if one is self-aware that is."

"Makes sense," Tree said as I nodded in agreement.

"Why can you only do magic here?" I asked.

Abigail's black and white gray hair was wiry around her face. She pushed some off her cheek and sighed. "Do you know when the cat's away the mice will play?"

I gave her a weird look. "I've heard that saying before."

"My hourglass is almost empty." She looked at Rex and smiled thoughtfully.

"Answer her question, Grams," Rex said, trying to keep a straight face. He leaned and whispered to me, "I told you so." He made a swirling gesture next to his ear like he'd done earlier. "No worries... she'll be able to help you." He winked, then planted his attention back on Abigail.

Yeah, right. I was beginning to have serious doubts. I chewed my fingernail again. Whatever, I guess. At least I got to experience her house and visit with a real witch, even though she was a bit batty.

Abigail's forehead wrinkled. She looked up and around, then at us. "What was the question again?"

You got to be frickin' kidding me?

"Why can't you perform magic anywhere other than here?" Tree asked.

I shifted next to Tree. He slipped his hand into mine and squeezed it in short spurts. Morse code. We used to use this tactic when we were younger, playing war with another group of kids. I was a bit rusty at it, but I got the meaning of what he was telling me: *Give her a chance. Have patience. She'll be able to help you.*

"Oh, yes. Now I remember." She let out a spirited laugh. "Knowing my great grandson," she said, eyeing him, "he offered up the truth about the nature of his existence."

"He did," I admitted, then quickly added in Rex's favor: "But I kept badgering him with questions, so he had no choice."

"There is always a choice," she said, the edge of her words biting through my admission. "But what is done is done. Rex knows I hold no ill-will toward him. I imagine he divulged you in other things as well."

She was fishing for details, so I took the bait. I figured I was here to learn from her and about myself, might as well start with a punch. "He gave us a vague detail about the drenths, but not much."

"What exactly did he tell you?" she asked.

I told her, and then Tree filled her in on the owl and the dog. He also opened up to her about Ayperos' short visit. As he was sharing with her his conversation with Ayperos, she made weird movements with her hands in front of her. The teapot lifted off the table and poured steamy tea into a teacup. Once it was settled on the table again, the silver cream container hovered above the cup, pouring a thin stream of white liquid into it. The cup then floated to her. She wrapped her small hands around it and took a sip. I couldn't help but stare in amazement at such an extraordinary event. She seemed unfazed by it, which made it even more awe inspiring. If I had the power to do the things she was doing, I'd be spared the mundane things in life, like dishes and laundry. That would totally kick ass.

"I'm going to start with answering your previous question," she said. "Magic has consequences. If you use an excess amount, you will suffer from overexertion and will temporarily lose your powers. Or if you go against the way of things, nature or the high council of witches from the other side will punish you in some form or another."

"Restricted to this house is your punishment," Tree said as more of a statement than a question. "You did something you weren't supposed to do. However, it must have not been too bad, because you're still able to practice your magic, only not beyond these walls."

"Correct. When Rex's human body died, I cast a spell bounding his spirit here with me. It was a selfish act, and I paid for it. I not only lost my granddaughter, who has disowned me, but my freedom as well. The magic dwelling in this house is my only source for living. But if I were to step foot off my property, it would no longer be."

"Is Rex's mom a witch?" I asked, trying to understand why she would kick Abigail out of her life.

"No," Abigail simple said.

"Then why—" I started to say.

"It's a long story." Abigail sighed. "Simply put, she blames who I am for everything and thinks I sold my soul to Satan."

"Why can't Rex appear in front of her like he does with us?" I asked, trying to come up with a solution for her. "I mean, if he did, she might change her opinion of you."

"She wouldn't see me," Rex answered. "She's too closed minded."

"Can you tell us more about the drenths?" I asked, thinking it might be a good idea to change the subject and save us from an awkward moment.

"What Rex told you about them was correct. They were part of a coven, and their high priestess cast a spell on them to escape persecution. I'm unaware of their size. I imagine their group ranges from three to thirteen in total, maybe more." Abigail shifted her gaze to the floor. Her face went slack and her eyes glazed.

I sent Rex a questioning look. He held up a finger and mouthed, "Wait."

"A pack is stronger than a lone wolf," Abigail mumbled. "Maybe not. A lone wolf must rely on his own instincts for survival and develops clever ways to be cunning."

"Grams?" Rex said.

Abigail slowly raised her eyes to us, her expression unreadable. "The drench you encountered in the canine form walks alone. The others are scattered."

Tree sat up and scooted to the edge of the couch. "I thought the owl might be a drench."

Abigail shook her head. "The owl is a bringer of wisdom and intuition. He's a messenger and has been placed in both of your paths to warn you when these entities are lurking."

"Why do you have one etched on your door?" I asked.

"He's my familiar and sends messages to me from the spirit world," she replied. "A lot of what I know regarding your current situation is from this owl you speak of. Although, Jade was able to lift the veil between our world and hers to request my assistance in aiding you."

Tree leaned forward on his knees, clasping his hands together. "What does the drench want from us?"

She pointed to Tree, and an ominous feeling rushed through me, causing my heart to race. "He doesn't want you near Carrie."

"Why?" I managed to squeak out, looping my arm around Tree's, hugging it for comfort.

Her eyes shifted to me, pouring into mine. The hair on my arms rose. "You harbor the spirit of his high priestess, Isadora, who was you in the 1600s."

Chapter Seven

Tree

Carrie gasped, and my blood ran cold. I turned to her. Her face was stark white, her brown eyes wide, brimming with tears. Her visit here had to be a mistake. Carrie could be ornery and blunt at times, but her spirit was gentle, kind, and caring. From what I gathered from Isadora's character, she was much like the dark spirits, choosing hedonism over everything else. Granted, she must have loved the people in her coven; otherwise, she wouldn't have spared them the horrors of persecution. Regardless though, hundreds of people died because of her. It was a little hard to swallow the assertion Carrie was Isadora. And what the hell had Grams meant by Carrie harboring Isadora's spirit?

"I can't be her," Carrie cried, choking back a sob. "How can this be?"

I wrapped my arms around her and pulled her close to me. "You'll be okay," I whispered. "It's probably a mistake anyway."

"It's not," Rex said.

I looked at him. "Why now? If it were true, the drenth would have appeared to Carrie long ago."

"Carrie was in an accident recently, was she not?" Grams asked, pulling my attention from the frown on Rex's face to her. She appeared calm and collected, not the least bit frazzled by Carrie's predicament.

"Yes," Carrie sniffed, wiping her nose with the back of her hand. "I was in a car wreck that put me in a coma."

A box of Kleenex's manifested in front of Carrie. Her muscles twitched against me, then relaxed. She pulled some tissues out of the box before the whole lot of them disappeared, and with a half-hearted smile she thanked Grams.

"I think we should go," I said, when the realization came that this stress might be too much for her. "Carrie is in a fragile state right now." I made a move to stand, but Carrie yanked me back down.

"I feel fine," she told me.

"Her health is in tip top shape," Rex reassured.

"And you know how?" I asked, raising my eyebrows.

He smiled. "I can see auras, and Carrie's has a healthy, bright orange glow."

"Hah." Carrie looked at me. "I told you I was okay." She gloated.

I pinched her nose and kissed her forehead. "Yes, you did." Her nostrils made a wet, squishing noise. I bunched up my face, feigning disgust.

Carrie pushed my hand away and sniffed. "Snot." She grinned

"You're good for her," Grams said to me, "which is why the drenth doesn't want you around. You see, you bring your light into her darkness or when she's feeling blue."

"He's an apprentice light walker, ya know," Carrie said.

Grams nodded. "I'm aware, and it will be your saving grace if he doesn't fail."

The theme song to *Buffy the Vampire Slayer* went off in Carrie's purse. She pulled her phone out. It was her mom and not a good time for her to call, I thought. I could tell by Carrie's hurried words that she felt the same way. I made up my mind right then to have Grams tell us what we needed to know in one shot. Our day was more than half over, and I knew Carrie's mom would want her home at a decent hour. As Carrie continued to talk to her mom, I watched Grams rise to her feet and slowly move about the room, gathering glass bottles from an apothecary cabinet. She placed them on a long, wooden table, then told us to join her.

Carrie said goodbye and with a sigh, tossed her phone in her purse. "I love my mom, but sometimes she can be so annoying. She wants me home by midnight." She rolled her eyes and followed us across the room. "Anyway, what were you saying about Tree failing?"

I raised my hand when Grams opened her mouth to answer. "We don't have much time, so I'd appreciate it if you filled us in on everything now," I said. "Not to be rude or anything," I added, thinking maybe I was.

Grams waved it off. "Don't trouble yourself. I take no offense at your desire to get straight to the point." She gestured for us to take our seats as she put some herbs in a stone mortar and then crushed them with a round pestle. "In order for Carrie to be part of the Devil's third and assist her friends, we need to execute an awakening spell to unlock Isadora's spirit attached to Carrie's soul. However, doing so can be disastrous, because Isadora is a separate entity, and the memories of her life might overwhelm Carrie."

"Um, I don't know about this," Carrie said, chewing her fingernail, looking pale. "I had Aosoth's memories from her possessing me, and I nearly went mad. Paige had to do her own magic to get rid of them. I don't want to go through that hell again."

"I agree," I said. "It's not worth putting Carrie through turmoil. The Devil's third or not. Her sanity is more important than us playing Indiana Jones and convincing the light walkers to destroy the magical tools they made before they get into the wrong hands."

"This situation is different than the one you endured," Grams replied, pulling a medicine dropper out of a tiny, thin, rose-colored bottle. She added a couple red drops to the mortar. "You were Isadora. Those memories are in a sense your own, and my spell will eventually help you two become one, like it should have been all along. So you need not to be concerned with going mad. Isadora is still connected to your soul. She just needs to join it."

"I don't understand," Carrie said, still chewing her fingernail.

I took her hand away from her face and held it in my lap, hoping it would stop her from gnawing. Nope. The tip of her finger on the other hand went straight into her mouth. I half laughed to myself and noticed Rex watching us from across the table with an amused look.

"Carrie," he said. "If you keep chewing on your digits, you won't be hungry for dinner."

Carrie's eyebrows pulled together, then realization of what Rex meant dawned on her. She pulled her hand away from her mouth and shifted her attention back on Grams. "I don't understand what you mean," she repeated.

"Think of it this way," Grams began, "we all have suppressed memories from our childhood. Sometimes something, or someone, will cross our paths to trigger a buried memory and resurrect it to the forefront of our brain. Isadora's memories are supposed to be yours, whereas Aosoth's memories were her own."

Carrie shrugged. "Then what's the big deal? I mean, they're my memories from a previous life, and now that I think about it, it would be cool to get lost knowledge back."

"I agree," Grams said. "But allow me to enlighten you on what knowledge I have of your current situation. As Isadora, you had too much power. Once you tired of the simple spells you would cast, you turned to dark magic. You thrived on its power. The only person who saved you from yourself was the one person you trusted the most... your lover. The one who murdered you and placed a locking spell on your spirit, so you couldn't be recruited by malevolent beings, thus turning into one yourself." She paused and then went on to clarify, "We are in a constant state of creation. We create ourselves on how we want to become through our experiences and free will. In each life we go through the person we are in that life, decides his or her fate. Jaegar stole that decision from Isadora. When her life here on earth expired, the person she was in the life before hers took the reins, so to speak, and the soul moved on. You see, each life we go through builds our soul. Isadora's life didn't have the opportunity. When she was alive, she was connected to all the previous experiences she had in other lives, but then her essence was sealed away by Jaegar. She is now a separate entity needing to become a part of your soul like she should have been. Once she does, you'll inherit her magical abilities."

"Let me get this straight," I said. I felt like I was missing something important, which annoyed me. My nerves were shot, and my mind was racing. "Carrie will still be herself, but she'll recall everything from her past life in the 1600s *and* have to deal with Isadora's spirit until it's able to become a part of her soul?"

Grams shuffled to the cauldron inside the stone fireplace. "Yes," she said. "The reason for the caveat of my earlier statement is quite simple." She hooked the cauldron on a metal rod and lit a fire beneath it. A whooshing sound filled the room, then reddish, yellow flames jumped to life. "There is a possibility Carrie will be in danger of reverting to Isadora's hedonistic ways and falling prey to the intoxicating feelings dark magic bestows on its possessor. But hope is not lost; otherwise I would not be proposing they merge." Grams half turned. In her hand was a wooden spoon, which she pointed at me. "She has you in her court... light walker. You can help her overcome hardships. Eradicate the blackness of that part of Isadora's spirit, leaving what we're aiming for."

"What's that?" Carrie asked.

"For Isadora to become part of your soul, so you'll have the ability to perform clean magic with a pure heart. It will aid you and your friends in your many quests."

"I'm not a light walker," I said, my stomach tensing from the thought of losing Carrie to darkness. "And what about the drenths?" I had a sinking feeling once Carrie reconnects with her emotions from the past, she would more than likely want to bring her coven back.

"Ah, yes. I did not answer your previous question about the drenths." Grams made a circle gesture with the tip of the spoon over the cauldron. Puffs of white smoke popped above the cauldron's lip in intervals. "After Carrie had her accident, her spirit was whisked away into another realm to recover from the trauma. During her stay she met Jade and Ashia—"

"That's her name!" Carrie blurted. She clapped a hand over her mouth and dropped it when she realized everyone was staring at her. "Sorry. I didn't mean to interrupt, but I've been trying to think who the other woman was I visited with. I can't remember everything we talked about, though."

"They told you about once being a powerful witch," Grams replied.

"I remember that part, but I thought Ashia gave me instructions on how to meditate. When I woke up from the coma, it was sharp in my memory, but now it's gone."

"She taught you how to center yourself through meditation, the power of a crystal and other stones, as well as earth magic." Grams smiled. "You, child, are a caster."

Carrie sat straight up, and her face glowed with excitement. "I am?"

"Yes, but we're going off topic," Grams said. "Back to the drenth. The spell they're under will alert and direct them to Isadora when the time draws near for her spirit to reawaken in the flesh. Neither they, nor she anticipated it being as long. In fact, she planned on evoking a transmigration spell where her spirit and soul would jump into another human and take over that body. However, her mate ruined her diabolical scheme by taking her life and conjuring his own devious magic upon her."

"Wow." Carrie held her cheeks in her hands. "Isadora... I mean, I was conniving."

"Tree is not a light walker, Grams," Rex said.

I threw him a thank you look. My stomach was now in a knot, and the back of my throat burned. I tried to swallow against the rancid taste edging toward my tongue, but my mouth was bone dry.

"Also, he needs water, pronto."

"How did you know?" I croaked. A tall glass of water appeared on the table in front of me. I gratefully took it and gulped it, enjoying the coolness streaming down my pipes.

Rex stuck his tongue out and pointed a finger in his mouth in a jabbing motion, making choking noises. After he pretended he was about to hurl, he said, "I can see in your aura you were on the verge of throwing up."

"Are you okay?" Carrie placed a hand on my forehead, worry creasing her face.

"I'm fine now," I reassured her, taking her hand in mine.

"You're not a light walker yet," Grams said while stirring inside the smoky cauldron. "But I addressed you as such because you're well on your way and have already conversed with Michael and Gabriel. Your case is a special one, and although I implied earlier you might fail Carrie, I have no doubt you will succeed. You will help her untangle the roots which might bind and entice her to do wicked things."

"Her roots, meaning Isadora's spirit," I said dryly, not liking her explanation one bit.

Grams nodded.

"I thought," Carrie said, sounding confused, "if you abuse magic, there are consequences. That's what you said earlier, and look what happened to you."

"Yes, there are," Grams said. "However, Isadora had allied herself with the dark spirits, which for a period of time cloaked her from the council of witches. But her overexertion from her excessive use of magic was on the brink of destroying her." Grams ladled some of the liquid from the cauldron and poured it into a tall silver cup. White smoke billowed out, as if a chunk of dry ice were dropped into it. "I need you to sit next to Rex," Grams told me.

"What for?" Carrie asked, her tone laced with panic. She tightened her grip on my hand.

"I need to sit in his place," Grams said to Carrie, "so I can assist you in this awakening spell."

My heart went out to Carrie. I wanted to comfort her as she looked up at me with wide, child-like eyes.

"Do you really want to open Pandora's Box?" I asked her. "I personally don't' think it's worth the risk."

She ran a hand down her face and tucked a lock of hair behind her ear. "I'm sure," she said. "I don't like the idea of having a spirit, who was in a sense me, attached to my soul like a parasite," she admitted. "It's kind of creepy."

I stood, kissed her hand and gently touched her cheek. Although I didn't want her to proceed, I understood her reasoning, and it was her decision, not mine. "Alright then, I won't let anything happen to you," I promised. "Besides, I trust Grams knows what she's doing." And I did. Otherwise, I would haul Carrie's ass out of here right now.

"I love you," Carrie said.

I softly kissed her, and when our lips parted, I whispered, "I love you, too." I released her hand and moved to the other side of the table. I took a seat next to Rex and folded my hands on the table, keeping a watchful eye on Carrie.

Grams claimed my seat beside Carrie, setting the cup down. She faced Carrie and took her hands. "Before I perform the ritual, I need your consent to do so. Do I have it?"

"What if I don't have a choice and darkness overpowers me?" Carrie asked.

"Darkness dwells in each and every one of us. It's up to the individual whether to give in or not," Grams told her.

"I don't want to be evil." Carrie bit her lip. "I want to be a good spell caster like you, and help my friends."

Grams smiled. "You're in exactly the correct frame of mind. Should we begin?"

Carrie nodded. "I give you my consent to work an awakening spell on me."

The room darkened.

Carrie gasped.

Doubt tainted with fear of failing her pierced my thoughts, my heart. But it was too late to stop it, because as soon as Carrie gave her permission, the energy around us shifted. It was thick, heavy, and fluid. I knew then Carrie's life would never be the same again.

Chapter Eight

Carrie

I sucked in a sharp breath when we were plunged into darkness, and at least a hundred lit candles appeared around the room. A warm, orangey glow bathed our surroundings, and the smell of Frankincense enveloped us. I watched strange shadows lick the walls, moving up, down, wavering.

"Carrie." Abigail's voice rose no higher than a whisper, but it was direct and caught my attention. "I want you to drink this." She handed me a silver cup.

White smoke swirled around the top, obstructing what the liquid inside looked like. I raised it to my nose and sniffed. "What is it?" It smelled like carrot juice. I hated carrot juice. I made a face and set the cup down. "Bleh. It smells gross. I don't think I can drink it."

"Hold your nose and chug it," Rex suggested. He mimed it, dramatizing the part after he swallowed the last drop by grasping his neck and widening his eyes. He stuck his tongue out and coughed. Tree elbowed him in the side, halting Rex's theatrics. "Just kidding," he said. "I'm sure it's not quite so bad."

I twisted my lips, contemplating on what to do. I had no other choice. This would probably be the only chance I'd ever get. So I had to drink nasty stuff with God knows what in it.

My stomach churned.

"The potion is magical," Abigail said, placing the cup back in my hands. "Every ingredient comes from the earth. I assure you, you will not get sick. Now drink, child, before the properties weaken."

I was afraid. What if it was created with bugs or frog eyes? I immediately pushed those thoughts out of my mind. I glanced at Tree. He was watching me closely with a protective gleam in his eyes. Taking comfort in him being here with me, I took a deep breath, pinched my nose, and drank the elixir. The texture felt like yogurt against my tongue and throat. It was thick and creamy yet easy to swallow. A warm sensation spread across my chest. Slowly, it crept through my body, relaxing every muscle. I set the empty container down and slumped in the chair, feeling deliciously buzzed and not having a care in the world.

Abigail dipped her fingertips in the stone bowl. "I'm going to paint a symbol on your forehead to further aid us in breaking the seal to release Isadora's spirit. Once it does, it will connect to your present mind and body, thus infusing you with the memories and knowledge from your life as her."

Abigail sounded like she was at the end of a tube. I could make out her words, but they were faint. My mouth tasted like cotton candy, reminding me of when Paige and I went to the state fair. I ate half my weight in the stuff while Paige ate hers in fried bread. The memory was fresh. I could smell the caramel corn and hear people talking, laughing, and screaming above us from the rollercoaster we were waiting in line for. Paige was smiling, her dark green eyes bright as she animatedly told me about a brown, spotted owl she saw in the forest behind her house.

"Carrie." Abigail touched my check with her free hand. "Try to keep focus. I need you to close your eyes and envision sitting in an empty theater in front of a blank screen."

"The owl," I said, sounding sluggish. "Is it a brown spotted one? I didn't get a good look when I saw him."

She nodded. "He is. Now, do what I said. The moon is full and rising. Time we cannot waste."

"Paige saw him two years ago," I whispered to myself, closing my eyes.

Abigail's finger was wet against my forehead. She drew a circle and a design that felt like several vertical loops, while chanting a spell in Latin. I could make out most of what she was saying, but instead of paying attention to her, I imagined myself in a dark theater instead. The flip up seat was well padded and comfortable. It rocked, and the armrests had holes for beverages. It was wild how clear and detailed everything came to me. I felt like I was there.

In the distance, I could hear Abigail's voice, strong and forceful as she repeated the incantation, moving her fingertip slowly against my skin. I shifted my focus to the large, white screen in front of me, wishing I had a pop and some buttered popcorn. I hadn't been to a movie in a long ass time. Tree and I should go tomorrow night. We'd have fun, but I doubt it would happen.

I felt myself sigh.

The meditation Abigail had me do wasn't working, nor was her spell. Maybe Tree and I were led to believe the things Abigail and Rex told us to keep us out of the dark spirits way.

How disconcerting.

I had to except the fact I would remain the not-too-bright sidekick who had nothing to offer but her loyalty and friendship.

How depressing.

Maybe I wasn't a part of the Devil's third. Actually, with Nathan it was four, but he wasn't the third—or was he?

It had to be a mistake.

I wasn't Isadora or harbored her spirit.

I possessed no magic.

I was useless.

I—

Something shifted.

Abigail's energy moved.

Fingertips pressed against my temples. Her voice was thick and forceful as she chanted an invocation. It surrounded me. A bluish, yellow spark erupted across the blank screen. A loud popping noise sounded in my ears, followed by a squirming sensation inside my body, like worms crawling beneath my skin. I tried to move but remained locked into place. Thankfully, the feeling disappeared in a matter of seconds. Pictures took form in front of me, as if a projector were displaying them. The landscape was gorgeous with dark green grass, hills, forest, and stone bridges arched over rivers and canals. I knew it was Bamberg, Germany—Isadora's home, my home. There were also Gothic churches crowning hilltops. I knew all about them, and though the architecture was stunning, a deep hatred boiled my blood.

The memories rushed in, setting camp in my conscious mind. I remembered Bamberg was ruled by Prince-Bishop Johann Dornheim. He was a vile, unscrupulous man who was known as *The Hexenbiscof* (the witch bishop). In 1627 he erected the Drudenhaus, which was a witch's prison. It contained torture chambers and cell rooms. Rumor had it, he'd built similar ones in the smaller towns nearby. He employed full-time torturers and executioners. He equipped them with the latest devices: thumbscrews, racks, the strappado used with weights, prayer stools fitted with sharp wooden pegs, among other sick contraptions. What set the motion for this wicked nexus was me, Isadora, and my beloved coven. But in truth, it was more than us casting a spell in an attempt to change the weather. It was greed, economics, misinformation, and Dornheim's insatiable need to line his pockets.

Yes, my past life was coming back. The part of me who was once Isadora sprang forth, aligning her essence with my present one to where we were both sharing memories. I decided not to push against her and allowed her presence access. Her ideologies attached to mine, causing me to second guess a thing or two. Her personality was strong and relentless, giving me a sense of powerful and uninhibited confidence, something I'd never felt before. I knew how to cast spells. Simple ones. Earth magic. But the dark magic eluded me at the present moment. Frustration knotted my fingers together in a fist, held tightly in my lap. I had to be clever and fool the inane I was associated with and regain the knowledge that escaped me to break the curse I had cast on my people.

I opened my eyes and closed them and opened them again. "It worked," I said, sounding nonchalant, almost bored. Maybe I should have said it with more enthusiasm, like I would have before my spirit was awakened. I tried it again, raising the pitch of my voice like I normally would as Carrie. "Omigod. The spell worked." I sat up. Wide-eyed I stared at the old woman in front of me. A smile crossed her worn face, bunching her wrinkles. An image of a sharpei dog flipped up in my mind. I pretended to cough to stifle the giggle rising in my throat.

"Are you okay?" Jack—Tree moved in front of me and knelt.

I touched his handsome face and told him I was fine in German. To my delight he answered back.

Ah, yes, Tree spoke fluent German. Thanks to Carrie's memories, I knew his family was from there and visited my homeland every other summer. Correction: used to be my homeland, I reminded myself. I was now part of Carrie Jacobson, the loyal and sometimes dim-witted friend to those superior. However, now things would be different— much different.

"You speak German?" the old woman asked Tree in surprise.

"I do," he answered, his attention still on me. He cradled my cheek in his big, callused hand. "Carrie?" he whispered.

"It's Isadora." The boy appeared next to me. "I can see it in her aura."

"I'm the same person," I said, still pretending to be Carrie, realizing I didn't have my German accent, and I spoke perfect English. In fact, I mimicked Carrie's speech perfectly. "Only now I remember everything from my life as Isadora," I added.

"There's something different in your eyes," Tree said. "A strong confidence I've never seen in you before." His thumb rubbed slow circles around the apple of my cheek, causing my heart to skip a couple beats.

He was a handsome guy and someone Carrie truly loved in her life. Her desires for him ran deep, reminding me of Jaegar. I had trusted Jaegar with my heart and soul, but he cast a locking spell on my spirit as he murdered me. I'd never expected he'd do such a thing. He was supposed to have assisted me with the transmigration spell, but instead he betrayed me and my coven. I would not make the same mistake twice, I vowed.

The old woman reached in her pocket and produced a lovely amethyst crystal charm with a thin piece of silver wire wrapped around it. The quartz dangled from a silver chain when she held it up to show us. "The crystal should help Carrie put some balance between herself and Isadora." She extended it to Rex and said, "Place the necklace around her neck."

"I don't think it's necessary." I half laughed and waved it off. "I can feel parts of myself from when I was Isadora, like what Jack... um... Tree said. I feel more confident and self-assured. I also know German now. I have no desire to be wicked."

"You still need to wear it," the boy said, unconvinced by my evasion. He was beginning to be a pain in my ass. "Frankly, from the things I've heard about Isadora, she was a bit nuts and not in the same kernel factory as Grams." There was a knowing glint in his eyes, like he knew he was talking to me instead of Carrie.

The old woman took no offense to the boy's insult. Instead, it fell on deaf ears. She probably had cobwebs in them and couldn't properly comprehend what he was actually saying. Or maybe she agreed with him and felt no need to chastise him. She was no longer in my line of vision, so I had to step away from those thoughts and tell myself maybe I made an inappropriate assessment on the matter. But nevertheless, I didn't appreciate his disrespect shown toward me, and I couldn't allow it to slide.

"Isadora's actions weren't bred from madness," I said, my temper flaring. "She had legitimate reasons for her actions. The history, or what you know of her and her coven, was tainted with outlandish tales from fools who knew *nothing* about the truth of the matter. Dornheim and his informers were the ones who perpetuated the stories. They were wicked beasts, who out of greed and power, stirred a frenzy of accusations, not only against us but others as well. Even the rich fell victim to it. They had their property and assets confiscated, which made Dornheim a wealthy man."

Jack's fingers unraveled my fist. They were gentle. His love and kindness flowed from him to me, dousing the heat percolating my blood. The tension strapped around my muscles unclenched, releasing a calming wave to flow through my body. The duality between Carrie and me clashed. An inward battled ensued as Carrie silently struggled to gain a foothold against my desire to dominate her life. A heaviness filled my chest and head. Carrie pushed me aside, surprising me with her stubbornness. And as she did so, I heard her wonder if Jaegar hadn't betrayed me, would she be much smarter and confident in this life? Would she be a practicing witch already?

Tree's gaze moved past me. "Put the necklace on her now. I can see a conflict going on inside."

Rex placed the crystal around my neck. Once it touched the space between my breasts, the strife dulled along with the sharp edges of thought and feelings, courtesy of my seventeenth century self. Lucky me.

I hugged Tree. "Thank you."

"Do you still know the German tongue?" Abigail asked.

"Ja, kann ich," I answered.

"Yes, I can," Tree repeated after me. He cradled my face in his hands and kissed me on the lips.

"Your aura is almost the same as before," Rex told me. "I suspect it'll never be back to where it was because the part of you that is Isadora has been freed."

"Tangled roots," Abigail said, causing us to look at her. She was holding a black book in one hand and a brown messenger bag in the other. "Don't allow the roots of dark magic and thought tangle you to where you will fall prey to what you once were."

"I have a choice, and I choose not to," I replied, even though I harbored doubts.

"How are you feeling?" Tree asked.

I shrugged. "I don't know. Weird, I guess. I mean, I was still there, but Isadora's spirit took the lead. I can only compare it to a closed off person losing inhibitions while intoxicated and becoming the life of the party. I hate to admit it, but I like the new sense of power, strength, and confidence I feel when she takes over."

"You will fully gain the things rightfully yours when Isadora overcomes the darkness in her spirit and can join your soul," Abigail said. She motioned for us to follow her out of the room. "Jaegar might have thought he was doing her a favor when he cursed her, but part of me is skeptical about his motives."

"Me, too," I said, trailing behind her into the hallway. An image of a dark haired guy with bluish gray eyes flitted through my mind. He had a dashing face and a rock hard muscular body. My heart fluttered. A scene began to play out showing Isadora in a hayloft with Jaegar. He was pulling the strings from her blouse. Abigail mumbled something. A soft, golden light bathed our surroundings, bringing me back to the present.

"Where are we going?" Tree asked when Abigail stopped in front of us and waved a hand over a black and white braided rug. It flipped over, revealing a trap door.

"The only place where the enchantments in this house are impotent. Carrie can practice casting spells down there," she answered. "I want to see what she can do on her own with the memories she now has."

Rex stepped ahead of us and unhinged the wooden door. A musky, earthy smell belched from its dark recesses. The temperature chilled, and I hugged myself to keep from shivering. Tree, noticing my discomfort, wrapped his arm around my shoulders. I loved how attentive he was. I encircled my arms around his waist and snuggled against him.

Rex disappeared. Shortly after, the square hole framed a golden light. Abigail dropped the book and messenger bag into the opening. Rex must have caught it because I didn't hear them make contact with the floor. Unless the room was deeper than I thought.

"The steps are steep," Abigail warned. "If you hold the railing, you'll be fine."

Slowly, she eased herself onto the first step. She swayed to the right. Tree and I moved to her. She took hold of the wrought iron railing to steady herself.

"Here, let me help you," Tree said, placing his hands gently around her upper arms as he positioned himself behind her.

Abigail released a nervous laugh. "I haven't been down here in ages. I guess I'm not as spry as I used to be." She turned to glance at him and almost lost her footing. Tree caught her before she tumbled backward. "Whoa." Her grip tightened on the railing. "Thank you, dear boy. I almost lost my head."

"No problem," Tree answered, cautiously guiding her down.

I followed behind, trying not to allow the vertical incline to mess with my equilibrium by focusing on each step I took. Having Tree in front of me helped. He was so tall his body blocked my view. As we descended, the air grew colder. Goosebumps scattered across my arms beneath my clothes. The desire to rub them came over me, but I wasn't about to risk losing my balance.

When we finally reached the bottom, Abigail released a tired sigh. She didn't look well, and it had me worried. Tree was also concerned and told her maybe we should try this another day. Abigail waved it off and said she was dandy, just old.

"This room reminds me of a dungeon," I said, eyeing the stone walls, blackened from age, and the lit torches anchored to them in cast iron holders. "I'm not comfortable here." My hands shook. I shoved them in my pockets. "I have memories from Isadora, of people I knew being held in one." I ran my hands through my hair. "God, this is so weird. I mean, her memories are mine. I was her, yet she's a separate entity because of what Jaegar did."—I pointed around the gloomy, gothic room—"And this cellar freaks me out."

"You need to work through those fears," Abigail said, opening the messenger bag and placing glass bottles filled with what looked like herbs on a table covered in a dark purple cloth. There was a design of a pentagram in the center of the material of an upright star. It was a good sign, meaning spirit over possessions whereas the inverted star meant the opposite. However, I could feel the objection squirming in the center of my chest. Spirit meant nothing to Isadora. It only caused heartache. But with power, she was no longer a victim. Her thoughts, I realized, were breaking through my consciousness. "Besides," Abigail went on, "there's no other place I can go but here to instruct you if need be."

"Instruct me?" Did she seriously think I needed her guidance? A cocky arrogance rushed from within. I almost laughed but bit my tongue instead. I turned and walked several paces away from everyone. The boy appeared in front of me, but startled I was not. Annoyed would be the appropriate term for how I felt at the moment. He was quickly becoming the bane of my existence.

The boy took my hand and placed it around the crystal. "Your evil twin is breaking through this charms' magical properties," he said. "If you incase it in your palm, you might be able to silence her."

He was right. The crystal became warm inside my palm. Its heat flowed up my arm and throughout my body, soothing every fiber of my being. Isadora retreated, and I no longer felt insulted by Abigail's comment. I remembered how to cast spells—simple ones. I even recalled which herbs to use. The information was right there, clear in my mind, like three times two was six. Elementary really. Something one could not forget, unless plagued by a diseased mind. However, the dark magic I once wielded as Isadora had escaped me, making me wonder if Jaegar had something to do with it. *Bastard.*

"Grams, I think we might run into a problem," Rex said, frowning.

Tree crossed the room in quick strides. "What?"

"I'm fine," I told them when Tree took my hand and checked me. "I'm not going to explode or cause unrest."

"Isadora's strong personality is overwhelming the..." Rex narrowed his eyes and studied me for what seemed like a long moment but was merely seconds. "Wait. She withdrew."

"Carrie will need to learn how to coexist with Isadora for the time being. But for now the crystal will have to suffice until I can get a hold of the council to see if there's something else we can do," Abigail said. "Come. Gather around the table and let's begin."

We moved to the table where a dozen small glass bottles with labels were laid out. A black leather bound book with straps, silver hoops and clamps rested next to them. I knew it was a *Book of Shadows*. I picked it up, feeling a stirring within and a welcoming energy that made me smile. The book was familiar to me, and I caught myself mentally saying, "Welcome home." Joy and warmth bubbled inside me. My smile grew.

Abigail pointed to the book. "That is a *Book of Shadows* and a grimoire in one."

Impressive. I'd never beheld nor entertained the idea of having both in one volume. Brilliant if you'd ask me. I also loved the wicked, medieval design.

"*The Book of Shadows* is an instruction book for magical rituals, and the grimoire is a textbook of magic, right?" Tree asked Abigail.

"Yes," Abigail and I said in unison.

"Each herb serves a purpose," Abigail told us and then turned to me. "You need to know about plants and the formulas to create the spells you want. In time you'll be able to design your own to fit your needs."

I used to be able to fashion my own brews, but I couldn't recall what they were. I wondered what happened to those memories, along with the one to reverse the curse I, as Isadora, had placed on my coven. Did Jaegar have anything to do with it? A flash of anger blindsided me. I glanced at the boy—Rex. He was studying me closely. I palmed the crystal, and as I did so a booming thought monopolized my musing: *The boy can see your aura. There is a spell to cloak the parts you want hidden. You can also cast a beauty spell to achieve the same effect.*

Isadora's thoughts were coming through loud and clear, and I felt an unexpected kinship forming.

"You have an intense look," Tree said to me. "Do you remember any details you didn't know before?"

"I do," I replied when all eyes shifted on me. I straightened my back and shoulders, feeling a confidence I'd never had.

"Well, then, child," Abigail said, curiosity dancing in her watery pale eyes, "by all means, tell us what you know." She stepped away from the table and gestured toward the contents. "Start with the herbs. Tell us their magical attributes."

I opened my mouth to begin rattling off information about each herb displayed on the table, when a warning signal went off inside my head. *Don't get too cocky. Pretend you have to struggle with recalling each one.* I told Isadora not to worry. I got this one handled. I would play the part well so I could move on to more important things, like finding a way to release the curse from the drenths. The name made me cringe. I loathed it. I meant *our coven.*

Tree's warm hand slipped into mine. "Are you okay?"

I offered him a reassuring smile. "I'm fine. I merely want to make sure I have each one right before I announce what they are and what they do."

"Why don't you say what comes to you?" Rex suggested. "Who cares if what you say is wrong? It's not like you're going to get ugly marks against you if you're incorrect."

"Okay," I said, taking a deep breath to add to feigning unsureness. Then I began, taking my time on each one when really I wanted to throw the information out as quickly as I could. I knew, though, the simple act of announcing what each herb's purpose in magic was only formed the beginning of a new and improved Carrie and a new life.

Chapter Nine

Tree

Carrie pointed to each herb and stated its magical properties. She struggled with most of them and had two more left.

Reading the label, she said, "Calamus." She shifted her weight back and forth and scratched her head. "Um, is used to control and dominate spells, right?" She looked at Grams for confirmation. Grams nodded, and Carrie continued. "You can also use it for luck, healing, and protection."

"Correct," Grams said.

Carrie picked up the last one. "Damina." She chewed on her lip while she thought. Her cheeks bloomed red. "Is Damina used in magic to intensify sexual passion?"

"Yes," Grams replied. "With the right ingredients, you can also burn the herb to produce visions."

"I should remember this stuff." Carrie sighed. "When will it come back to me?"

Grams patted Carrie's arm. "In time it will. Be patient."

I felt bad for Carrie. I knew she had high hopes to acquire all of her past knowledge regarding magic, but maybe failure was a good thing. She seemed to be having a hell of a time controlling Isadora's spirit. Thankfully, the crystal seemed to be helping her deal with it. Personally, I thought it would be best for her to concentrate more on Isadora's situation than being a practicing witch. Her present limited knowledge of how she could create enchantments might be a blessing in disguise. It would at least give me a chance to help her cope and sort things.

Grams reached into her messenger's bag and produced a large, folded piece of parchment. "Here is a map of my house and the surrounding area," she told us. She smoothed it on the table so we could take a look. "Aesop is somewhere in the vicinity, and Carrie is going to attempt to cast a locator spell."

"I am?" Carrie asked at the same time I asked who Aesop was.

"Aesop is the owl you and Carrie saw," Rex told us.

"I don't know how to perform a locator spell," Carrie said. She glanced at me, and something sparked in her brown eyes. Mischievousness? She looked away before I could be sure. I must have imagined it, or maybe Isadora was poking through again.

"The formula is in the grimoire section," Grams told her, undoing the leather straps and silver clamps. She placed the book next to the map in front of Carrie and opened it to where the locator spell was written. The pages were yellowed from age, and the penmanship was elegant. "Here's a feather from Aesop." She handed it Carrie. "To place a locator spell on a person or animal, you need something from the individual."

I remembered Nathan telling me about when Jade had done the same ritual to find Paige. He gave Jade a letter Paige had written. I was curious to discover if this spell would work in the same manner as Jade's.

"Did Nathan or Paige tell you Jade performed the same incantation to find Paige?" I asked Carrie. I couldn't recall if they had and wanted to know for sure. If so, the spell might be easier for Carrie to cast.

"Not really," Carrie answered. "I mean, Paige mentioned it to me, but she wasn't there, so she couldn't give me any details."

"It doesn't matter," Grams said. "You can't learn until you perform it yourself."

I watched Rex cross the room to a wooden cabinet. Each shelf had a glass door with a tiny knob at the bottom. The dust was so thick I couldn't see what was inside. He lifted the door in the middle and slid it back, revealing two small brass bowls, empty potion bottles, and candles. "Do you need these?" he asked Grams, pointing to the candles.

"No," Grams answered. "Carrie, in her life as Isadora, executed the locator spell countless times, so it won't be necessary."

Carrie narrowed her eyes. "How do you know?" I could hear the caution in her tone, as if she began to realize Grams knew more about Isadora's abilities than Carrie thought, and she didn't like it.

"Jade, of course," Grams replied, taking the bowls from Rex and arranging them on the table. "This is natural spring water." She showed us a glass vial and then gave it to Carrie. "Pour it in one of the bowls." After Carrie did as instructed, Grams pointed to one of the herb bottles. "Put a pinch of crushed lavender into the liquid." Without hesitation, Carrie followed Grams orders. "Now, focus your mind on Aesop. Close your eyes and visualize him while holding his feather in front of you. Once you have his image solid in your mind, open your eyes."

Carrie frowned. "I don't know what he looks like. When I saw him, he was in shadow, so I can't picture him."

"I'll be right back," Rex announced, then vanished.

"Pardon me for my lack of forethought," Grams said to Carrie. "I should have been more prepared and considered you never met Aesop."

"It's fine," Carrie reassured her. "I tend to be forgetful, as well."

"Same here," I chimed in. "My mom gets annoyed with me when

I forget to do the dishes, take the garbage out, and—"

Carrie laughed. "You don't have forgetfulness. You have selective memory."

Grams smiled. "I think Carrie has you figured out."

Carrie pinched my arm. "I know his game."

"Here's a photo of Aesop," Rex said, appearing next to us. He handed it to Carrie.

The photograph was a good close up of a large, brown spotted owl with yellow eyes that looked ancient and wise. He was perched on a low branch in a huge, thick gnarly elm. The orange sky made the perfect backdrop, giving the image of Aesop a mystical feel.

"He's cute. I love the picture," Carrie said. "Can I have it, or is it rude of me to ask?"

Grams patted Carrie's arm. "You may keep it. I have plenty of photos of him. Now, let's get busy."

Carrie stared at the picture and closed her eyes, holding the feather in front of her. "Okay, I have his image in my mind," she said, looking at Grams.

Grams nodded. "Your next task is to focus on locating him while chanting this incantation." She pointed to an open page in the book. "Once the feather begins to smoke, drop it in the empty bowl."

Slowly, Carrie read the incantation. Her voice stumbled on a couple words, but then it was as if a switch flipped inside of her. Her tone became confident and powerful. She looked up from the grimoire and recited the spell, no longer needing to read it. Wisps of smoke curled from the edges of the feather. She tossed it in the bowl. A small flame ignited.

"Dip your fingertips in the other bowl," Grams said, "and—"

Carrie plunged her fingers in the liquid, chanting as she did so. She lifted her hand, flicked drops of the potion onto the fire and a loud "pop" issued from it. The flame died. Carrie picked up the bowl and dumped ashes onto the map. I leaned in to get a better look, amazed at how capable and confident she was. The ashes gathered and formed a straight line. It slithered across the map until the tip touched a room marked "Greenhouse."

Carrie stopped the incantation and glanced at me. I'm sure my eyes were wide and filled with wonder because I felt the emotion on my face. She smiled. She looked happy, but I saw smugness in her expression before she turned her attention on the others. Isadora? We wanted to have Carrie's memories from her past work in correlation with her present self, though. I saw no reason to be alarmed. Carrie seemed in control now and showed no signs of submitting to her former self. Maybe things would turn out better than we thought.

"You did a great job," I said. "The memory must have come back."

Carrie's smile turned into a grin. "It did. How awesome is that?"

I pulled her into a hug. "Pretty awesome."

"Excellent," Grams said. "Your performance leads me to believe it will be the same way with the other enchantments." She gathered the herbs and began placing each one in her bag.

"Are we done?" I looked at my watch—7:30. Where did the time go? No wonder I was hungry. I bet Carrie could eat, too. I thought about how much money I had—fifty-three dollars. I decided then where to take her for dinner, all in a matter of seconds.

"Yes," Grams replied. "Time is slipping away, and this old woman needs her rest. I expect to see you two here tomorrow around six p.m."

I thought about if we had any plans to interfere with the suggested time. "I should be off of work by then... wait, now that I think about it, seven would be better. I have an engine to tear down, and I don't know how long the project is going to take me."

"Then you get here when you can." She gave me the spell book. "I'm not going anywhere," she half-laughed and pointed to my hands. "Would you please carry *The Book of Shadows* for me?"

"Certainly," I said. There was no way she'd be able to climb those stairs carrying this hefty book. She looked worn out anyway. Haggard was a better description. I wondered how old she was and marveled at how well she ambled around, despite her age.

"Can we see if Aesop is in the greenhouse?" Carrie asked, admiring his picture in her hands. "I would like to meet him."

"Yes, dear." Grams was struggling with her bag, trying to slip the strap over her shoulder. It slid off her arm and fell to the floor. The bottles clinked against one another. "Fiddle sticks." She sighed and bent to pick it up, but Carrie stopped her.

"Here, allow me to carry this for you." Carrie snatched the messenger bag.

"Thank you." Grams sent Carrie a grateful smile. "I must be more tired than I thought."

"I'll help you up the stairs," Rex said, moving to Grams' side, looping his arm around hers.

"You can tell a child time for bed, but he won't sleep until he's damn well ready to," Grams mindlessly said.

"C'mon," Rex said, coaxing her along. "I'm sure once your head hits the pillow, you'll be fast asleep.

Grams slowly moved beside him, her slippers scratching against the floor. "You can wait for the right moment to do what you desire and watch the time go by, or you can grab it by the balls and yank it toward you."

Carrie and I laughed. The visual in my mind was too clear not to. Grams may be a few fries short of an order, but she was entertaining and knew her shit.

"Grams!" Rex exclaimed, trying to keep a straight face.

"One word I have to say. *Ouch*," I said.

"Totally," Rex agreed, snickering.

As we made our way up the stairs, I realized how much I enjoyed being around Rex and Grams. They were good people, and I was looking forward to visiting with them again tomorrow. I didn't know how I could ever repay Grams for guiding Carrie in the right direction, but I'd find a way. For now, though, my top priority was Carrie and to make sure she had all her ducks in a row. If she were to submit to Isadora, I'd have a serious problem on my hands. A problem I had no idea how to solve.

Chapter Ten

Carrie

The greenhouse was attached to the back of the house. The slanted ceiling and curved walls were constructed of plastic. When we entered the spacious room, the thick smell of soil and herbs enveloped me. I breathed it in, and an immediate calming sensation ebbed beneath my skin. I sighed. Quickly putting two and two together, I had an answer for my sudden Zen feeling. In my life as Isadora, my family made a living farming. I had a lovely kitchen garden my father built out of stone, separate from our house. A sad longing tugged at my heart. I palmed the crystal hanging from my neck and moved on.

There was a small counter with gardening tools and potting equipment across from me. Beside it was a sink. Scattered plants hung above us and against the wall were rows of herbs. There were several buckets filled with soil, displaying plump red tomatoes on dark green vines. I was admiring them when Tree tapped me on the shoulder and pointed to the far corner of the room. I had to crane my neck to the side to see past the hanging foliage. Right where Tree indicated was a branch with a large, brown spotted owl perched on it.

Aesop.

He was magnificent. I stepped into his view, and like a dork, I waved. His yellow eyes glanced at my hand moving in the air, and then they settled on me. He nodded.

"Did you see what he did?" I asked to no one in particular, grinning.

"Yes," Tree answered, slowly stepping closer to Aesop, as if afraid he might spook him.

"He's acknowledging you, dear," Abigail said. "He knows all about you and Jack."

"Aesop is cool," Rex said, moving beside me. He elbowed my side, and when I looked at him, he continued. "He loves classical music like Mozart and Beethoven."

"How do you know he likes it?" I asked, picturing a cartoonish version of Aesop pretending to be a conductor, leading an orchestra by moving his wings up and down to the rhythm of the music. Of course he was wearing wire spectacles in this animated fantasy of mine.

"I can tell by the color of his aura," Rex answered, "and by how relaxed he becomes."

"What's his aura like now?" Tree asked, inching his way closer to Aesop and stopping directly in front of him.

Rex tilted his head to the side and stared at our feathered friend. "Green, which means he's calm."

I hooked elbows with Tree and leaned into him. Aesop seemed like he was studying me. His yellow eyes danced around my form, as if he were sizing me up. Though I continued to hug Tree's arm, I felt Isadora bristle inside. *Who does he think he is? He has no right to judge me or go to the council of witches and rat on me. The dirty, rotten scoundrel is their spy. But maybe...*

"He appears to be interested in you," Tree said, poking through Isadora's mental tirade.

I blinked and focused my attention on Tree. His handsome face held an amusing smile. I wanted to kiss his luscious lips and fall into him and become one with him. Isadora's aggravating thoughts lifted, but as they did so, one suggestion whispered through me: *Aesop will let us know when one of our own is around. Yes, he will be useful after all.* I returned Tree's smile with an uneasy one. "I hope he likes me."

"Don't trouble yourself with such silliness, child," Abigail said, causing us to glance over our shoulders. She was bracing herself on a cane she must have had tucked away here. "He knows the plight you're in and has no means to pass judgment on you. His wisdom and intuition stretches across the boundaries of countless worlds, much like a light walker's does. Therefore, he harbors no malice toward you. He's simply getting acquainted with your essence."

"Why does he seem disinterested in Tree?" I asked, sounding slightly annoyed.

"He's not the one in jeopardy," Rex said in a matter-of-fact tone. When I shot him a look, he raised his hand as if he wanted to shield himself from my glare. "No offense, but Isadora's spirit was more or less forced into cryosleep onto your soul, and she has been awakened. You now have a powerful witch as a second consciousness to contend with. It's up to you to get her to merge with your soul. If she doesn't, things could get ugly."

I turned to Abigail and asked, "Is there a spell to unite her essence with mine?"

She nodded. "Yes, but we're not allowed to perform it."

"Why?" Tree asked. I looked at him. His brown eyes were filled with interest, but I could see a hint of irritation in them. He wasn't pleased with our current situation.

Abigail released a tired sigh. "We'd have to use dark magic and that would go against nature. However, I will contact the council. I'm sure they're already aware of Carrie's unfortunate situation and are probably pondering a solution as we speak."

"What do you think happened to Isadora's old flame, Jaegar?"

Tree wanted to know. "What he did to Isadora deprived her from moving on to the next realm, get counseling from her guides, and help from the light walkers." The corner of his eyes tightened, along with his lips. His tone became harsh as he continued. "Because of his dumbass mistake, Carrie is the one who has to correct it. He basically stole a life from Carrie."

"I have no doubt," Abigail replied, "there were consequences to Jaeger's insubordination." Slowly, Abigail turned and inched her way toward the door, using the cane to support her weight.

Anger swept through me, then sorrow, catching me off guard. My hand fluttered to my neck as an image of bluish gray eyes, welling with tears, came to me. I could almost feel Jaegar's strong grip around my neck and smell the alcohol on his breath. I knew that he had to be intoxicated in order to have the balls to end me. And as he choked the life from my body, he tearfully begged for my forgiveness.

His masculine voice dominated my thoughts, wheeling me back to the last words spoken to me in the year 1630 in an empty barn where we met in secret to cloak our relationship.

"Please forgive me, Isadora. I love you. I'm risking my soul to save yours. Do you not understand? Dark magic has bewitched you, my love. I cannot stand idly by and watch Dornheim send you to the Drudenhaus, where you'd be tortured beyond repair, then executed. I also can no longer bear the silence I have taken regarding your friendliness with wicked beings. I need to protect you from them and save your soul. I must eliminate this body and your spirit."

He tried to kiss me on the lips, but my struggle prevented him from doing so. Something inside me broke.

My heart.

I stopped fighting him and stared into his watery eyes, projecting my thoughts through my gaze:

Why must you do this?

I had a plan of escape.

I trusted you and gave you my heart.

Why?

My vision blurred, but I continued to gaze upon him and silently repeated why?

He kissed my lips with a fierceness that stilled my thoughts. "Forgive me, my love." His grip tightened around my throat, and he began to chant. My mind whirled with gibberish thoughts as I tried to pry his hands off my neck, desperate for survival. He backed me against the wall, next to the barn door and pressed his legs on mine, preventing me from kicking him. I went to claw his face, but weakness took hold of my limbs. I could no longer fight. I turned my head toward the window beside us and silently said goodbye to the star-filled night and full moon. Then a dark, empty space possessed me, and that was the last I could remember.

"Are you alright?" Tree asked me, pulling me into his arms.

I hugged his waist. "I'm... I'm fine."

"You had a distant look in your face, and you began to tremble." He cradled my cheeks in his hands and gently tilted my chin up with his thumb. "Were you remembering something?"

"Yes," I answered. "I don't want to talk about it, though."

He kissed my forehead. "I think it's time to leave. Carrie has had enough for one day."

I dropped my arms and took his hand, interlacing our fingers. Aesop appeared to be sleeping, but when Tree and I looked at him, he opened his eyes. His yellow orbs darted between the both of us, then rested on Tree.

"He's recognizing Jack as a future comrade," Abigail said from across the room. "My old eyes cannot see him from here, but he sent me this message and wanted me to share it with you."

"Interesting," Tree murmured.

"Did he say anything about me?" I asked, watching Aesop shift his attention to me.

"He's concerned about you."

I didn't comment. I knew the situation; we all knew. The vivid memory of Jaegar snuffing the life from my body kicked me into a somber mood. We made our way back upstairs and said our goodbyes. I didn't say much as Tree and I headed to town in the Scout. The moon was full and bright, like it was the night I took my last breath. I stared out the window, watching the forest whiz by as we drove beneath the towering cliffs. There was a lot I needed to process, and I was thankful Isadora had curled away somewhere inside me and gone silent. I could feel her sorrow though; it was part of me now, like it should have always been. I rubbed my neck and wondered if I'd have issues with it now. Would I be able to handle wearing a turtleneck or a choker necklace? I recalled reading about a woman who was deathly afraid of water. She went through a past life regression, only to discover in a previous life she drowned.

"Does your throat hurt?" Tree asked.

"No, why?"

His eyes shifted to my palm resting on my throat. "You were rubbing it."

I dropped my hand. Hugging myself, I peered out the windshield to admire the ocean. The watery surface resembled black glass, capturing the silver moon's round image in its dark, aquatic web. I had a sudden urge to get skyclad and dance under this gorgeous ball.

Skyclad?

I'd never heard of such a word before, let alone thought it, but I knew what it was now. The term stood for nudity, ritual nudity to be exact. Those thoughts of being naked beneath the moonlight with my bare feet hopping and skipping against the earth in a witches' dance were foreign to me, yet appealing.

"Carrie?"

"Hmmm?" I glanced at him. Worry marred his features. "I'm fine. I'm just... I don't know." I shrugged.

"You don't know what?"

"I'm changing, and I don't know if it's a good thing." I sighed. "I want to experience something I've never thought of before, and the idea fills me with joy."

"Like what?"

I laughed, though nothing was funny. "Do you really want to know?"

"Yeah. In fact, I want you to tell me everything. I can't help you if you don't."

"Okay, well..." I shifted in my seat so I was facing him. "I have the sudden desire to dance under the moonlight naked."

"Like, Paige," he said, unfazed by my admission.

"Like, Paige?" I echoed, trying to figure out why he would mention her. He opened his mouth to elaborate, but I beat him to the punch. "Yes, like Paige; however, she never attempted it before, at least not that I'm aware of." I paused and then asked, "How do you know this about Paige?" I was sure she never told him. It was our little secret. I then recalled how Tree knew, but he said it before I could stop him this time.

"Remember before your accident? You and Nathan were arguing, and you told him how Paige always wanted to dance around a bonfire naked while playing her whistle beneath a full moon."

I nodded as a stirring sensation entered my solar plexus. I could feel Isadora's consciousness riding next to mine, like it did earlier. A partnership between us was taking place, and because of the memories I now had of her life, I welcomed it. I listened to her, took her direction, and allowed her to influence my actions. She was attached to my soul, so I was still in control. Not to mention the crystal helped subdued the sharp edges of her personality.

Paige is one of us.

A burst of energy slammed into me, causing me to sit straight. Paige and I would certainly make a great team, but I already knew that. However, once I remembered how to break the curse I placed on my coven, I could introduce her to them. They would love and accept her with open arms. First thing first, though, I needed to figure out the damn counter-curse.

A blazing thought punched through my consciousness, dismantling all others.

One word.

Ayperos.

My mind stretched for the importance of his name, for the shadow of words which lurked and trailed behind it. But grasp it I could not. The faint memory sifted through the sieves of my spirit and faded away. Instant frustration took hold of me, but I recovered quickly when the realization came: I had a lead. Soon the rest would follow. I had no doubt.

Tree glanced at me. "Are you hungry?"

"I am," I admitted. A few moments ago, I would have said no, but now I was famished. I pulled my cell phone out of my purse to check the hour—9:18. I still had plenty of time before I was expected home by my overprotective mother. "I'm in the mood for some seafood."

Tree smiled. "You read my mind. I know just the place."

* * *

The white, clapboard restaurant sat on the pier overlooking the Columbia River. The structure reminded me of a large, one-story, 1930s house, with tinted windows lining the front. The red door with an anchor attached to it more or less told you this was a seafood joint. If you were too thick to get the hint, the wonderful smell of fried cod would surely give it away.

"I love the food here," I gushed, sitting in a red vinyl booth across from Tree. "I think it's cool how Max's dad bought this joint, and someday Max will own it." I looked at the wide chalkboard hanging above a glossy, dark wood bar. Tonight's specials were written on it. "I think I'm going to order the shrimp basket. What about you?"

"I'm feeling like clam strips, beer-battered cod, and chips," Tree answered, shrugging out of his coat. "So are you going to—"

"Max!" I waved my hand in the air when he spotted me. He was delivering food to another couple two tables over. I was surprised to see him still working here because Paige told me he planned on going to culinary school to become a chef. I wondered if his plans fell through.

"Hey." He smiled, revealing cute dimples. I always thought he was adorable with his short, black spiky hair and blue eyes. "How are you two?"

Tree shook his hand. "Great. What about you?"

"I thought you'd be in Paris or somewhere else, studying the culinary arts," I said.

His smile slipped into a frown, and sadness entered his eyes. "My dad has pancreatic cancer. He..." Max looked away and cleared his throat. He swiped a hand across his face and focused his attention on the salt shaker. "He knew he wasn't well a while ago, and I think that's why he bought this restaurant... for me... for my future. He knows how much I love Astoria, and I also think he wants me close by to help my mom when she needs it. He's never confided in me about those things, but he doesn't have to."

"Omigod, Max." I took his hand and gave it a comforting squeeze. "I'm so sorry about your dad. I know you two are close."

"If you ever need anything," Tree told him, "let us know. We're here for you, man."

Max tried to smile, but failed. "Thanks. Watching my dad's health decline has been tough, but we'll get through it. I have a good crew here and the doctors are doing everything they can for him."

"Good," I said. "Maybe he'll beat it."

"My mom is a nurse," Tree told him. "She's the best. If you don't mind, I can give her your phone number, so she can talk to your dad. There may be a new experimental treatment that might work."

"Thanks. I'll have my mom call yours. I think that would be best." Max glanced over his shoulder. There were two middle-aged men waiting at the cash register. "I'll be right back." He stepped away from our table, then stopped when his waitress spotted the gentlemen and rang up their order. "Never mind." His gaze shifted on us. "Do you need a menu?"

Tree shook his head. "No, we're cool. We already know what we want."

Tree and I gave Max our order. A few minutes later, he arrived with our drinks—Pepsi for me and root beer for Tree. After he left to go check on our food, Tree asked me if I was going to get naked in the forest and dance around. If so, he wanted to be there to make sure no one else would be around, and he'd love to see it. Waggling his eyebrows, he took a deep drink of his pop.

I laughed. "What if Paige was with me or..."

My coven?

"Or what?" He set his glass down and leaned forward, resting his forearms on the table.

A sudden boldness took hold of me. "My coven," I said, repeating Isadora's words. I gave him a challenging stare and slowly stirred my Pepsi with the red straw. The thought of once again being with my people brought such a joyous elation to me that it was difficult to contain. I held back a smile.

"Ah, you mean the drenths?" He said, raising his eyebrows, meeting my challenge.

"You say the name as if it's poison on your tongue," I said, even though he hadn't, but I wanted to test his reaction to such a simple accusation.

"No," he replied, watching me closely. "I don't even know what drenth means, but the name doesn't sound good. Why don't you tell me?"

I glanced away from our table and saw Max coming toward us with two plates. He looked tired, and his eyes held a somberness that caused my heart to ache for him. If only there was a way I could help him. An idea came to me, and I latched onto it before thinking it through.

"You look like you could sleep for a hundred years," I said to Max, catching Tree watching me from the corner of my eye. I glanced at him and winked.

Max set our food on the table. "I'm whipped," he admitted. "Between working here twelve plus hours a day and taking care of my parents, it's running me thin." He yawned and rubbed the side of his face.

I tilted my head to the side, a mischievous smile forming on my face. "What if I told you I could give you a boost of energy?"

Tree shifted in his seat. The vinyl moaned and squeaked beneath him. "I'm sure Max has tried large doses of caffeine to ward off the fatigue."

"I have," Max said. "I've even been drinking Red Bull."

"Humor me and give me your hand," I said, offering mine.

"Why don't you show Max the cool crystal charm Grams gave you?" Tree suggested.

I ignored him, knowing if I touched it I'd go back to being my boring useless self. Besides, I was curious to see what would happen, and I was enjoying this sense of power uncoiling inside me. I was still in control. I knew right from wrong. My identity was intact. If I could master these small tasks without going rogue and blasting everything in my path, I would no longer need the necklace and Isadora would join my soul.

A playful expression entered Max's face. "Are you going to try something on me you learned from *Buffy the Vampire Slayer*?" He laughed. "I know how much you love that show."

"We all do," Tree said, flashing his goofy grin, but the nervous glint in his eyes betrayed his easygoing manner. "Don't embarrass yourself, Carrie. Please."

Embarrass myself? Hah! We'll see about that.

I took Max's hand. "Close your eyes." He hesitated, then complied. "Imagine a time when you had the most energy and how alive you felt," I instructed and concentrated on blocking the chattering noise surrounding us. An image of Max playing baseball floated through my mind. Other kids I knew were in this vision, including me, Tree, Brayden, and Paige. We were fourteen. The sun was shining, and the green grass was so bright, it almost hurt our eyes. The image shifted on Paige gripping a bat and Max behind her, adjusting her elbow to show her how to hold it properly. I stilled the picture in my mind, narrowed it on him, and chanted under my breath. I recycled the energy from that time and transferred it into him now. My hair gently lifted off my shoulders, strands tickling my cheeks. An electrical current flowed through my veins, down my arm, straight to my palm against his. The lights flickered, and a loud "snap" issued between us, zapping us. Reflectively, our hands jerked apart.

Tree half stood. "Just a parlor trick, folks," he announced to the customers who were staring at us, wide-eyed and open-mouthed. "No need to gawk." He sat back down and shook his head in disapproval. "Carrie, you can't—"

"Wow, Carrie. How in the hell did you do that?" Max asked. He laughed. "I feel great. This... this is amazing!"

I wanted to squeal and clap my hands. I didn't. A strong sense of power and pride overtook the need to do so. I had to compose myself. The simple spell I performed on Max was only the beginning.

I shrugged. "What I did was easy. We're made up of energy, which is eternal. With meditation and concentration, anyone can achieve the same thing." There was more to it than what I was letting on, but my answer would quench his curiosity... or maybe not. I turned my attention on my shrimp basket and chowed down.

"What do you mean?" he asked.

"Think about it. Google it, and do some research," I told him between mouthfuls.

"I will." His gaze swept toward the kitchen, then on me. "I have to go back to work. Thank you so much, Carrie. I don't know if the burst of energy I now have is in my head or what, but I feel like I can run a marathon. You rock."

"My pleasure," I replied, taking a drink of my Pepsi so a hundred watt smile wouldn't break across my face. Truth be told, I was sharing in his elation on so many levels. In this life, I possessed no outstanding or extraordinary abilities. Sure I was good with hair and accessories, but other than those two things, I was yawn-worthy and nothing more. But now... now Isadora's spirit was alive and active inside me. We were one and the same, and I was enjoying it.

"Dinner is on me," Max said, spinning around and jogging to the kitchen.

"Hey, thanks," Tree said.

"Thank you," I called out. "He's so nice." I reached across the table and stole one of Tree's clam strips. "Ya know, he's carrying a torch for Paige." Tree was staring at me. His lips were in a tight line, his eyes all squinty. I stopped chewing. "What?"

"You need to control yourself," he said in a low voice. "Nobody can know what you're capable of." He gestured toward where Max was standing a few moments ago. "What you did for Max was irresponsible."

"Maybe so," I said, bored. I hovered my fingertip over my straw and slowly moved it around, imagining it going in a circle. To my delight, it stirred my pop without me even touching it. This was fun. "But Max deserves to get a little boost of energy, considering the enormous amount of stress he's under. Don't you think?" I pulled my attention from my drink, onto Tree. He was glaring at my finger. In one swift move, he reached across the table and pushed it away from my glass. "What the hell?"

"Enough," he said, his tone sounding like a deep growl. He slid out of his seat across from me and moved to my side of the booth, making me scoot over. Before I could object, he took my hand and wrapped it around the crystal. "You need to resist these powers cropping up inside you. Do you understand? If you don't, they will destroy you."

He kept his hand on mine. My palm grew warm. My heart raced. Chaotic thoughts impaled my ability to reason. My head swam. I closed my eyes and slowly breathed in through my nose and out my mouth. A promise blew into my consciousness, sweeping aside the confusion, lifting the debris so my focus was now clear.

I will not make the same mistake as before.

I sighed and opened my eyes. I kissed the back of Tree's hand. "I'm fine. I got carried away, and I'm sorry."

His hand went to the back of my head. He gently pulled me to him, embracing me. "I don't want to lose you, Carrie," he whispered in my ear. "You must think things through before you act."

I touched his face. "Don't worry. I will think before I act. Okay?"

He nodded but didn't look convinced.

He was the love of my life, just like Jaegar was. Jaegar had betrayed me. This time around, I would do what I should have done hundreds of years ago with Jaegar. This time around, I would not fail.

Chapter Eleven

Tree

C arrie had me seriously worried. I didn't think the amethyst she wore was working worth a damn. I took my last thought back. The crystal was working in a sense. It tamed Isadora's strong personality and kept her at bay. However, her presence made frequent appearances, and Carrie seemed to enjoy having Isadora around. I understood the allure and excitement in being able to do magic. Hell, in all honesty, it fascinated me. But if Carrie didn't get a grip on herself soon, we were in deep shit.

I still needed to figure out my part in all of this. I had no idea how I was supposed to help her. Grams had too much faith in me. Sure, I was an apprentice light walker. Sure, Michael and Gabriel blessed me with their presence. Yeah, my case was a special one. But so what? Those things were of no use to me since I don't have the foggiest idea on what the hell to do. The only tools I knew I had in my arsenal were my perception, and I could keep a relatively clear head. Although I feared my love for Carrie would gloss them over and obstruct my judgment on the matter at hand, I prayed it would not.

When I took Carrie home, I reopened our discussion about the drenths. She never answered my question about why the strange name.

I was curious about it, along with everything else in her prior life. I also wanted to observe her reaction to this matter.

"Dornheim was the one who gave my coven members that despicable name." Carrie stared out the windshield. Her hands balled into a fist in her lap.

"Why? What does it mean?" I was driving through downtown, past the theater, coffee shop, bookstore, and café. The golden hue from the streetlamps poured through the windows. Carrie looked at me, and something dark skittered across her face. Her eyes turned hard. I paused at a crosswalk to allow a young couple, each carrying bags in one hand and a coffee in the other, to cross in front of us. I turned my full attention to Carrie as I waited.

"He did it to put fear and loathing into the hearts of others," she said in disgust. "The name derives from his invention. He created a dark fairy tale, which bloated the people in our village and the ones nearby with filthy lies about us."

"The name stuck," I said more to myself than her, thinking of Rex yelling the same name earlier today.

"Yes," she said, looking away and watching the pedestrians in front of us stroll across the courthouse square beneath the large skeletal oaks.

"Was any of it true?" I turned my blinker on to make a right.

"Of course not," she snapped. She took a deep breath and sighed. "At least, not all of it."

It didn't take a rocket scientist to realize Isadora was the one conversing with me. Yes, it was Carrie, I reminded myself, but she was allowing Isadora to take center stage. Not good. I decided to carry on with our conversation to get to know Isadora much better and to see what I was up against.

"Do you mind telling me about it?" I asked.

She unzipped her purse and pulled her phone out. "I'm going to text Mom," she said when I sent her a questioning look. "She'll love the fact that I'm keeping her posted on my whereabouts, which I rarely do." Her thumbs slowly moved across the keypad like she was afraid she would hit the wrong letter. "Maybe this will ease her off my back."

"What are you telling her?" I was definitely talking to Isadora; she was just using Carrie's memories to portray her. I knew it without a doubt, because Carrie was a whiz at texting and would never be so awkward.

"I'm telling her we finished eating dinner at Max's dad's restaurant."

She set her cell on her lap. "I'll answer your questions," she said. "However, I don't want you to take me home yet. For a conversation such as this, a much more suitable place is in order."

My heart skipped several beats. I couldn't deny the fact I was both intrigued and fascinated by her. However, my awareness of those feelings allowed me to take a step back and have the presence of mind to act in a reasonable manner. "Where do you suggest we go?"

Her cell made a tinkling noise, alerting her of a text. She picked it up, but answered me before she read it. "I want to go to the woods behind Paige's house. I've always loved it there." She read the message and a triumphant smile crossed her face. "Last minute change of plans. Dad is taking Mom to see a midnight movie. She said she doesn't know when they'll be home." Carrie answered her back. I noticed she was texting fast this time, then she placed the phone back in her purse. "She lifted my curfew and told me to be home at a reasonable time."

"Sweet," I said. "She must be having a wonderful time."

Carrie nodded. "When Dad wants to, he can be such a romantic."

"Do you want to hang out at the treehouse?" When we were eleven years old, me, Carrie, Paige, and Brayden built a bitchin' treehouse, half a mile away from Paige's house, deep in the forest. We all had fond memories of our special place, so I thought maybe Carrie wanted to revisit it. I was wrong.

"No," she replied. "I prefer to stand among the trees beneath this wonderful moon." She leaned forward and peered out the windshield, up at the sky. The moon was full and bright. Its white light stretched across a dark canvas, illuminating the wispy clouds floating across the twinkling stars. "I think it would be grand if we could light a bonfire while we're there."

"Do you plan to get naked?" I tried to sound nonchalant, but my thoughts were throwing images of her beautiful, bare body at me. I felt a stirring in my jeans and abruptly halted those racy images. "The temperature is too chilly to be nude outside."

"Ja. Schade, weil ich es gern möchte." She flopped against the seat and sighed.

Startled by her shifting to German, I translated what she said. "Yes. Too bad because I would like to." Yup, I was definitely talking to Isadora again.

She crossed her arms and nodded.

"I don't have a lighter or matches on me," I said, thinking about how I would start a fire and wondered if our old pit remained there. The last time we used it was over a year ago, the summer before Paige met Nathan.

"Don't worry," she said. "I think I might have that part handled."

I raised my eyebrows, and a mischievous grin formed on her face.

Carrie's grin.

Now I was confused as to whom I was talking to. Regardless though, she piqued my curiosity, and I was anxious to see what tricks she had up her sleeve. She was still my Carrie, I reminded myself, and I'd be a dumb ass not to take the opportunity to listen to what she had to say about her life as Isadora, as well as witness whatever magic she remembered how to perform. What happened back at the restaurant was flat out carelessness on her part. There was no question about it. However, I had to give her the benefit of the doubt. Carrie was probably overwhelmed with the memories and dealing with Isadora's spirit. Granted, I had my suspicions about her allowing Isadora to speak for herself, but then again, maybe I was wrong. Maybe she was struggling to control a part of herself, who seemed to be quickly introducing things to her she once knew, which ultimately was impairing her judgment. Whatever the case may be, I would have to reaffirm to her it wasn't cool to display her powers in public. She would be making a huge mistake if she did.

"Carrie," I said, pulling onto Paige's street, which was thickly forested. There were only three houses on this road. Each was spread evenly from the other, with cathedral trees in rows separating them. Paige's two-story gray and white bungalow was at the end in a cul-de-sac, nestled among the timber. "Or should I say, Isadora?" I parked in Paige's driveway, turned off the Scout, and gave Carrie my full attention.

She ran a straight line with her fingertip down the front of my chest and looked at me through long lashes. "Who do you want me to be?" Her voice was low and seductive. I must have had a blank look on my face because she threw her head back and laughed. "It's Carrie, silly." She playfully shoved my shoulder. "I'm just messing with you."

I wasn't amused and took hold of her wrist. I placed her palm on my chest over my heart. "What do you feel?"

Her lips twisted sideways. "Your heart is beating fast."

"Why do you think?"

She pulled her hand away and shrugged.

"Because, right now, I have no idea who I'm talking to. My perception may be far superior than it was before, but it seems to be impotent when I'm around you. I would—"

Carrie giggled. "Impotent. I hope that's the only thing impotent around me."

I shook my head and despite my frustration, I cracked a smile.

"Okay, poor choice of words. Seriously though, I can't help you if you fuck with me. It's not cool."

"Okay. Okay," she said, raising her hands in surrender. "I'm sorry. I didn't realize you couldn't tell the difference. But ya know, because that part of my spirit is now free, I am changing. I mean, if Jaegar wouldn't have performed that vicious spell, I'd probably be a lot smarter, have more confidence and already be a practicing witch in this time." Her hands rested in her lap, but when she told me this, she dug her nails into her thighs. The moonlight, streaming through the windows, allowed me to see the tears glistening in her eyes. "He basically took a life from me, and I hate him for it. But at least now I'm gaining what was once stolen from me."

My heart went out to her. It killed me to see her so unhappy. I understood Jaegar's reasoning behind his actions. He didn't want her to be tortured or become a dark spirit afterward. In his mind, I imagined he thought he was doing the right thing. However, he had no right to take her free will away, and although I could see his side on the matter, I thought he made a terrible mistake.

I cradled her cheek in my hand and wiped away a stray tear with my thumb. "I promise you," I vehemently said, "I will never betray your trust and..." A disturbing thought crashed through the words I was about to say, dispersing them and forcing me to focus my attention on it instead.

Carrie is walking on thin ice. Don't make promises you might not be able to keep. The battle has not been won yet, and you may have to betray her in order to save her.

I closed my eyes and leaned my forehead against hers. Silently, I told myself I would never in a million years betray her like Jaegar had done to Isadora. I'd find a better way, I vowed.

"And?" Carrie prompted.

I opened my eyes and leaned back. "And I will help you through this," I said, tucking a lock of hair behind her ear.

She bit her lip and nodded.

I wanted to kiss her, but before I could make an attempt, she turned and hopped out. I followed her around Paige's house to the back, into the forest where our fire pit was.

"Do you still want to know some things about Isadora's coven?" Carrie asked, halting next to the boulders circling a pit of dirt and dried leaves.

I picked some sticks up off the ground and tossed them in the center of the stones, wondering how we were going to light the bark. "Yes. I want to know everything."

She gestured for me to sit on one of the large logs facing the pit. "I don't have a lighter or matches," I reminded her. I sat down, anxious to see what she was going to do.

"Don't worry, my love. I have this one handled."

My love?

She threw her hands out, palms facing the branches in the circle, and she chanted in Latin. I recognized some of the words, but not all. She was saying something about earth, fire, and blessings. A flame in the shape of a thin, vertical line shot up in the air, well above the trees. I jumped to my feet. An umbrella of sparks rained down around us, lighting the dark sky, reminding me of fireworks. I grabbed Carrie's wrist and pulled her to me. As we backed away, I heard her repeating the word shit in German.

I took hold of Carrie's arm and turned her to me. "You need to stop this now; otherwise, the forest and Paige's house, might go up in flames."

"Omigod!" Carried shrieked. Panic entered her face. "I don't know if I can." She turned away from me, looking at the sparks arcing in the air as the fiery tube kept shedding. "Why is this happening?"

"Do you remember a water or wind spell to put it out?"

"I don't understand," Carrie said to herself, dumbfounded. "I performed the fire spell plenty of times in the 1600s, and I never received these results before."

"Carrie." I took her hand, and when she faced me, I lightly shook her. "You need to stop this now. Do you understand me?"

She blinked, her eyes round and haunted. "I... I."

I cupped her face in my hands. "Focus. Think."

The sparks hitting the branches fizzled, probably due to the moisture clinging to them from last night's rain. Time was running out, though. The unknown was upon us. For all I knew, the fire could result in an explosion or some similar shit, and then we'd be toast. Literally.

Carrie stared past me, dazed. I wasn't sure if she was trying to remember an antidote or what, but I couldn't wait for her any longer. I had to do something. I kicked dirt into the pit, but the blazing tube didn't waver. Instead, a shimmering light of orange and yellow snaked up it, discharging crackling sounds as it did.

Holy hell.

Whatever the thing was, I think I pissed it off. I stepped away and clasped my hands behind my head. I watched as it slithered upward, my heartbeat thumping in my ears. An angry spark flew out, landing on the ground nearby, making contact with some underbrush. A flame ignited, engulfing the shrubs and twigs in one fell swoop. An owl hooted, but I couldn't see him.

Aesop?

I looked at Carrie. She stood with her feet apart, her arms raised above her head, palms skyward. Once again, she chanted in Latin.

Something caught the edge of my vision. Between the dark pockets of trees was a pair of glowing eyes.

Drenth. I was sure of it.

I stuck my hand in my pocket where I kept my knife and wrapped my fingers around the handle. A gentle breeze blew across my face. Carrie's voice grew louder and stronger as she continued to recite the incantation. A fierce wind kicked up, lifting dirt, broken sticks, and debris off the ground.

"Make it rain," I shouted, knowing the fire was going to spread even more, because the blowing sparks would cause other things to burn.

Carrie stopped what she was doing. Her hair whipped her face. She held it back and glanced over her shoulder at me. "What?"

"Rain," I yelled. "We need rain." I pointed to the burning shrub, which must have ignited another one when I wasn't looking. Now there was a growing path of fire, catching any dry item it could latch onto. The flaming tube in the pit seemed impenetrable. It never once faltered and continued to make popping and crackling sounds. The only good thing was it stopped producing sparks.

Carrie nodded and resumed her previous stance. In a powerful voice, she chanted a new spell. The wind abruptly stopped. A peal of thunder broke across the sky. I looked up. A web of blue and red lightning flashed in intervals through the clouds, followed by a loud rumbling sound, reminding me of when I was a child. To ease my fear of storms, my mom would tell me the angels were bowling.

The thick smell of rain pressed down upon me. I watched as the clouds formed an inverted funnel, displaying a brilliant gold color in its center. Then, as if some unknown force, pushed down on its apex, pancaking it, the clouds flattened and rain fell. The vertical line of fire disappeared.

"Woo-hoo! I did it!" Carrie said, jumping up and down.

I bent over and rested my hands on my knees, not caring about the rain pouring off my face. I breathed a sigh of relief, trying to calm my nerves and steady my heart rate. "Thank you," I whispered to God, the universe, to whomever had a hand in saving our asses. I stood and through the sheet of rain, I spotted Carrie on her knees hugging and petting a drench. When I approached her, a low growl issued from him. I stuck my hand back in my pocket and halted. I didn't want to kill him, and Carrie would be pissed if I did. Hell, she probably would never speak to me again, but if I had to, I would. There was no way in hell I was going to die in an attack if he went all Cujo on my ass.

"He's a good guy," Carrie said to the dog.

"Let's go." I stuck my hand out, so she could take it. "We're both soaked. Time to leave." I wasn't in the mood to deal with her stubbornness and hoped she would zip it. We both had a long day, and this night was edging toward a nightmare. I had enough.

The canine's eyes darted to my hand and then my face. His lips curled over his sharp teeth, but no sound came from him. I stared him down, silently warning him to back off.

Carrie released her arms from around his huge body and tenderly rubbed his face. "He's not going to hurt us, Driscol." She must have seen something in his eyes, because she laughed and kissed him on the head. "Yes, I know it's you. I missed you." She leaned over and whispered something in his ear. Whatever she said, it set his tail wagging like crazy. He licked her face and ran off into the trees.

"Who's Driscol? How did you know it was him, and what did you say to him?" I asked, pulling her to her feet. Or was it Isadora? Despite her wet hair sticking to her face and water dripping off the tip of her nose, she looked happy.

My gut twisted.

Something wasn't right.

Nothing in the world meant more to me than Carrie's happiness, but I felt a darkness attached to her elation, and I didn't know why. Maybe because of all the events transpiring today, or because it bothered me that she'd reunited with one of the drenths. As soon as my mind thought of the name, a heaviness settled in my chest. I wonder if she was going to—

"Driscol," she said, interrupting my train of thought while we headed out of the forest, "is part of my coven. I knew it was him because on his side in small brown dots is the letter D. Each one of my members has the letter of their first name on their side like his." Carrie gathered her hair into a ponytail and squeezed the water from it before stepping into the Scout. After I settled in the driver's seat and started the engine, she continued. "As for what I told him"—she flashed me a clandestine smile—"that's between Driscol and me."

I gripped the steering wheel and flexed my jaw. "You've got to be joking, right?" I could hear the annoyance in my voice and did my best not to get pissed off, but my tolerance was wearing thin at the moment. Ever since Grams did the awakening spell on Carrie, it seemed like her whole persona was nothing but a clustered fuck. How in the hell was I supposed to help her sort this out when she was working against me?

She made a zipping gesture over her lips and smirked.

I ground my teeth and pulled off the road into a wooded playground. I parked but kept the engine on so the heater would run. "You made some dumb ass mistakes tonight," I said, trying my best to keep my voice steady. "You may be remembering how to perform some magic, but obviously you're out of practice. Don't you realize you could have burnt up the whole damn forest and Paige's house?"

She sighed. "I realize what you're saying is true. It is clear I need to focus more."

"It's clear," I said, "that you need Grams' guidance to help you learn how to focus."

"Hah! I don't need that old bag of bones to teach me such things," she scoffed. "I can teach myself. All I have to do is retrain my brain through meditation on how to center myself. I will make it a nightly routine from now on, so I will not make the same blunders I have tonight."

In one swift move I unzipped Carrie's jacket, throwing her off guard, revealing the crystal necklace hanging over her sweatshirt. I grabbed her hand, pressed the stone into her palm, and closed her fingers around it. Stunned, she blinked and gaped at me.

"I'd like to speak to my girlfriend please, instead of a bullheaded and prideful witch," I announced. I made up my mind, then. I'd have to make a personal visit with Grams and air my grievances.

"I'm sorry, Tree," Carrie said. "I was so scared when the fire got out of hand. I didn't know what to do. I was so sure of myself, but then my thoughts ran away from me. I would have died if something happened to Paige's house and to the forest."

I embraced her. "I know. So would I."

"We are the same person," she said. "Isadora and me."

"Doesn't seem that way," I replied, releasing my arms and sitting back so I could look at her. "Like now, I'm talking to you instead of her."

Carrie poked her chest and forehead. "Isadora is here and here." She shrugged. "I can't really explain it."

"But she's separate from you," I pointed out. "Therefore, you have another entity dwelling within you."

Carrie shook her head in protest. "The situation I'm in now is not like when Aosoth possessed me. Isadora is attached to my soul, so I have control and know what's going on. I do sometimes give into her and allow her to respond on her own accord."

I frowned. "Bad idea." I didn't like this one bit.

"Why?"

"Because when you hold the amethyst like you are now, you're back to being yourself. When you're not, Isadora's strong personality filters through yours and monopolizes it." I rubbed the side of my face and yawned. "We need to fix this soon before I lose you to her."

"You're not going to lose me," she reassured. "I'll be okay."

I yawned again. I was beat and needed to sleep. I was to the point where I was too tired to care about anything. We would deal with the situation in the morning. I pulled out of the playground and headed to Carrie's house.

"Don't you believe me?" she asked.

"Believe you about what?" I was lost. What was she talking about?

"That everything will be okay. You didn't answer me."

"I don't know. I hope so. I'll let you in on a little secret, though." I glanced at her, and she made a gesture with her hands, urging me to continue. "I'm fascinated by the magic you can do and intrigued by your past life as Isadora in the 1600s. I want to know everything about it."

"Well, then," she said with an endearing smile, "I will tell you what I remember from that century, including about my coven or drenths as that bastard Dornheim so wrongly labeled them."

"Awesome," I replied.

I must have gotten a second wind, because I was now alert and anxious to hear what she had to say. I pulled into her driveway. Her house was dark, which told me her parents weren't home yet. Her mom did tell her they'd be out late, I reminded myself. Carrie invited me in, so we could talk in the comforts of her living room. Her parents wouldn't mind. Hell, they'd known me most of my life and were good friends with my folks. As we settled in on her couch, my mind spun with all the events we went through today. I couldn't help but wonder if we made a huge mistake doing the awakening spell and if what she was about to tell me would change the way I felt about her and our relationship.

Chapter Twelve

Carrie

I really didn't know what to tell Tree. Should I let him know my father was a farmer, my mother died from some horrid plague, and I had a younger brother whom I adored?

Wait a minute.

I had a brother?

Yes, you did... we did. His name was Niklas.

I suddenly knew what was going on, why I couldn't remember everything. The problem was the amethyst Abigail gave to me. The charm hindered my conscious mind from recalling finer details of my life as Isadora. In fact, the crystal kept parts of her at bay more than I realized. The memory of Niklas happened to sift through me, and Isadora confirmed it. I should have remembered him right away. It irked me that the memory of his existence didn't come to me sooner. I'd have to remedy the situation soon. I knew a solution and would have to test it once I was alone.

I'll help you tell Jack what he wants to know. We can enlighten him together.

"Niklas," I said, when his name rolled through my mind again after I silently agreed with Isadora to team up with her on satisfying

Tree's curiosity. Tree raised his eyebrows and waited for me to clarify. "He was my younger brother and only sibling. I loved him with all of my heart. We were close."

"What happened to him?"

"He's... I hate saying this word." I made a face. "He's a drenth now."

Tree shifted in his seat and narrowed his eyes. "You cursed him like the others?" His tone wasn't accusing. It sounded more curious than anything, although I felt a stab of judgment on his part. He thought I made a foolish mistake, I imagined.

I swallowed against the lump forming in my throat. "Yes." I had no choice, was what I wanted to say. Underneath our noses, Dornheim had apprehended my father and detained him in the Drudenhaus where he was tortured relentlessly before he was burned at the stake. I'd be damned if I would have allowed Niklas to suffer the same fate.

"Was he a witch like you?"

"He was learning the craft," I said. "He pestered me for years to teach him what I knew. You see, the women in my family were witches. The men were farmers and known not to have an ounce of magical abilities. One day, after our mother's death, Niklas approached me. I was in my greenhouse seeking refuge from the sorrow I felt due to her passing. Niklas wanted to become the first male witch in our family. He believed he had a gift when it came to herbology because he was an excellent farmer. His skills in agriculture, along with his deep interest in learning the magical properties in plants, fueled this belief. It weighed heavily on him that he didn't think of it sooner. He had no doubt he could have saved our mother if he had the knowledge he now craved. I assured him our mother's demise wasn't his fault. None of us could have saved her. The gods needed her more than we did, so they claimed her. It was that simple. He couldn't accept my answer, and in a fit of rage, he cursed the gods. I chastised him for throwing such ugly words at them. His anger wasn't worth their wrath. He needed to bite his tongue."

"Wow," Tree said. "What happened? Did you decide to teach him what he wanted to know?"

I nodded. "I did. His ability to retain the knowledge needed for him to become an asset to my circle was impressive. Unfortunately, time was not on our side. A witch hunt exploded in neighboring villages, and before Niklas could discover if he was a caster such as myself, we heard of the Drudenhaus Dorheim erected."

"A witch's prison, right?" Tree asked.

"Yes," I said. "The Drudenhaus was where Dornheim and his henchmen tortured hundreds of people, including children as young as six months old." I held my stomach, feeling nauseous just thinking about the horrific acts during that time.

"Jesus Christ," Tree whispered, his face losing color.

"They used all kinds of horrid devices and inhumane tactics to get the confessions they desired," I went on in a low, careful voice. The subject we were on was difficult for me to talk about, and I really wanted to move past this conversation. "They didn't care that the stories were fictional, created by the rambling minds who sought relief from the suffering and agony bestowed upon them."

"What started it?"

I rubbed my eyes. They were burning. I was exhausted and needed to go to bed soon. I told myself I would after I shared what I thought Tree should know. It was important for me to get him to understand my life in the 1600s. I would like to have him in my court or at least derail his suspicions of me and my actions. I didn't need him to shadow my every move and spoil my plans.

"War devastated our area," I replied. "What followed after that were crop failure, hunger, and plagues. People blamed these misfortunes on the supernatural world, instead of taking a good look at our politicians. Dornheim took advantage of this opportunity for purely selfish and greedy reasons. He took charge of a network of informers. Once the hounds were let loose, no one was impervious to the frenzy of accusations that ignited. Even rich and powerful people fell victim to it. Dornheim and his officers would confiscate their properties and assets and divide the loot among them. Needless to say, they became extremely wealthy men from their devilish behavior."

"What about your father? Where was he in all of this?"

My gaze fell to my lap, where I twisted and untwisted my fingers.

Now would be the perfect time to play on his sympathies. Remember blind magic? Ayperos had taught us that. You compel people by dazzling their minds and dulling their reasoning.

Ayperos.

I used to dislike the guy, but now that I was remembering the role he played in my past life, my opinion of him was changing. Not all dark spirits were bad, hedonistic maybe, but not evil. Ayperos may not be as wicked as I once thought. I wasn't one hundred percent sure, but he seemed harmless. He had helped me—as Isadora—out of some sticky situations and also taught me dark magic. He was the one who—

"Carrie?"

I looked up to Tree's questioning eyes. "Huh?"

He touched my arm and gave it a gentle squeeze. "If you don't want to tell me about your father, I understand." He rubbed the side of his face and sighed. "I didn't realize how horrific and awful that time was for you. I feel bad for Isadora... for you both."

"He was taken from us," I blurted. I honestly had no intention to manipulate Tree's feelings to gain sympathy like Isadora wanted me to. It just happened. Tree was an empathic person, so my hands were clean on this one. "He was purchasing supplies when they apprehended him. Niklas and I didn't get word of our father's arrest until hours later." An overwhelming feeling of despair washed over me. My throat tightened.

I covered my mouth to block a sob. Tears spilled down my cheeks.

Tree embraced me. "I'm sorry. We don't need to talk about it. I can fill in the blanks to what happened next and why you cast a spell on your loved ones." He rocked me back and forth like a parent would to console a child.

I clung to him as clips of memories whizzed through my mind. A desperate need to get them to stop consumed me. The only way I knew how was to mention each one out loud, regardless if I sounded like a rambling fool. "Jaegar was the one who informed us about the matter. I wanted to use my power to free my father, but Dornheim's officers were coming after us. There was no time to do anything but quickly gather our effects and flee. Whatever we could shove into a bag and carry on our backs, we took, being mindful to take the most important of all our possessions. We exited through the back of my property, keeping to the shadows of the night, darting behind trees. I learned soon after..." I pulled back from Tree, wiped the tears off my cheeks, and cleared my throat. "I learned soon after that some of my coven members were snatched from their homes and beds: Margaretha, Tobias, Simone, and Ulrich. I was devastated and enraged. They pissed off the wrong witch, and I was ready to do battle with them to save my father, my friends, and all the innocents those monsters held captive. But in order to make it to safety, I had to swallow my fury and smash my lips together. For all we knew, there might be informers lingering by the stables and houses we had to past. Thankfully, we didn't have to go through the village in order to reach the forest. A thick fog had blanketed the ground, which was a tremendous help. For some reason the gods were favoring us. Why, I had no idea, but I thanked them nonetheless. Once we were deep within the woods, I could no longer keep silent. Jaegar, being the sensible and clearheaded one, talked me down."

Tree brushed a stray tear off the side of my chin. "What did he say?"

"He said, 'Anger accomplishes nothing,'" I answered. "My rage would only cause me to make foolish mistakes. I needed to think up a detailed plan that could take them down."

"Smart man."

Something snapped in me. Heat rose up the back of my neck. "Maybe, but he was a wolf in sheep's clothing. I was an idiot for relinquishing my heart to him," I spat.

Tree held his hands up, palms facing me. "Sorry. I didn't mean to rattle your cage. I know he was an ass monkey for what he did to you. What I meant was," Tree said, carefully choosing his words, "what he said is true. Allowing your anger to get the best of you and acting on it is not a smart idea. You need to have a level head, if you want to see the results you're aiming for."

The heat subsided from my face. I released a big yawn. I knew Tree meant well. He wasn't like Jaegar, I told myself and Isadora. He'd never betray us. My eyelids felt heavy. I closed them and said, "I know. I didn't mean to get so defensive."

"I understand." He shifted in his seat. The couch creaked with his movements. "Before you fall asleep on me, I need to ask you a question."

"I'm not falling asleep," I said. "I'm resting my eyes. But go ahead. Ask away."

"Yeah, okay... resting your eyes." He laughed. "Anyway, did you align yourself with the dark spirits and perform black magic?"

"Yes," I answered, "long before my father was charged with witchcraft." My mouth ran before I realized what I was saying. I was so tired that I didn't care what I told him. "Jaegar knew of my dealings. I trusted him with my most intimate secrets. Not all dark spirits are evildoers. Ask Nathan and Paige. They're quite chummy with Ameerah, who is one."

"You have a point," Tree said, surprising me.

"They're hedonistic, yes, I'll admit, but aren't we all? The thing is," I went on, my words drifting between half awake and half asleep. "Because of my connections with them, I was able to save Niklas, Driscol, Jorsten, and Lukas from being tortured and burned to death. I might have suffered the consequences, but it was worth it to save their hides."

I felt myself being lifted and held against a muscular frame. I submitted to it, allowing the dreams that were forming grasp me. They were about the last days of my life as Isadora. I was lowered onto something soft and comfortable. I turned on my side and sighed. Something gentle touched my forehead. Lips? Then sweet words reached my ears.

"I love you."

Chapter Thirteen

Tree

Thoughts of Carrie, Isadora, and everything that had happened today devoured me. After I tucked Carrie into bed, I went home. I was expecting to see the drenth—Driscol, I corrected myself—but I saw nothing out of the ordinary. My ride home was uneventful. When I entered my house, I went directly to my room, peeled off my clothes, only leaving my boxers on, and flopped on the bed. Sid jumped up and lay beside me, kneading the pillow.

"Hey, buddy," I said, my eyes half closed. I reached to pet his head. He was purring. The sound reminded me of a 1972 Ford Cleveland engine. It was a deep, choppy noise. My mind drifted to Brayden's car, a black 1970 ½ Rally Sports Camaro with two white racing stripes down the middle of the hood and trunk. The front had a split chrome bumper. God, it was a sweet ride. I wondered where Brayden was. After Paige told him her heart belonged to Nathan, Brayden took off. None of us heard from him since. His association with Bael was questionable; however, Brayden did defy Bael by snapping his neck. I imagined he wouldn't be stupid enough to join sides with the dark spirits.

Isadora.

Her name popped in my head. My mind scattered as sleep took hold of me. Isadora's actions were justifiable. I couldn't fathom being in a time like hers where you had no rights and could be brutally tortured or burned to death for no apparent reason. She couldn't trust anyone, though she trusted Jaegar and look what happened. She had relations with the dark spirits. *Not all of them were bad,* Carrie had pointed out. True, but the black magic Isadora learned from them must have gotten out of hand and tainted her spirit. I was guessing at this because Isadora held things back from me. She had said something to Driscol. Why wouldn't she share what she told him? Her brother Niklas must be alive—a drench.

My mind sank into a fitful sleep of chaos, death, and a gathering of lost souls. In the end, two words tied them all together.

Holy hell.

I woke with a start, the bed sheet plastered to my sweaty body. I clapped a hand on my chest, feeling my heart thumping wildly against it.

The reaping.

* * *

I had a lot of work to do today, and my dad made sure to remind me. He called me first thing in the morning from Vegas. I could hear the slot machines dinging and lively conversations buzzing around him. I assured him not to worry. I was a big boy. I knew what needed to be done. I had to pull an engine off a '69 GTO, tear it down, and inspect the crank shaft, pistons, rods, and main bearings. Not to mention search for excessive wear on the cylinder walls and check for metal shavings in the oil pan. Then, I had to take the engine to a machine shop. He thanked me and said they'd be home in four days. They wanted to visit my older brother Ren, who lived in Flagstaff, Arizona. I told my dad to send my love before we said goodbye.

Now, as I took the engine apart, I thought about calling Carrie, but it was only 7:48 in the morning, and I knew she'd still be asleep. I'd give her a couple hours and then call her. As I took off the air cleaner, I thought about yesterday. Carrie tried to convince me she was fine, but I wasn't so sure. Something didn't sit right with me, and every time I pondered it my gut twisted, like it did now. I hated to admit it, but there were a couple times when I didn't know who I was conversing with—Carrie or Isadora. However, there were some occasions when I could tell the difference by the way Carrie did things, like when she was texting her mom. I knew it was Isadora and not Carrie sending the message. The thought of her buddying up with Isadora entered my mind. Carrie did admit she sometimes gave into Isadora's spirit and allowed her to respond.

Hold up a minute.

I bet Grams knew all along there was a good possibility Carrie might empathize with Isadora and become her ally, rather than try to get Isadora's spirit to join her soul. However it was supposed to work. Hell, I didn't even know.

Dammit!

It hadn't even crossed my mind to ask Grams about the whole spirit-joining-the-soul process before she performed the awakening spell.

I stepped away from beneath the hood of the car and wiped my hands on a shop rag. I needed to speak to Grams now but had no way of doing so. I didn't have her phone number, and I couldn't bail on this job. I decided to focus on Rex and callout his name. It was a lame idea, and I'd feel like a jackass doing it, but I had nothing to lose except a few minutes of my time.

"Rex," I said, imagining his messy brown hair, his Suicidal Tendencies band T-shirt, and his Vans skater shoes. "Rex, I need to speak to you. It's important. Are you there?" This was ridiculous. What was I thinking? "Rex! Dude, I need your help."

"I haven't been called dude since like... forever," Rex said behind me.

I spun around and saw a grinning, freckle-faced twelve-year-old, dressed as I imagined him to be, hovering above the floor. Relief poured over me, and I smiled. "Thanks for showing. I wasn't sure if you'd hear me."

"Oooh, I heard you." Rex stuck a finger in his ear, a painful expression on his face.

"Huh?" I asked.

"I said..." Rex began, and then caught what I did. He closed his mouth and shook his head. Laughter danced in his amber eyes.

I pointed at him. "Hah. Hah. I gotcha, sucker."

"Aw, you got lucky. You caught me off guard."

"Yeah, whatever," I responded in a lighthearted tone. "Anyway, I need your help."

Rex did a sweeping bow. "I'm at your service."

The kid was a natural comedian. I wondered if he were alive like me, what sort of life would he be living? Too bad his mom never gave Grams the opportunity to help her communicate with him. What a shame the only family Grams had now was her ghostly great grandson.

"I need to speak to Grams, but I have a ton of work to do today, so I can't leave," I told Rex, gesturing toward the engine behind me.

"Do you want her phone number?" His eyes moved past me, and they lit up. "Wow. What a totally rad car."

"You should see my friend Brayden's. It's badass." Rex opened his mouth, but before he could peep a word, I continued. "I need my hands to work, and if I want to make it to her house with Carrie this evening, I need to use my time wisely."

"Then get to work." Rex clapped a couple times. "Chop. Chop. And tell me what you want to ask Grams. Maybe I can answer your question instead."

I turned my attention back to the engine and got busy. "I think memories of Carrie's past life are intoxicating her to give into Isadora's spirit."

"There's a good possibility she is," Rex said. "But I'm not sure. I haven't been around her as much as you have. If you think about it, though, since Carrie now has those memories, it stands to reason she'd have sympathy for Isadora's situation." He scratched the side of his nose and went on. "She *was* Isadora until Jaegar cast his spell on her spirit. I wouldn't be surprised if Carrie did submit to Isadora's consciousness."

"Is Grams aware of this?"

"She's concerned about it."

I clenched my jaw and had the sudden urge to throw the air cleaner lid across the room. Instead, I set it aside on a cart next to the vehicle and took some deep breaths. If we would have known there was a possibility of this happening, there was no way in hell we would have chanced it. Grams had said not to worry. Carrie wouldn't go mad because Isadora's memories were essentially Carrie's or were supposed to be Carrie's. She was correct on that aspect, but she had to have known all the risks involved.

Son-of-a-bitch!

I should have paid closer attention to what Grams told us beforehand. She said when Isadora was alive, her spirit was connected to the soul, which is now Carrie's. Grams didn't say it in those exact words, but it was basically what she said. When Jaegar performed the locking spell, sealing Isadora's essence to the soul, he stole her spirit's opportunity to join it. Now the soul has two entities attached to it: Carrie's and her former self—Isadora's. Man, this was some deep universal, equation shit. But I understood it perfectly well and was mad at myself for not being sharp enough to have caught the warning signs.

At the time, I was too wrapped up in worrying about how Carrie was feeling, so I totally overlooked the most important thing. I remembered thinking I was missing something, but then dropped it. The whole situation royally pissed me off.

"Are you okay?" Rex said, interrupting my mental rant. "You look like you're going to blow a gasket."

Despite my anger, I laughed to myself at his metaphor associated with my job. "I'm pissed," I said, grabbing the tools I needed to drain the fluids, so I could take the manifold and carburetor off and get to all the other happy horse shit I had to do today. "Why didn't Grams flat out tell us this could happen?"

"She wasn't sure," Rex said. He was to my right beside the hood of the car, floating above the floor, his shoulders level with mine. He shrugged and looked at me. "But it had to be done."

"Why?"

"Carrie was robbed of a life, which needed to be reclaimed." Rex moved back a few paces, as I bustled about to get the liquids drained. "She was also a powerful witch, and those skills could be used to outsmart the dark spirits. Our hope was Carrie could handle Isadora's presence, and with Grams guidance, her spirit would merge with Carrie's soul."

"It's not," I said. "Carrie did magic last night and screwed up. I think the power she once had as Isadora is in the process of bewitching her. I also had a disturbing dream last night about a gathering. The reaping is what rang through my head. I suspect with Carrie's help, Isadora is going to attempt to break the curse she had placed on her coven."

"Aesop told Grams about the fire last night," Rex said, frowning. "Bad deal."

"I know, and I have no idea what to do." I dropped the wrench. It clattered to the floor, making a clinking noise. "I feel so helpless."

"All you can do is keep a close eye on her and help her fight against the dark part of herself."

I had a sudden strange feeling Rex was withholding information. My spidey senses were going off like crazy. "What aren't you telling me?" I asked, turning my full attention on him.

He ran his fingers through his hair and sighed. "Fine. I'll tell you." He moved closer to me, his feet dangling high above the floor and looked me straight in the eyes. "You're not going to like what I have to tell you," he warned.

My mouth got bone dry. I tried to swallow but couldn't. All I could do was nod and brace myself for what he was about to tell me.

"You're going to have to kill Isadora, get her spirit to the crossover point, and hand her over to another light walker. He or she will take it from there. Afterward, Isadora will be able to join Carrie's soul."

I gaped at him. I didn't think I heard him right. "Wh-what?" Then it sank in. I shook my head. "No. I won't do it." I paced the shop, kicking empty boxes and oil bottles that were in my path. "Not in a million years will I harm Carrie's body. If I kill Isadora, I'd be ending Carrie's life. There has to be a better solution."

"The dream you had," Rex said, "is a bad omen. If Isadora breaks the curse she placed upon her coven, she's going to unleash a powerful force that hasn't been around for centuries."

"How do you know?" I asked. "Maybe the drenths aren't bad people. She told me about her brother Niklas. He seems like a nice guy. I mean, you can't really blame her for wanting to correct her mistake and reunite with the people she loves." I was rambling, I knew. Probably talking out of my ass, but I was freaked.

"I don't know for sure," Rex admitted, "but it's logical, considering the circumstances."

"What are my other options?" I turned to him, crossing my arms over my chest. "Dark magic?" I recalled Grams telling us yesterday it would go against nature to use it, and she was sure the high counsel of witches wouldn't be pleased. There would be consequences.

"You don't want to use black magic," Rex said. "That would be a huge mistake."

I threw my hands up. "Then what am I supposed to do?" My voice rose in frustration. "I'll be damned if I'm going to kill Isadora and Carrie."

"Carrie only has to be dead for a minute or so," Rex said. "You can bring her back after you help Isadora crossover."

I grabbed some of my tools and got back to work, hoping if I kept my hands busy I wouldn't haul off and break something. "No. The risks are too great to take a chance. I won't do it."

Rex hovered next to me, watching me work. "I understand; however, if Isadora's spirit takes over Carrie's life, it's going to be catastrophic."

"Carrie told me she has control over Isadora," I said. "She does like the confidence she feels when Isadora is present, which anyone who lacked it would. Maybe we're not giving Carrie enough credit. Maybe the dream I had last night was only that... a dream, nothing mystical about it at all." I knew I was in denial. I knew there was a big possibility we were in trouble. I didn't care at the moment, though. I had to push it away. I needed to refocus. I wouldn't give up hope there was a better solution than the one Rex gave me.

Rex watched me unbolt the carburetor. He didn't say anything, though his silence spoke volumes. He disagreed. Fine. I wasn't about to convince him otherwise. He was entitled to his own opinion, but I wasn't about to fold the cards I was dealt. I had to relax my mind and get all the bullshit out of the way. When we stepped back from our problems long enough to clear our minds, a solution would present itself. I knew it to be true. I'd done it many times. The trick was to get the original emotions out of the way because they clouded all reasoning.

As I continued to overhaul the engine, concentrating on the task at hand, while Rex silently observed what I was doing, an idea came to me. The striking thought wasn't the answer I'd wished for; however, it might lead to one.

"Can you spy on Carrie?" I asked as I checked for debris in the fluids I drained from the engine.

"I tried."

"And?"

"I can't."

"Why?"

"Because."

"Because why?"

"I'm not free to roam without Grams' permission. She doesn't want me to get too closely involved, because she's afraid the dark spirits might harm me."

Rex's situation was clear to me now. The charm Grams used when he passed away bound him to her, which gave her complete control over him. I liked Grams, but in my opinion, what she did and continued to do was selfish. She was a bit mad, though. Maybe her madness drove her to cast the spell. I didn't know, since I only met her once.

"How come you can only be around Carrie when I'm around?" I asked, wanting more information. It didn't make sense to me.

"Because you're on the righteous path to becoming a light walker. You're halfway there, if not more since you know about it." He shrugged. "Or so I'm guessing."

I cocked an eyebrow. "You're not sure?"

"I'm positive about your connection with the other light walkers and you being an apprentice and all," he adamantly said. "That's why Grams feels like I'm safe if you're around. She thinks the goodness inside you will defeat Carrie's dark side if it were to come out. What I'm not sure about is how much longer you have until you're a light walker."

"She has too much faith in me," I said with a heavy sigh. "I have no idea what to do, and I will not," I stressed, pointing a finger at him, "harm Carrie or Isadora. There has to be another way."

"Why not ask Gabriel?" Rex asked. "He might know what to do."

My heart skipped a beat as a sudden rush of hope pumped through my system, but then reality set in, crushing my optimism. "I have no idea how to reach him. I mean, he told me my energy has to be in direct accordance with theirs to activate the universal thread to reach them. Then, it's a matter of if one of them will answer me. He told me my desire to know the situation and your presence was how he was able to come to me."

Rex scratched his head and screwed up his face. "I would think he would have already appeared to you while I'm here now."

"You would think," I said, getting back to work. "Maybe he can't or doesn't want to help me."

"Your frustration and anger might have influenced the connection," Rex suggested. "I can still see those emotions in your aura."

He was right. Those negative feelings served no purpose but to hinder me in what needed to be accomplished. I had to calm myself and refocus. I decided sometime today I would attempt to contact Gabriel. Right now, he was the only hope I had.

Chapter Fourteen

Carrie

The dreams were vivid, revealing more about my life as Isadora. When my phone went off, startling me awake, I had to take a couple of deep breaths to calm my racing heart before I could answer. I snatched my cell from the nightstand. The time displayed on the screen said 2:22 a.m. The caller was my mom.

"Hi, Mom." My voice came out thick with sleep.

"Oh, my. I'm sorry I woke you," she said. I could hear music in the background and what sounded like billiards knocking against each other.

"Don't worry about it," I replied, sitting up. "Are you at a bar playing pool?"

"Busted," she giggled, sounding more like a teenager than an adult. "I'm calling to tell you your father and I decided to get a hotel for the night. We'll be home sometime in the morning."

A thought of my parents doing the nasty in a hotel room entered my mind.

Gross.

I pushed the disturbing thought aside and said, "I could have stayed at Tree's house so you and Dad had some privacy."

"No. I prefer you to be at home."

Of course you do.

"Okay… well, have fun," I told her.

"We will, sweetheart. Love you bunches."

"Love you, too."

I ended the call and lay back down to collect my thoughts. My room was dark, except for the moonlight glaring behind the white mini blinds, illuminating them. I turned on my side and stared at the window, replaying the dreams Mom woke me from, starting with Jaegar.

My love for him was born from lust and admiration. His talents were not only in the bedroom, but as a sharp business man, as well. He owned a bakery in town and was well known for his exquisite pastries and cakes. Dornheim and his death dealers had a penchant for sweets and were Jaegar's most prized customers. Every day, they would enter his store with their false charming demeanors, striking pleasant conversations with Jaegar. There was a silent agreement between them: Jaegar continued to produce his mouthwatering baked goods and provide them with their favorite treats. In return, he'd be exempt from persecution.

Many fights erupted between Jaegar and me due to his traitorous behavior. Each time, he assured me his scruples were intact. He was engaging in the perfect ploy by being cordial with those vile men and pleasing their palates. He received inside information from them and promised to pass it along to my family. Our relationship, of course, was kept secret. He couldn't be seen with a farmer's daughter whose beauty and curves would most certainly bewitch anyone.

Yeah, I was hot. Too bad I wasn't in this life. When I was Isadora, I had long, dark hair that fell in loose waves down to my waist and eyes the color of the ocean. I was five feet six with a rocking hourglass figure. A scene of Jaegar and me had played out during my slumber.

We were lying naked on a couple of bedrolls in a hayloft within a circle of lit candles. The flames cast us in a warm glow against the darkness of the abandoned barn. Slowly, Jaegar's hand traveled down my bare skin. Arching my back, I softly moaned, inviting him to continue.

He propped himself on his elbow and gazed down upon me. His gray-blue eyes were filled with hunger. "You are a vision, my love. You're always ripe to my touch and ready to offer me the nectar of your sweetest desires."

The dream was so vivid I could feel his strong hands on my body. I was sure I recreated the movements in my sleep as the scene played out. Thinking about it now turned me on.

Yes, Jaegar was crafty with his hands.

Without resistance, my mind sought to relive those moments where Jaegar's fingers slid down my stomach. A chorus of moans issued from my lips, which he eagerly kissed as he parted my legs and used the tip of his thumb to manipulate my body. His fingers slipped easily inside me; at the same time, his tongue flicked against mine. The deeper his kiss, the deeper his fingers went. Slowly, he moved them at first, until my hips rocked against his hand. My deep breaths quickened. My moans grew louder. Right when I was about to reach pure ecstasy, he pulled his hand away and positioned his body on top of mine. His lips made a trail of soft kisses down my neck to my breast. He took a nipple between his teeth and lightly grazed around its tip before taking it into his mouth. He entered me and rotated his hips, back and forth. Ahhh, I could see why I was so entranced by this man. He was an expert lover who possessed a gift of how to bestow pleasure upon a woman.

Guilt pulled me out of this delicious scene. I bit my lip. Was I emotionally cheating on Tree for longing to experience that moment? I flipped on my back and released a heavy sigh. Wow. Jaegar was good. He was more than good. He was... fantastic. But I loved Tree. He was great in everything. I shouldn't be fantasizing about Jaegar. Or was I? Shrugging it off, I turned on my side again. Tugging the blanket up, I bunched it next to my cheek, getting more comfortable to allow a different event in my life as Isadora play out.

I stood in a clearing deep in the forest with four followers. My fellows: Driscol, Jorsten, Lukas, and my baby brother Niklas. All of them had on the same dark, hooded cloak I wore. The torches we held blazed, casting us in a reddish orange glow against the night sky. The full moon was white, like marble glass. Its rays filtered through the canopy of trees, throwing layers of beams to the right and left of us, crisscrossing, as if the Moon Goddess was sheltering our coven from outsiders. Every cell in my body buzzed with magical energy from what I took from the earth when I made the elixirs I now carried in my pocket.

"As you know," I said to the group, "Margaretha has been accused of causing frost on the crops in a diabolical plan to destroy her competitors, resulting in crop failure, plague, and malnutrition. Because of the loss of wine and grain, a period of hyperinflation ensued. We all know the accusation are false and misleading. Margaretha did nothing of the sort. The only guilt that weighs upon her shoulders also lies on ours: practicing control of the weather. But by no means were we the perpetrators of such stressful times. By no means did our weather- making practice stimulate the vicious nexus of supernatural beliefs and common reasoning. Nature is beautiful and ugly, temperamental even. From its bosoms, it bears wondrous gifts, but her misgivings grow beneath the surface and can erupt at any time and for any reason." I paused long enough to look at each one of my fellows. They nodded in agreement. A fierce, affectionate love for them warmed my heart. "Margaretha," I continued, "is innocent of all charges, so are Simone, Tobias, Ulrich, and my father."

"Why don't we save them?" Lukas asked.

He was the most adorable one out of the bunch, with his golden hair and eyes to match. However, he was the youngest and lacked common sense. He favored his emotions over reasoning. We were lucky to have reached him before he made a foolish mistake.

"Why ask something you already know the answer to?" Niklas asked. "Your magic is no longer effective due to your excessive use and possible punishment from the high counsel of witches."

"But Isadora still has her magic," Lukas countered. He met my eyes with his. There was no malice in them, only curiosity. "Why won't you free your father and our friends? You have the power to do so."

"My power is waning," I told him. "I must conserve it to protect us."

"But—" Lukas started to say, but Niklas elbowed him in the side and gestured for him to listen.

"When Jaegar told Niklas and me about the fate of our father and friends, I wanted to do nothing more than bring Hell's fury down upon those involved in these witch hunts." I pointed to Niklas. "He can confirm the truth I have just spoken." Niklas nodded, and I went on. "Thankfully, Jaegar had the presence of mind to quell my wrathful state, so I could think clearly on the matter. After he departed to attend his store, I formulated a plan which would surely guarantee our survival."

"An immortality spell," Driscol said, a grin crossing his handsome face.

Ah, he possessed many enticing qualities that had more than once sent me in a tailspin of unvirtuous thoughts. Countless nights, as I lay skyclad beneath the moonlight, I'd envisioned straddling his tall, muscular frame and riding him as we paid homage to our ancestors. Jaegar was a skillful lover, but Driscol was a bit of a rogue—edgy and a trusted ally. Jaegar, on the other hand, I harbored reservations for. However, I was drawn to his touch and had given him my heart before

I'd realized I did so. In truth, I knew it would be my undoing. There was no future for us, yet I gravitated to him like bears to honey.

"Correct," I said, sending Driscol a flirty smile. He winked and brushed his brown hair out of his eyes. They appeared darker green than normal, and a hungry need filled them. Was it for me or for outwitting our oppressors? My body warmed at the mere thought of him touching it. "Well... theoretically speaking."

"What do you mean?" Jorsten asked, shifting his weight, rubbing the stubble on his face. He was the rugged, beastly type in our group, with his dark, shoulder-length shaggy hair and dark eyes. He loved his ale and to have a grand time. He never cowered from a challenge or authority. I admired those qualities about him.

"All spells have a loophole," I told them. "I plan on casting a transmigration spell after I see Jaegar tonight. Once this nightmare is over, we'll meet here, and I'll break the enchantment you'll be under. If for some reason I run into some trouble, you my friends will live on, unless you choose to die or some accident befalls you. You will heal from your wounds quickly, sickness won't touch you, and you will be the same as you are now, only in canine form. Your humanity will still be intact."

"Why not turn us into wolves instead of a hunting dog?" Jorsten asked.

"People are more apt to slaughter wolves than a house or work pet," I answered. "My choice will give you the freedom to be seen in public without the fear of being harmed. You can use it to your advantage and play on the sympathy of others. They'd surely give you food and a warm place to sleep."

All of them made agreement sounds.

"As you all are aware," I said, "Ayperos is my consultant. The things we were able to do beyond casting simple enchantments were because of him. He possesses grimoires that date back to ancient civilizations, now lost to this world and will never be discovered.

Ayperos and all the other dark spirits are limited to what magic they themselves can perform. Nonetheless, they are the owners of these treasured books, and we were fortunate enough to get a taste of their powers."

"The whole witch craze is our fault," Lukas said, his tone thick with guilt. "Hundreds of innocent people are suffering and dying horrible deaths because of us. If we had never toyed with black magic and attempted to manipulate the weather, this would have never happened. We deserve to burn in hell. Maybe I should turn my—"

I flicked my hand at him. His mouth kept moving, but no words came out. "Silence," I said, enjoying watching his eyes bulge from their sockets. The element of surprise always made magic fun. I couldn't help but smirk.

"You need to conserve what magic you have left instead of wasting it on this fool," Niklas said, glaring at Lukas.

He was right. Our excess use of magic had rendered everyone powerless but me. But even I knew I was pushing my luck. I may be more powerful than all of them, but I wasn't impervious to the high counsel of witches or nature's will.

"Duly noted," I said, flicking my hand at Lukas again.

"What I was trying to say," he persisted until I held my hand up to shush him. A startled look contorted his face, and his hand flew to his neck.

"Please. I understand your concern," I told him. "But there's no need to trouble yourself over matters you're clearly uneducated about. Allow me to enlighten you." I threw my torch down a few feet behind me. The flame ignited the ground and commenced a half moon crescent of fire around me. The others mimicked my movements. We were now standing inside a flaming ring.

"Do you want me to tell him?" Niklas asked.

"If that is your wish to do so. Please, explain to him how foolhardy his statement was," I said.

Niklas gave me a half nod and turned to Lukas. "These witch hunts have been going on long before we practiced weather-making and other crafty tricks. Have you forgotten about Prince-Bishop Aschhausen? He's responsible for torturing and killing three hundred alleged witches. And as I speak, a witch craze is going on in Wurzburg."

"You know what they're calling Margaretha?" Lukas asked and continued before any one of us could respond. "A frost witch."

"Imbeciles," I spat. The flames jumped, flickering around us. "Unseasonable weather is what caused the frost. There was nothing supernatural about it. Dornheim and his henchmen are using this natural occurrence as a construct for their twisted agendas to put fear in the hearts of others with dark fantastical tales of witchcraft. People were demanding an explanation for the economic crisis and plague, which you have so conveniently forgotten," I said to Lukas, focusing my blazing eyes on him, "killed my mother. In no way are we responsible for her demise. Dornheim and men like him poisoned the masses with these tales to answer their questions."

"I apologize," Lukas said. "It wasn't my intention to imply you or anyone of us had a hand in your mother's death. I know how much you and Niklas adored her, and the same affection applies to your father, as well. Please forgive the hastiness of my tongue."

I inhaled through my nose and slowly blew out the air from my lungs, releasing the tension from my chest. The wall of flames lowered. He was the youngest out of our group, I reminded myself. One who mimed high drama and was enslaved to his emotions. Regardless, though, he was one of us, and I cherished him.

I placed my hands on his cheeks, tilted his chin down, and kissed his forehead. "You're forgiven."

"Thank you, high priestess." He took my hands and kissed the backs of them.

I stepped away and positioned myself in front of everyone, pulling four glass vials from my pocket. I held one between my index finger and thumb and raised it before me so the others could see the purple elixir. "Because of Ayperos' continuous generosity, I was able to create this potion for you to take. A drop of my blood is in each one, which will bind you to me. What this means is you'll be aware of my presence and location. The transmigration spell I'll cast, will allow my spirit to inhabit another body. Your eyes will say it's not me, but without a doubt, you will know that, yes, indeed it is your high priestess."

"But you're so beautiful," Driscol said. "Is it really necessary for you to abandon your present form for a lesser one?"

"Unfortunately it is," I told him. "Jaegar informed me that Margaretha and Simone were forced, under extreme torture, to confess about us and our engagement in the dark arts. It is now believed that I made a diabolical pact with the devil himself. Therefore, I must take swift action before they apprehend me and do unspeakable things to this body." I handed each one of them a vial.

Lukas looked at me. Fear reigned in his eyes. "Will this hurt?"

"I imagine so," I said, watching the color drain from his face and sweat break across his forehead. He opened his mouth to speak, but I placed a finger on his lips. "Fear not. Your high priestess has already thought this through." I lifted a leather cord over my head. Attached to it was a suede pouch filled with enchanted herbs. "These herbs will sedate the pain." I opened the bag and dipped my fingers inside, taking a hearty pinch. "Stick your tongue out," I ordered. Lukas did as he was told. I gave him the substance and proceeded to do the same with the others. "Now, free your cloaks from your bodies." I stood back and watched as they dropped the only article of clothing they wore onto the ground. I'd seen them skyclad many times, but Driscol's muscular frame and impressive endowment had always taken my breath away.

My eyes lingered on him longer than I intended. When I looked up, his lopsided grin was silently daring me to touch him. My skin grew hot, along with other parts of my body.

"What do we do afterward?" Lukas asked, nervously shifting his weight back and forth, pulling my attention onto him.

"You run from here," I answered. "Get used to your new form. Go to the abandoned cottage Niklas and I took you to. There's food and a brook nearby. You'll be free to do what you wish. Tramp around the villages if you would like. Make friends with a child. Be creative."

Jorsten removed the cork and raised his tiny glass vial to me. The others did the same. "Cheers. Until we meet again, high priestess. Thank you for saving our asses."

"Cheers," they all said in unison.

"I love each one of you," I said, feeling an ache in my heart that sent tears to my eyes. I was doing the right thing, I told myself. It was better to be apart from them for a short period of time than to have them suffer and lose them forever. "I promise you this: we will reunite once the madness has ended, and I will break my spell so you can return to your present form."

"So mote it be," Niklas said. He drank the elixir as did everyone else.

I released the cloak from my body and threw my arms above my head. "So mote it be!" I repeated in a strong, powerful voice.

Clouds blotted out the moon, and a bolt of lightning flashed red, then blue across the star-filled night. The ground shook as a loud rumble rolled through it, swaying me. All four members fell to their hands and knees. The flames that encompassed us leapt twenty feet. A sharp, cracking noise of thunder sounded above us. Then a gust of wind blew through the clearing, rustling the leaves, swaying the tree tops. My hair flew out in front of me. I held it back, surprised to find the fire remained stationary, as if it were a solid wall protecting us from the elements. The moon broke through the clouds, its rays spotlighting us. For a brief moment, the world became silent. I envisioned the Gods holding their breaths in anticipation.

"Balls," Jorsten said, his tone deeper than normal, his fingers digging deep into the earth. His body was shaking. Drops of sweat rolled down his forehead, dripping off his contorted face.

I watched in amazement as his skin rippled. His muscles bulged and moved. The sound of bones cracking made me flinch. None of my fellows appeared in much pain, which comforted my troubled spirit. There was no turning back now. I had forced nature to bend to my will by going against it. There would be consequences, I was sure, but I was willing to take the risk in order to save what family I had left.

My gaze swept over to Driscol. He looked at me. His eyes were now golden brown instead of hazel. The muscles in his face shifted in a grotesque manner, then elongated, forming a snout, widening his mouth. Fangs broke through his gums, blood coating them. His hands and feet stretched, popping and cracking more bones, and then reforming to tissue and muscle. His bubbling skin exploded into fur. A brown tail emerged from his backbone, and his canine body continued to fill out and grow. All four of them were enormous in size compared to a normal German shorthaired pointer. Each one was different in his coloring, but they all had the same broad high-set ears that hung close to their heads. Driscol's coat was a liver color with a small letter D on his side. To my delight, the others had the first letter of their name in the same spot Driscol had his.

I pulled out of those memories and flipped on my back. My heart grew heavy. I knew what followed. I had hugged and kissed them, not realizing that would be the last time I'd see them. What came after was the memory I had earlier of Jeagar and me making love, then him squeezing the life out of my body.

I failed my coven, and I missed them terribly. Driscol found me though. My Driscol. He was the one I should have been with, not Jaegar. I wondered where the others were. They could still be in Germany for all I knew.

Ayperos.

I had to find him, which I didn't think would be too difficult. Now that I knew what he'd done for me in my life as Isadora and my coven, I was starting to like him more and more. I was still me, Carrie, I reaffirmed to myself, but now that I knew the story behind my past life, I felt a strong connection to it.

Yes, a strong connection to it, I repeated in my mind while closing my eyes. I fell back asleep. There were no dreams this time, only darkness. A few hours later, I woke up in a cold sweat, my breathing fast and heavy, as if I were running from monsters. I was guessing that was what it was like for Isadora after Jaegar cast the locking spell on her spirit—a black existence of nothingness.

Bastard.

Your assumption is correct.

I took a deep breath and released it. Tears formed. I blinked and hastily wiped them off my cheek. "I'm sorry," I whispered. "He stole so much from you... from us."

No more being under subjugation!

I sat up, thinking about the memories Isadora shared with me and took the necklace off, welcoming her spirit to come forth full throttle. It was *our* promise we needed to fulfill to *our* coven, and I wasn't about to hinder it by keeping her at bay with the crystal necklace Abigail gave me. We weren't going to play by their rules anymore. Now was the time to make our own decisions and not be under someone's control.

I yanked the covers off me. "You're right," I said aloud and stepped out of bed.

Something shifted in my solar plexus. A confidence and a strong sense of determination engulfed me.

Isadora's.

I loved it, along with the power I had because of her. It totally rocked. I was still in control, and Isadora knew it, but in order to accomplish our goals, she would have to take the driver's seat—until Tree came around, at least.

"Let's do this," I said, feeling Isadora's personality push to the forefront of my mind. I laughed. Insecurities I used to have were gone, and my mind was a lot more focused instead of scattered like it normally was. We were going to make some changes, starting right now.

Chapter Fifteen

Isadora

A rush of adrenaline went through my system. Elated, I glanced at the digital clock on the nightstand and skipped to the bathroom. It was ten after seven. I had plenty of time to shower, get dressed, eat, and see if I could locate the herbs I needed to cast a spell before Jack picked me up and took me to that crone's house. If my luck held, I'd cross paths with Ayperos. I was Isadora. Being a dark spirit, he would sense me taking the lead while Carrie stood aside in observation mode.

Today was going to be glorious, especially if Driscol had stayed around. I'd tell him my plans, which would delight him, I was sure. I leaned over the sink and looked at myself in the mirror. Shoulder length dark hair with red tips, brown eyes, and a splatter of freckles across the bridge of my nose.

Boring!

Carrie thought her eyes and face were nothing special. She wasn't ugly, but then again, she wasn't gorgeous like I was in the 1600s. Why couldn't she at least have my blue eyes in this life? Sure, I could get colored contacts, but Carrie didn't like anything in her eyes. I shrugged. So be it. The doe eyes were fine, I guess. They were more cutesy than alluring, like the rest of Carrie's attributes. However, I planned on working a beauty spell before Jack arrived to change those things.

He goes by Tree, because he's tall and used to have an awesome Mohawk.

"Right. I will not make the same blunder again," I said under my breath.

I knew why Carrie and her friends called him Tree. Her memories and life was like an endless landscape of information and details I could wander through, but I thought it was utterly preposterous to disregard a lovely, masculine name like Jack in favor of a plant.

It fits him. Move on.

I never took too kindly to orders, but we were in this together, and I had no interest in a petty quarrel. I thought his nickname was amusing, though, and giggled before I could contain it.

"Moving on," I announced to the empty bathroom, while stripping my clothes to take a shower. I was looking forward to the hot water beating on my skin and to what this day might bring.

* * *

Driscol's presence was scarce. Maybe because it was raining cats and dogs. The weather had me concerned about where he had escaped to for shelter. I hoped it was warm and comfortable. Carrie's basset hound Odell had it made. He lived a far superior life than I had in the 1600s—a dog with his own bed in the corner of the living room. Only the wealthy had such luxuries in my time. Odell wouldn't come near me at first. With a wary eye, he observed my every move while I pillaged the refrigerator and then ate a slice of bread, a hunk of ham, and cheese at the kitchen table.

"Come here, boy," I said after I had my fair share, kneeling a few feet in front of him. With my hand extended, I offered him a piece of meat. "I will do you no harm." I always had a soft spot for animals and waited patiently while he crouched, his belly touching the floor. Looking up at me with his adorable, droopy eyes, he slowly eased his way toward me. "Here you go, my friend." Timidly, he took it from my fingers and chowed down, as Carrie would say. Afterward he stepped into my open arms. I wrapped them around his stocky frame and kissed him. "See, regardless of what others think, I'm not such a bad person." Wagging his tail, he licked my face and made me laugh.

He's such a sweet boy.

Carrie's soft voiced sighed through me. I stood, silently agreeing with her, and followed Odell to the sliding glass windows in the kitchen. I knew what he wanted by his antsy behavior, but I hated for him to get soaked in the rain. He looked at me and whined, his backside dancing. I unlatched the door and slid it open. He bolted. I watched as he relieved himself and then hurried back inside.

"Do you feel better now?" I asked, as I bent and dried him with a kitchen towel. He rewarded me with another sloppy kiss on the cheek. "Why, thank you, King Odell," I said. "Now you can go to your bedchamber and enjoy an afternoon of relaxation."

I had a lot to accomplish today, so I got busy once Odell scampered away. I needed to find a place where I could purchase the herbs required for the spell I planned to cast before Tree entered my presence. There had to be a shop in Astoria that stocked such items. I could feel Carrie mulling it.

Alternative newspaper.

A memory of Carrie grabbing a free newspaper as she and Tree were leaving a café came to me. *Bare Bones* is what the paper was called. Carrie only thumbed through it once and had tossed it in her room. The following day, she was in a car accident.

I went to her room and searched the computer desk scattered with notebooks, pens, and candy wrappers. The newspaper wasn't there. I glanced at her bureau. A display of Disney figurines surrounding a whitewashed jewelry box in the shape of a castle were the only items there. A memory of Carrie sitting on the floor against her bed flashed in my mind. I dropped to my knees, lifted the bed skirt, and voila, there it was—a large magazine newspaper. I slid it in front of me. Crossing my legs and leaning forward, I scanned it. There were ads about underground bands, plays, art, and a brilliant full page advertisement of a zombie apocalypse party in Portland, featuring a group of people who appeared undead. I kept flipping the pages, until toward the end, I found what I was searching for. The Mystical Path was the headline. Beneath it psychics in Oregon were advertising their services: palm reading, channeling a loved one, tarot cards, and medallions to ward off evil spirits, among other things.

"No. No. No," I said, tapping the tip of my finger down the row of useless rubbish. "There has to be some sort of mag—"

On the following page was a list of magic shops. At first glance, my hope faltered. The listing of merchandise was for parlor tricks performed in front of an audience: trick coins, cards, the breakaway wand, and so forth. Then a triple moon symbol caught my eyes. A full moon was in the center and on either side was a crescent. I remembered this quite fondly. The first one represented the waxing moon, which meant a youthful maiden developing into a woman. It was the phase between the new and full moon. When it reached its apex, the magnificent orb represented a mother and powerful goddess. Artemis was her name. The other crescent was the waning moon, which occurred between the full and new moon. It symbolized the crone who was wise and guided souls into the afterlife.

"Abigail," I whispered.

Suddenly something profound struck me between the eyes. I could feel Carrie's spirit buzzing alongside mine in zeal. Her thoughts overwhelmed mine, staggering me to where I could do nothing but pay attention to her. She was the maiden, and once my spirit would merge with her soul, we'd become the goddess. As for the crone, Carrie imagined herself old, with the ability to help souls crossover to the next plane of existence. I thought her perception on the matter to be juvenile and snorted at its absurdity.

I shifted my attention back on the newspaper, feeling her retreat when she realized I wasn't enthused with her idiotic idea. The significance of the moment slipped away. I shrugged it off. I had more important things to focus on than a fleeting epiphany. Below the triple moon was an advertisement for a shop called The Witch's Corner. The store was located north of Cannon Beach and south of Astoria. There was a category of items on the left hand side of the page: herbs, athames, candles, incense, and other useful accessories.

Excellent.

I ripped the page out, thankful Carrie and I were connected enough to where coming from the seventeenth century to the twenty-first wasn't shocking. Because of her memories and our odd predicament, it was as if I'd always lived this way. I could even drive. I found nothing exciting about it. The moving contraption got me from point A to point B, like when I used to ride my horse. However, I'd have to admit, I preferred a horse over driving in a metal coffin any day.

Metal coffin?

Yes, the vehicle robbed people from being a part of the earth. There was no true freedom in being enclosed inside a can with wheels. The car was a brilliant invention with lots of advantages, like keeping the weather off our backs, but it also added to the desensitization of the human spirit. Our true nature wasn't designed for such luxuries. No wonder a plague of madness had gone rampant in this new age of technology.

You sound like Bael.

Ah, Bael. The king of dark spirits. The "old one" who had fallen from grace. I'd heard many things about him and would like to personally meet him. I never had the pleasure to do so in the 1600s. I admired his ideologies, for they were wise and raw. No sugar coating a turd and calling it a delectable treat, then selling it to the masses as so. Not Bael. He wouldn't do such a thing—at least, from what I knew of him from Ayperos and some of the other dark spirits.

You're brutal. I like it.

I laughed at Carrie's response as I took what I needed out of her purse and slipped them inside the many zipper pockets of the black, baggy pants I wore. In a rush, fueled by excitement and anticipation, I went to the kitchen, grabbed the car keys, and wrote a short note to the parents, informing them I was shopping in town.

I'd been told and chastised countless times for crudely voicing my opinions. I'd never paid any mind to the objections of others on how I should behave as a proper lady. If they couldn't deal with my boisterous attitude, then they shouldn't be in my company, I silently told Carrie.

A sudden feeling of admiration warmed my spirit. I smiled and reminded her essentially we were the same. She was me, but because Jaegar had cast that wretched spell, he divided my spirit from her soul. Our soul. Thus, making me a separate entity.

Snatching a black jacket off the kitchen chair, I shrugged into it and pulled the hood over my head. I stepped out into the gray, gloomy world where it was still pouring rain. The thick smell of dirt and dried leaves overwhelmed my senses, triggering a memory of me dancing bare footed in my white dressing gown. The temperature was too cold to reenact the witches dance now, but nonetheless, it was a fond memory to behold.

While darting to the red Ford Focus in the driveway, I pushed the button on the key ring to unlock the doors and quickly stepped inside. The fierce pounding on the roof and the water flowing in waves down the windows sent me in a bit of a panic. It spurred an instinctual reaction out of me, like a feline swatting at her enemy to keep it at bay. Words spewed forth from my lips. I was chanting in a deep, forceful voice, my chest drumming in time to each syllable. The spell was in Latin. It was like revisiting an old friend and welcoming him into my life again. I realized then that the enchantments I once knew were all coming back to me. With a grin, I made a swishing gestured in front of me. Water disappeared from the windshield. I turned in my seat. Despite the torrent of rain outside, the rest of the windows were also bone dry. Silence surrounded me. I squealed in delight and clapped my hands, which wasn't like me.

Carrie.

The annoying behavior was her reaction, not mine.

Omigod! How frickin' cool.

Her glee was contagious, though, and I couldn't help but give into her excitement. Grinning, I headed to The Witch's Corner without one single drop of rain on the windshield. Each time I approached a red stop light, I imagined it to be green and said, "Lucem." The device would then blink green, allowing me to keep going. I was having a grand time getting reacquainted with the powers I had hundreds of years ago. Last night's blunder must have been a fluke. However, I knew I shouldn't overexert myself and use too much magic. My powers were like a battery. There was only so much juice I could use. Once I bled them dry, I'd have to recharge in order to cast spells again. Excessive use could also lead to death if I weren't careful. I decided to hold off on casting anymore spells until later today when I had the ingredients I needed to outwit the boy and dazzle Tree. Glamour was the only way to keep him from interfering with my plans. Besides, I knew Carrie would be pleased with the results and with Tree's ultimate reaction to my work. Tonight was going to be a night for her to remember and for me to gain a strong foothold in this world.

* * *

The shop was one of many set inside a brownstone building. It surrounded a cozy cobblestone courtyard with a couple benches and wrought iron café tables that were conveniently displayed for privacy and leisure. Tall Douglas firs dwarfed the area, giving the grounds an ancient European vibe. As I walked the stone path, longing and sadness swept through me. Jaegar's bakery came to mind, along with the other merchants at the marketplace long ago in Bamberg. I could almost smell the fresh bread baking and the sweet mingling scent of apples, which created a mouthwatering mixture of aromas that would reduce any respectable gentleman to a beggar.

When I approached the entrance, I couldn't help but admire the dark, thick wood outlining a nook that housed the oak door. Above it, hanging from a black iron post was a sign that said, "The Witch's Corner." On either side were tall, round, dusty windows with strips of dark metal in a grid pattern holding the panes together.

A twinkling tinker bell sound alerted my presence when I opened the door and stepped inside. I breathed in the heady smell of sandalwood and felt immediately in my element.

"I'll be right with you," a lady called from the back room.

"Take your time," I answered, grateful to have a spare moment to myself so I could browse.

The shelf on the north wall was lined with herbs in glass containers, shiny brass bowls, and pewter chalices, some engraved with a crescent moon pentacle. There were also soapstone mortar and pestles and a selection of books on witchcraft and divination. A round black table was but a few feet away from where I stood. A medium size open wooden box sat on top, revealing its treasures of candles, incense, anointing oil, a ritual bell, blood stone, and a small packet of Balsam used for burning during a ritual.

"May I help you?"

I looked up to a set of emerald eyes cast in a lovely heart-shaped face. She smiled. The lines around her mouth deepened. Her ash blonde hair was in a low ponytail. She tucked a loose strand behind one ear and crossed the room. Her calm energy brought me comfort, putting me more at ease.

"You have a wonderful shop," I replied. "I never realized such a place existed near my hometown."

"Thank you," she said, the warm smile still on her face. "I opened The Witch's Corner a month ago."

"Your selection is quite impressive," I said. There was an area with all sorts of candles and accessories such as holders, snuffers, lighters, a carving set, and the like. They were displayed on a black, squatty, wooden shelf. Above it was a matching sign, tacked to the dark purple wall, with witchy letters hand painted in red that said, "Candle Magick."

She nodded, following my gaze. "The inventory took me several years to accumulate, but I have to say, it was well worth the wait."

"Indeed," I agreed.

"Are you looking for anything specific?"

"I am." I half turned toward the herbs. "I need some of those, and do you have rose oil?"

The woman picked up a wicker basket from a stack next to the front door and handed it to me. "Yes, we do," she answered. "There's a nice selection of essential oils over there." She gestured toward an antique white washed hutch across the room. "There's also material to make sachets, different types of incense, charcoal, soaps, and lotions."

"Wonderful," I said, flashing a pleased smile. "I need rose oil, gold material, three pink candles, and"—I wandered back to the herbs and picked through them—"witch hazel tincture, ginger root, lavender... among a few other things." I carefully placed the glass bottles of the four herbs I mentioned into the basket.

"My name is Georgia," she said, giving me three pink candles and offering her hand.

I noticed the silver moonstone goddess ring on her index finger. The light caught the gem exactly right to where a rainbow of colors danced before my eyes. I returned her gesture, and as soon as our palms touched, mine began to tingle. "Isadora," I said, pleased she was an actual witch instead of an imposter. "But some people call me Carrie."

"Which name do you prefer?" she asked. The surprised look on her face told me she realized I, too, was a witch.

"Isadora." I released her hand and continued to search through the merchandise, adding what I needed to my basket.

"Well, Isadora," she said. "If you have any questions, or if I can be of any assistance, don't hesitate to ask."

"Actually," I said, as I continued looking through the herbs, not sparing her a glance. "I need a six-inch square golden cloth, a one-inch square green lace, a red ribbon, one piece of rose quartz, and one garnet. If you would collect those items for me, I'd be most grateful."

I could feel her presence moving away from me, the wooden floorboards creaking beneath her feet. "Certainly."

A gust of cold air stirred my hair and a twinkling sound followed.

"Good morning, Ayperos," Georgia said in a pleasant voice.

My heart jumped in my throat. I spun completely around. A striking man with shoulder-length black hair tied back filled my vision. He was of average height and wore a dark trench coat over his lean body. "Ayperos?" I whispered. I knew it was him but still had to physically confirm it to myself to fully register I was in the company of an old friend.

"Isadora," he said, smiling. He crossed the room at the same time I set my basket on the floor.

We embraced. The smell of cherry tobacco filled my nostrils.

I had the sudden urge to cringe away. Carrie wasn't keen on this intimate moment. I hugged him tighter, pulling up memories of him assisting me and my coven in a bleak world where hope was quickly being lost. The feeling of resistance lifted. I smirked, enjoying taking charge of Carrie's weak and pliable emotions.

He kissed me gently on the cheek and released his arms. "We finally meet again after all these years."

"I dare say," I answered, "I had no doubts of making your acquaintance once again. However, I must admit, regardless of possessing such a notion, I'm guilty of being stupefied the moment you entered this shop."

He softly laughed. Amusement filled his chestnut eyes. "You still are as charming as ever."

"Is there anything else I can help you with?" Georgia asked, picking up my basket and placing the merchandise I told her I needed into it. "I remembered the rose oil."

I turned to the shelf and took a mortar and pestle from it. "Thank you, Georgia," I said, facing her and Ayperos. "I think I have everything."

"My pleasure." She turned, and I followed her to a shiny oak counter where she rang up my purchases and placed them in a black bag. "If you ever need anything," she said, handing me a business card after I paid her, "don't hesitate to ask."

I slipped the card inside my pocket and took the bag from her. Ayperos was waiting near the entrance. I had a feeling he wanted to tell me something, and I was anxious to discover what. "I won't, and thank you again for your assistance." I turned on my heel and headed out.

"Anytime," she said.

Ayperos opened the door for me, and we stepped into the gray world. The rain had completely stopped, but there was a cold, dampness in the air that seeped into my bones. I shivered and pulled my jacket tighter against me

"Would you be interested in having a cup of coffee?" Ayperos asked. "There's a quaint sho—"

The theme song to *Buffy the Vampire Slayer* went off inside my jacket pocket.

"Excuse me," I said, reaching for the phone. The purple case around it with black and red rhinestones was pleasing to the eyes. I'd always been fond of turning dull items into something fancy. I glanced at Ayperos. "It's Jack... I mean Tree."

Ayperos frowned. "You should answer it. Otherwise, he won't leave you alone."

"I'm afraid he's not going to anyway," I said. I could feel Carrie's presence squirming inside me. Silently, I assured her I could handle this. I cleared my throat and adjusted the tone of my voice to sound more like hers. "Hi, darling."

I would never say that. Great. You just tipped him off. Way to go.

I made a face. She was right. I needed to sift through her memories, so I could use them as a cheat sheet to fool him. I would fix my mistake.

"Carrie?" he carefully said.

"Yes, it's me." I laughed. "Gotcha! You thought I was Isadora, huh?"

"Um, yeah. I told you not to mess with me like that. All of this is confusing as it is."

"Sorry. I won't do it again. What's up? Are you done with your work?"

"Not yet." He paused, as if he were considering his words. "What are you doing?"

"I needed some retail therapy, so I'm shopping."

"How are you feeling?"

"I'm fine. Why?"

"You're supposed to take it easy, and last night was more than we bargained for."

I sighed. "Don't coddle me. I'm fantastic, so *back off*," I barked. Shit, I shouldn't have said those last two words.

Silence.

"You're right," he finally said. "I'll try not to baby you. My bad."

"Forget about it. I know you worry, but I'll be okay."

"I better get back to work. I should be at your house around six."

"Sounds good."

"I love you."

"I love you, too. See ya in a bit."

I ended the call and released a lungful of air. Trying to impersonate Carrie was harder than I thought. I wasn't sure if I succeeded, but it would have to suffice.

You should have let me talk to him.

I ignored Carrie and shifted my attention on Ayperos. "I would love to have a cup of coffee with you."

"Wonderful. There's a lovely café not far down this walkway." He stuck his elbow out, offering me to loop my arm around it. I did and leaned into him while we stepped over the puddles of water on the cobblestone path. "I have a couple of surprises for you," he said.

"You do?" There was a mischievous glint in his eyes. "What?"

"I will tell you one of them in a moment. The other will have to wait until later."

My stomach did several flip flops. He was going to help me break the curse I cast on my coven. I could feel it. I wanted to jump up and down and beg him to tell me, but those were Carrie's emotions, not mine. She was equally as intrigued and excited as me. But I chomped on the bit and refrained from allowing her emotions to take over. I didn't want them to ruin this moment, not when I was close to getting what I wanted.

Chapter Sixteen

Tree

The situation with Carrie was getting real. When I called her, I wasn't sure if I was talking to her or Isadora. Maybe she was messing with me again. However, my spidey senses alarmed me when she told me in a shitty tone to back off. Isadora? But afterward, I began to second guess myself. The night before Grams performed the awakening spell on Carrie, she did get upset about me wanting to take precautions regarding her health. So maybe I was talking to Carrie and not Isadora. I tried to remember what the light walker chick said to me the other night. Her message was something like using my observation to sharpen my intuition. But how in the hell was I supposed to rely on my inner voice, when I had no idea what was really going on with my girlfriend?

In a sudden burst of anger and frustration, I threw the screwdriver I held across the room. It bounced off the wall and clanked against a metal drum. "Dammit!" I cast my eyes skyward. "What do you want me to do? This is bullshit! And for your information, I will not kill Isadora or Carrie."

Silence.

I could feel my heart beating in the side of my neck. No one was going to answer me or come to my aid. I was relieved Rex left before I called Carrie. I needed this time alone to process everything. But the reason Rex bailed had me concerned. Grams wasn't doing well. He told me her health was already in a fragile state when she performed the spell on Carrie. Since then, it seemed to be rapidly deteriorating. My world was unraveling at its seams.

"Deep breaths," I told myself, breathing in through my nose and slowly releasing it out of my mouth.

I needed to calm myself. Maybe Rex was right about my anger stifling the connection to get an answer from Gabriel, Michael, God, or any higher being for that matter. Hell, I wasn't picky. I'd settle for the hookah smoking caterpillar in *Alice in Wonderland*. What was his name? Absolem?

I decided to turn the radio on to a station dedicated to '80s rock. My nerves were too frazzled to attempt anything other than completing the engine job. Nine times out of ten, music would snap me out of a bad mood. I was hoping it would this time. When I heard the fast tempo of guitars and drums beginning Metallica's "Master of Puppets," the heaviness in my muscles lifted. The chaotic thoughts in my mind vanished. I focused on the task at hand and allowed myself to get lost in the haunting rhythm of the instruments.

* * *

I dropped off the engine and its components to a machine shop we did business with. I was ahead of schedule by two hours, which made me happy. Now I had more time to ponder my next move. The first thing on my agenda, though, was taking a shower. I had grease caked under my fingernails and past my elbows. I also stank like oil and gasoline. I picked out a pair of black jeans, an army green long sleeve steampunk skeleton shirt, a brown zip up hoodie, and Batman boxer shorts. I tossed them on my bed and proceeded to discard my clothes, pulling my T-shirt over my head.

"I need a favor."

I started when I heard Rex's troubled voice and yanked my shirt off. I was going to give him shit about popping in without warning and almost causing me to fill my drawers, but his forlorn expression stopped me. "What's wrong?"

"I need you to call my mom."

My eyebrows pulled together as I tried to reason why he'd want me to. "What for?"

"Grams is dying, and I think Mom should see her."

"But your mom doesn't want anything to do with her. In fact, she thinks Grams sold her soul to Satan." I wanted to help him, but I didn't see the point. His mom had severed ties with Grams long ago, and from what I understood, she said hurtful things to her, as well.

Rex sighed and shifted his gaze to his feet. "I know, but Grams is her grandmother. Will you at least try? Please." He looked at me, his amber eyes shiny with tears. "Please."

My heart sank. He was torn up by this whole ordeal. How could I say no to him? Besides, he was helping Carrie and me out. Despite my reservations, calling his mom was the least I could do.

I grabbed my cell off the dresser. "What's her name, and what do I say to her?"

"You're going to call her?" Rex raised his eyebrows. A hopeful look entered his face.

I lifted my hand with the phone in it. "Yeah."

He smiled. "Awesome. Her name is Jane. Tell her who you are and Grams is dying."

I took a deep breath. I hated calling people I wasn't acquainted with, but in the long run she deserved to know. If she decided not to make peace with her grandmother, then it was on her and no concern of mine. "What's her number?"

Rex told me and wrung his hands as I thumbed the numbers. It rang five times. I was expecting it to go to voice mail when a female answered.

"Hello."

"Yes, can I please speak to Jane?"

"This is she."

"Hi, my name is Jack. I'm a friend of Abigail's. She's your grandmother, right?"

"I don't have a grandmother... not anymore." Her voice sounded hard and distant.

"Okay, well, I just wanted to tell you Abigail's health is rapidly deteriorating, and she won't be with us for much longer."

"How did you get my number?" she demanded.

"Excuse me?"

"I said... How. Did. You. Get. My. Number?" she asked in a snotty, patronizing tone.

I bristled. She had no right to talk to me in such a manner, and it instantly pissed me off. Before I could think my words through, I ran my mouth. "Look, lady. You have no right to speak to me like I'm an idiot. I'm not. I thought I'd give you an opportunity to make peace with Grams, so you wouldn't regret it later. She may be a few fries short of a happy meal, but she's still your grandmother. She loves you."

"Why did you call her Grams?"

She caught me off guard. I blinked and pressed the phone against my ear. "What?"

"You called Abigail 'Grams.' Why?"

I didn't know what to say. I didn't anticipate her to ask that, so I said the first thing that came to mind. "I guess because Rex calls her Grams."

"How do you know Rex? Were you friends with him? How old are you?"

I could hear panic, sadness, and frustration in her voice as she rattled off those questions. If she could reach through the phone and shake me senseless, I think she would have. I hated being in this awkward situation. I looked at Rex. He had an anxious expression on his face. I was sure he heard her, the pitch in her tone was elevated enough.

"I'm eighteen," I answered. "And yes, I'm friends with him."

"For your information," she spat, her anger quivering each word, "Rex died years ago. How dare you call me, you sick asshole, and tell me a bunch of garbage about Abigail. It was her fault my Rex died, and if she set you up to this to—"

"She didn't," I interjected. "I know you don't believe this, but Rex's spirit hasn't moved on. He's been with Grams all along. In fact, he's here with me now and was the one who told me to call you. I'm only trying to help and honor his wishes, so maybe you can make amends with your grandmother before her body fails."

Click

"She bailed," I said, tossing the phone on my pillow. "I'm sorry."

"It's not your fault." Rex sat on the bed and hunched his shoulders. "Her reaction doesn't surprise me. I was hoping since she's older now and probably has grandkids of her own, she would have a change of heart. I guess I was wrong."

"She said it was Grams' fault you died. Was it?"

He shook his head. "The accident was my fault, not hers."

"What happened?" I never really thought about how Rex actually died, but now that the subject had been brought up, I was interested in finding out.

"I was riding my BMX bicycle and was hit by a car in town. I didn't die right away. I was in a coma four days."

"Did anything weird happen to you during that time?"

Rex scratched his head and tilted it to the side. "You mean

supernatural stuff?"

"Yeah."

"Not at first," he said. "I don't recall the car hitting my bike, but I do remember being in a deep sleep and having hardcore dreams about my life and what I suspect were my past lives. Then my consciousness shifted..." He rubbed the spot above his eyebrow. "It's hard to explain."

"You're doing fine," I assured him. "I'm following what you're saying."

"Anyway," he went on, "I could hear people talking, but not with my ears."

"Telepathically?"

"Yeah." He nodded. "Their voices were distant, yet I knew what they were saying, and I could feel their joy. They were happy to see me. I sat up in the hospital bed when a brilliant, ray of white light streamed through the window and swiped clockwise across the room, erasing everything in it. Beads of sparkling colors, rained around me. I realized at that moment my spirit had shed the body, then an overwhelming feeling of freedom and excitement came over me. I could see a silhouette of a man and woman, beyond the glittery shower."

"A veil," I blurted, thinking out loud.

He blinked. "What?"

"Sorry. I was thinking there was a veil around you that separated our world from theirs."

"You're right," he said. "Because the next thing I knew, everything turned black, as if I were in a box and it collapsed on me. Then I heard Grams chanting, and I was standing next to her."

"Crazy. You had quite the experience, but why would Jane blame Grams?"

"Because I was sacking out at Grams' house while Mom was on a cruise. Grams was supposed to be watching me, so Mom places my death on Grams' head."

"Wow," I said, rubbing the side of my neck. "I'm sure guilt is playing a role in her behavior."

"I think so, too." Rex stood and floated the short distance between us. He raised himself to my height. "Thank you for at least trying to get through to Mom. I appreciate it."

"No problem," I replied, feeling bad for him.

"I'm going to go check on Grams." He drifted backward.

A thought occurred to me I had to voice before he left. "What's going to happen to you once Grams passes from our world?"

He shrugged. "I don't know. I imagine I'll have a choice whether to stay or move on."

"What do you want to do?"

He pulled in his lips and tapped them with the tip of his finger. "I'd really like to stay and help you and your friends; however, it's not safe for me to do so with the dark spirits around."

"But there are other entities who roam here without any problems from them," I pointed out. I thought it would be cool to have Rex around. He'd be an asset to have on our team, and I enjoyed his company. Yeah, the kid was growing on me.

"True," he answered. "But they're not meddling in the affairs of malicious beings. If they were, it would be a different story."

"I suppose you're right," I said.

"But whatever." He shrugged again. "I'm good with transitioning to the next realm with Grams if I have to."

"Have you ever seen what it's like on the other side?"

He shook his head. "Not really."

"I had a glimpse once when Paige's grandmother Kora visited us."

His eyes widened. His interest immediately peaked. "Really? What did you see?"

"The realm was beautiful," I told him "In fact, Carrie cried. I saw a plush, green meadow with brilliant, gorgeous flowers. The sky was a lilac color, and in the distance were snow-capped mountains."

"Awesome," he said, grinning. "The place sounds totally rad."

"It was," I admitted.

"See ya later. Gotta go check on Grams." He waved and vanished.

"Later," I said to the empty room and went to take my shower and get cleaned up.

A half hour or so later, I decided to lie on my bed and try to contact Gabriel. I had no idea what I was doing. I was lost in more ways than one, but I wasn't about to throw in the towel. It wasn't my style to give up so easily. Besides, Carrie was my world. One way or another, I would find a way to help her.

I closed my eyes and silently called out to Gabriel, visualizing him in my mind and my desire to converse with him. After a couple of minutes, my focus slipped and skipped to Grams and Rex's mom. I wondered what would become of their situation. I wondered—

Dammit.

I shouldn't be thinking about them right now. I redirected my thoughts to Gabriel. Then, I pondered about Carrie, Isadora, the reaping, and Rex telling me I'd have to kill Isadora and in the process, Carrie, too. My heart raced, and my desire to speak to Gabriel or anyone who could help me, peaked exponentially. A feeling of weightlessness overcame me. My mind and consciousness rose. The experience was like having poor vision and seeing clearly for the first time. The muck placing a film over our human eyes lifted. I was no longer a spirit looking from the inside out. I was simply a spirit no longer housed in a meat suit.

I stood in a vast field full of radiant wildflowers. The sky was lilac, exactly like I told Rex. The temperature felt like seventy degrees. Perfect.

"Jack," a male voice said behind me.

I turned and smiled. "Gabriel." He stood tall in all his glory, looking sharp in black slacks and a white button up shirt. "I was afraid I wouldn't be able to reach you."

"Your desperation and need to contact one of us stimulated the connection," he told me. "I happened to receive your call, and you were fortunate enough to have accomplished it. Your future attempts will not always be so."

He mentioned this to me before. I was well aware there would be times when my message for assistance would go unanswered. Regardless, it didn't matter to me now. What mattered was the dire situation I found myself in.

"I need your guidance," I said. I opened my mouth to continue, but closed it when he lifted his hand.

"The council of witches has already enlightened me regarding the nature of your troubles," he informed me.

"And." I gestured for him to continue.

"They're not pleased with the results of the awakening spell," he said in a matter-of-fact tone, like we were talking about the stock market and how lousy the stocks were doing.

"Why won't they do something?"

"As I'm sure you already know they will only step in when a crime has been committed, such as when Abigail bound Rex's essences to your world, or when another witch kills her own. There are laws in witchcraft that must be followed."

"Wait a minute," I said, furrowing my brows. "I thought when a witch uses dark magic or too much, she loses her power as punishment from the council of witches."

"Your assumption is incorrect," he said. "Magic is rooted in nature. Nature has its own laws. If one abuses it, the consequences can be catastrophic. However, it's true that excessive use of it can deprive one of the ability to perform."

"What if a person goes against nature while using magic?" I was thinking about when Isadora turned her coven into dogs. Her intentions for casting the spell weren't sinister, but it probably didn't matter either way.

Gabriel raised his eyebrows. "You're referring to Isadora cursing her friends?"

I nodded. "I am. Her heart was in the right place but..." I trailed off.

"But she used black magic and forced nature to do her bidding," he finished.

"Yeah." My stomach knotted. I thought about the reaping and knew without a doubt Isadora would attempt to do the same thing again in order to break the curse she cast on her coven. If she succeeded and lived, she would be facing the wrath of both Mother Nature and the council of witches, which meant Carrie would as well. Not good.

"Do you understand what's really taking place in terms of Carrie and Isadora?" Gabriel asked.

"Their situation is confusing." I rubbed the back of my neck and rolled my head around to loosen the tightness in the muscles. Strange I was in—I was guessing—Summerland and still had to deal with my human body. In the back of my mind, the movie *The Matrix* popped up. My neck probably wasn't hurting, but my brain told me otherwise. "Jaegar cast a locking spell on Isadora's spirit when he murdered her," I continued carefully, thinking this through as the words rolled off my tongue. "Isadora's spirit remained attached to her soul, like a parasite. The soul moved on and reincarnated." Gabriel nodded. "The spirit of the next life after Isadora became part of the soul, so on and so on... building it through the experiences of those lives. Now we have Carrie's spirit. It's attached to her soul and will become a part of it when she dies." I scratched my head and frowned. "Am I understanding the process right? When I say it out loud, it sounds weird to me."

A small smile formed on his lips. "It's difficult for the human brain to encompass the ethereal process of the soul. Too complex, I suppose. However, you my friend have a grasp on the concept that's quite impressive." He placed his hand on my shoulder. "Every one of us has a common enemy, which is oneself. If you allow doubt and fear take root inside your heart, it will lead you astray." He released his hand and continued. "You're an apprentice light walker, who is in constant training. The plight you're in is a lesson to be learned. Neither I nor any other light walker can meddle in your affairs, so you can cheat your way into becoming one of us."

"I'm not asking you to," I said, my face burning from embarrassment. Maybe I shouldn't have contacted him, because he had the wrong idea about why I did. "I plan on earning my wings... so to speak... on my own," I added.

"I'm aware," he said. "I wasn't suggesting anything less. I was only informing you on the matter."

"Rex told me I'd have to kill Isadora, so she can crossover and eventually join Carrie's soul." I tightened my jaw. "I'm not going to. I refuse to harm Carrie."

His expression displayed nothing but understanding and kindness, but then he told me something that threw me for a loop. "Isadora's spirit won't be merging with Carrie's soul." I gaped at him, and he went on. "Jaegar ruined any such opportunity for her. As we speak, Isadora is piggy backing on Carrie's spirit. In truth, she's a separate entity dwelling inside of Carrie but has the ability to share memories and possible thoughts with her. As far as we know, Isadora is unaware she's no longer connected to the soul. If she discovers the truth of her reality, we believe she will attempt to take full possession of Carrie."

"It gets better and better." I sighed, the back of my neck heating up. "Grams assured us Isadora wouldn't be able to monopolize Carrie's body, yet in truth she can. If we knew there had been even the slightest possibility she could, we would have never agreed to the awakening spell."

"Carrie would have," Gabriel said, nonchalantly.

"How do you know?"

"She was already seeking answers to connect with her life as Isadora."

"So what will happen to Isadora?" I asked, not wanting to get into whether Carrie would have made the same decision or not. It didn't matter anyway. She made it, and Grams opened Pandora's Box. "And didn't the council of witches know there was a possibility Isadora's spirit might be severed from Carrie's soul?" *What a stupid ass question*, I silently chastised myself. Of course they didn't know. However, basically they were betting the farm, so to speak, it would work.

"She will—"

"Wait a minute," I interrupted. "I thought of something I need to ask before I forget."

"Go ahead," he said, unperturbed.

"The soulless humans on earth... do they have spirits?"

"No."

"Okay." I gestured for him to continue. "Please tell me about Isadora's fate."

"The council of witches was hoping Isadora's essence would integrate with Carrie's soul." His eyes dimmed, the sandstone color dulling. He glanced away and then back at me. There was a disagreeable look on his face. "They underestimated Jaegar's cleverness. When Abigail executed the awakening spell, it severed Isadora's spirit."

"What's going to happen to her?" I asked again, wanting to kick Jaegar's ass for doing this to her and Carrie.

"She's now a spirit without a soul," he simple stated. "Since she's a witch, she'll have to stand before the council. Otherwise, I have no knowledge of what will become of her."

"I'm not going to harm Isadora," I reaffirmed. *If they expect me to, they can piss off.* "So what can I do to get her to release her grip on Carrie?"

"Since dark magic is what created this mess, the council is deciding as we speak on how to take care of what's become a delicate and volatile matter," he answered. "All you can do is be there for Carrie and help prevent her from being intoxicated with Isadora's consciousness."

"Hold up." I raised my hand, palm facing him. "You said earlier the council won't get involved unless a witch kills her own. Jaegar was a male witch."

"Yes," Gabriel confirmed. "He wasn't part of Isadora's coven, but she knew he was a solitary wizard."

Gabriel's form began to fade. A sharp pain ripped through my head. I recalled it didn't happen the last time I visited with him and wondered why it was happening now. There were still questions I wanted answered, but the sudden debilitating pain took precedence over them. "Why is my head hurting now? It didn't hurt before," I cried out, grasping my temples, my hands clenched around my noggin.

"At the time, you were in the company of a good spirit," he said, disappearing before my watery eyes. "Rex's energy prevented it from happening."

The world around me spun. The ground fell out from under me. I spiraled downward. A loud dinging erupted in my ears. I sat up in bed, held my head in my hands, and groaned.

Chapter Seventeen

Isadora

"Are you going to keep me in suspense for much longer?" I asked, taking a sip of my cappuccino, loving the frothy milk on top. I added a couple of packets of raw sugar, making the bold flavor sweet and heavenly.

Ayperos eyes darted around the charming coffee shop, as if he were searching for spies who would interrupt and ruin our plans. There were about a dozen people, much like ourselves, enjoying the intake of caffeine and the coziness of this place. We were fortunate to lay claim a table next to a window. The young lovebirds who were sitting here earlier when we were ordering our drinks decided to relocate themselves on the maroon loveseat in the back, leaving this table unoccupied. I looked past Ayperos, to them. They were reading a magazine together, pointing at a page and laughing. They had to be in their early twenties, I thought.

I focused my attention back on Ayperos. "Well," I prompted, raising my eyebrows. "I'm waiting." The harsh, sucking and spitting sound from a cappuccino machine drowned out my voice. Ayperos heard me, though, because his gaze shifted to me.

"I have good news and bad news," he said.

My heart slipped, but I told myself I was bound to run into some trouble. "What's the bad news?"

"The grimoire with the spell to break the curse was stolen from Volac's lair," he told me.

I knew the name, thanks to my connection with Carrie. Volac was a dark spirit who had quite a following, and he didn't believe in Bael and Ayperos' agenda to change the world back to how it once had been. Their plan had entailed controlling all malevolent beings like themselves and building an army to create mass genocide on the humans they felt unworthy. Paige destroyed their scheme, and now I imagined they were cooking up another one.

"Do you have any idea who stole the spell book?"

He took a sip of his coffee and slowly set it down. He frowned. "No."

I sighed and shifted in my seat, annoyed. The theft had to have been by another witch. I drummed my fingers against the mosaic tile table. The caffeine was definitely kicking in. "What's the good news?"

A slow smile spread across his handsome face, making the corner of his eyes crinkle. "I still have the potion you created to break the enchantment you'd cast on your coven."

I sat up and leaned forward, my wide eyes on his. "You do? I don't recall creating one." I stared past him at nothing in particular, stretching my memory in an attempt to remember me concocting the counter curse. Bits and pieces of me brewing a spell in Ayperos' company came to me, but I wasn't sure if it was the one he spoke of. I guess it didn't matter. He had the potion, and that was marvelous news. I had the urge to squeal but grinned instead, silently telling Carrie her schoolgirl reaction wasn't appreciated. She had to be more refined in order to be taken seriously and have control over a situation. A strong feeling of embarrassment and humiliation fluttered through me. I ignored it, refusing to allow Carrie's insecurities to diminish my cheerful mood.

A smug expression entered Aypero's face. "I've kept it under lock and key for hundreds of years, in hope you would return someday." He folded his hands on the table. "I always have a backup plan." He took a drink of his coffee, eyeing me over the rim.

"You're brilliant," I said, still grinning like a fool. "Now, we have to find Driscol and the others and bring us all together." I would create a locator spell, I decided. But then reality quickly settled in, and a dark cloud overcast my sunny mood. I had nothing from them to perform it with. The only hope I had was them finding me on their own like Driscol had. They were bound to me, so it stood to reason they would. But how long would that take?

"What's troubling you?" he asked, setting his mug down and pushing it aside. "Mere moments ago you were beaming, and now you appear crushed, as if your world caved in on you."

"I thought I could use a locator spell," I shared. "However, I'm unable to." I slumped in my seat and crossed my arms over my chest. "I have no idea how to track my coven's whereabouts. Driscol is here, but the others might still be in Germany for all I know."

"There is no need to trouble yourself with such matters." Mischievousness sparked in his eyes.

I gasped and sat up. "You know where they are?"

He smirked. "Of course."

"Where?"

"If I were to tell you, you'd stop at nothing to go to them now. Am I correct?"

"Absolutely," I answered. "Wild horses couldn't keep me away from them."

He nodded slowly and reached into his pocket. "I thought so." He produced a folded piece of paper and handed it to me. With eager fingers, I opened it, surprised to see directions that would take me deep into the woods.

Omigod! This is the cabin where Aosoth and Roeick would meet when they wanted to be alone and have dirty monkey sex.

I laughed out loud at Carrie's lewd remark.

I no longer have her memories, but I recognize the address, because Nathan had written it down.

"You find this amusing?" Ayperos asked, cocking an eyebrow.

"Not at all," I said. "Carrie informed me these directions lead to Aosoth's cabin, and then she said something I found quite comical."

"And what might that be?"

I told him, and he guffawed.

"Is Carrie right?"

"Yes," he answered, clearing his throat. "Though Aosoth and Roeick are no longer occupying the premises. Their spirits were forced to leave earth."

I tapped the paper with the tip of my finger. "My fellows are here?"

"At the moment, they are not. But tonight they will be."

I folded the paper and shoved it in my pocket. "I want to see them now," I demanded.

"Now is not the right time," he calmly told me. "You still need to deal with Jack and Rex, so they will leave you alone tonight."

Ayperos had the upper hand, and I didn't like it. I needed him, though, and he went far beyond his loyalty in regards to me and my coven. But then I wondered why. What could he gain from our situation?

I drank the rest of my cappuccino and licked my lips. "I gather my coven's presence in Astoria is the second surprise you mentioned earlier?"

"Yes." He was studying me, probably trying to determine what made my demeanor shift from annoyance to a reserved, almost bored attitude.

"What's in it for you?"

He feigned surprise. "You don't trust me?"

"It's more of a matter of curiosity than trust," I countered.

"I have my reasons, and that's all you need to know." He placed his elbows on the table and leaned forward. "I'm helping you get what you want." A dark shadow passed over his face, and his lips tightened. "I have no obligations to you, so don't ever question my intentions."

I bit my lip and sat back in an attempt to get enough space between us as possible. My heart pounded painfully against my chest. I'd pissed him off, something I shouldn't be doing right now. I collected myself and raised my hands in a halting manner. "I'm sorry. I didn't mean to anger you."

"Apology accepted," he said, scooting the chair back, scraping it against the wooden floor. "I will see you tonight at eight."

"My coven will be there?" I asked, rising from my seat.

"Yes, and I will have the potion. As you already know, since you're the one who cast the spell, only you can break it."

"I'm aware," I confirmed, picking up my bag from The Witch's Corner and following him outside.

"I suggest you don't expend too much of your magic beforehand. Otherwise, you might not be able to perform tonight," he advised me.

"Shit," I blurted. "Overexerting my powers never occurred to me. I was planning on casting a spell this afternoon. Do you think it would interfere with breaking the curse?"

"No. One little charm won't ruin your chances tonight." he said. "However, the decision is yours, not mine." He pushed the sleeve of his jacket up and glanced at his fancy gold watch. "I must be off. It's been a pleasure." He turned on his heel and in quick, long strides, he headed in the opposite direction down the cobblestone path.

* * *

I managed to have minimal contact with Carrie's parents when I arrived back at the house. Luck had it they were on their way to the antique shop her mom owned. They wanted to take care of some things and start on inventory. They were happy to see their daughter, hugging her and making sure she felt okay.

A deep sadness tugged at my heart. Carrie's parent's affection and concern for her well-being made me realize how much I missed my own mother and father. I pushed those feelings away so they wouldn't break through my easy expressions while I continued to play the part of Carrie. I pulled it off quite well, thank you very much. Carrie didn't even try to force me aside. Instead, she allowed me to take charge, and I could sense her amusement as I impersonated her.

Now that I had the house to myself, I unloaded my purchases on the kitchen table. Odell was sitting at my feet, staring at me with his brown, droopy eyes. I patted his head and handed him a treat. He devoured it and wagged his tail, giving me anxious looks.

"Alright, big boy," I said, half-smiling as I gave him another biscuit. "No more until later. I have work to do."

When he realized I wasn't budging, he left the kitchen. The dog tags rattling around his neck were the only sound in the house. Returning to my project, I got busy placing herbs in the soapstone mortar for the beauty spell. This enchantment would charm others enough to where they wouldn't look past it, and it would cloak my aura from the boy. As I crushed the ingredients with the pestle, I focused all my energy on visualizing what I wanted. Once I was satisfied with the results, I added rose oil to the concoction until the consistency became runny.

"Perfect," I said to the empty room, pleased with the outcome.

Gathering the items, I took them to Carrie's bedroom and stored everything I wasn't using in an empty shoe box at the bottom of her closet. While shoving it to the far left corner, where it would be hidden among countless shoes and scattered handbags, the hairs on the back of my neck prickled. I had the distinct feeling of being watched. Slowly, I turned around. A sharp gasp escaped my lips when my eyes met Jaegar's. He stood next to the bed, expressionless, wearing dark breeches that stopped below his knees, a matching jacket, and black leather boots. Automatically, my legs pushed me backward, thrusting me against the wall of the closet, behind a curtain of clothes, obstructing my view of him. With a shaky hand, I pushed the material aside. His image vanished. Reluctantly, I crawled out, my eyes frantically searching the room.

Nothing.

I saw no further evidence his presence still remained. Pushing myself off the floor, I held onto the wall to prevent my wobbly legs from buckling. I could feel Carrie's fear, or was it mine? Her thoughts rushed in like a mass of people trying to outrun a giant.

Okay, now I'm freaked. Was that really Jaegar? What the hell does he want? What are we going to do? Maybe we were seeing things. What do you think?

I took a deep breath to collect myself and told her to remain calm while I tried to think events through. Jaegar's image had to have been an illusion. Maybe I was subconsciously thinking about him, considering what was about to take place tonight.

You did share with me your memories of him and what he'd done.

She was right. Thoughts of him and his treachery had plagued my mind. I released a lungful of air and decided to meditate to center myself before I performed the spell. Sitting on the floor cross legged, I closed my eyes and focused on relaxing my muscles, starting with the toes. As I worked my way up each limb, I could feel the tension lifting. Afterward, I felt much better.

"Are you ready for our adventure?" I asked Carrie out loud.

A burst of excitement energized me. My surroundings were clearer and brighter. This was the state of mind I needed to be in and was aiming for. With the three pink candles and mortar in hand, I crossed the hallway to the bathroom and placed them on the counter. The tapered candles needed holders to keep them erect, so I took a few from the bottom drawer in the kitchen. Back in the bathroom, I turned the light on, closed the door, and discarded my clothes. There were no windows, which was a blessing, considering the beauty spell needed to be cast in darkness in front of a mirror.

After the candles were placed in holders, I hovered my hands over them and said, "Incentia."

The wicks ignited. I couldn't help but smile.

Pointing to the switch on the wall, I said, "Decido."

The lights went out.

My smile grew into a gleeful grin. The magical abilities I possessed were flowing a lot easier and working correctly since last night's blunder with the bonfire. I noticed it this morning how simple it was to perform a spell and how it worked effortlessly. I'd finally arrived. Soon I'd be with my coven.

I proceeded to anoint my body with the potion I created in the mortar: forehead, breast bone, belly button, and the pulse points on my wrists and behind each knee. As I went through the motions, the flame on the candles flickered wildly, casting eerie shadows on the wall behind me. I could see them in the mirror. They stretched and bended, as if an elongated being was hovering over me. I wasn't troubled or frightened, though involuntarily I shivered. Ignoring Carrie's sudden fear of having an audience of unknown spectral beings, I stared at my reflection in the mirror. The orange glow around my face made my features standout against the darkness—well, technically, Carrie's features, but I had control, so for the time being, they were mine.

Concentrating and visualizing on my intent, I chanted the incantation in Latin. The image in the mirror wavered. I continued reciting the enchantment, pleased it flowed from my mouth so easily. My reflection rocked back and forth, slowly at first. As my voice gained rhythm, becoming stronger with each word I spoke, the process quickened. A picture of me—the real me—flashed in the glass: long black wavy hair, ocean blue eyes framed by long, thick lashes. I sucked in a sharp breath. My heart raced. I was dangerously close to fouling the spell. However, I managed to keep my composure.

"So mote it be!" I cried out, arms raised above my head.

A loud spitting noise erupted.

The flames went out, plunging me into darkness.

Flicking my hand toward the light switch, I was suddenly bathed in false illumination. Remembering what Ayperos said about conserving my magic, I told myself no more tricks. Tonight was too important to toy with the powers endowed upon me.

Staring at myself in the mirror, I could make out an energy field expanding twelve inches away from my body. There were glittery particles sparkling and shimmering inside its perimeter. What I was observing would compel others to be enraptured by my very presence. The glamour would last for roughly twenty-four hours. I could have made it longer; however, the spell would require more energy to do so, and I didn't want to press my luck. Besides, I only needed the charm long enough to distract Tree and the boy, so I could carry out my plans without them intruding in my affairs.

Feeling both cocky and sensual, I traipsed through the house skyclad. After taking a wineglass from the antique china cabinet in the dining room, I went into the kitchen and poured a glass of wine from the bottle Carrie's mom kept in the refrigerator. It had a deep red color and a rich grape aroma I loved. Retracing my steps to the restroom, I set my alcohol beverage on the sink and twisted the faucet in the bathtub, adding two capfuls of lavender soap to the stream of water. To set the mood I was aiming for, I decided to burn incense Paige had given Carrie. The thick smell of sandalwood filled the room. White, foamy bubbles were rising to the edge of the tub. Humming an old German lullaby, I stepped into the steamy liquid, enjoying how it felt against my bare skin as I sank into it.

* * *

I spent the rest of the afternoon lounging, painting my nails dark blue, and putting makeup on, which included black glitter eyeliner and some smoky eye shadow. Since I was the one who created it, I could see through the glamour. I had to admit though, the extra cosmetics on Carrie's face applied to the right spots made her more attractive. Carrie was pleased with the results. She was thrilled with the beauty enchantment and wanted me to perform more magic, so she could master it through me. We both believed each time I used witchcraft, it left an imprint on her spirit. Also, having my memories was a huge benefit to her. I reminded her we needed to refrain from casting anymore charms until tonight. I tossed her the memories she'd already seen of when I used black magic to turn my coven into canines, and why I chose such drastic measures. The fear of persecution and innocent people being relentlessly tortured fired Carrie's imagination. She was reminded of my mission and why. She calmed down, and a strong determination flowed through me. She was still on my side, and her captivation with the black arts was an added bonus. Like myself, Carrie was anxious about tonight, and I found myself glancing at the clock countless times. We had four more hours to go until eight. The trip would probably take about forty minutes to reach our destination.

While I was pondering things, a knock at the front door caught my attention. I went into the living room and peeked between the curtains covering the front window. It was Tree. He looked worried.

My heart skipped several beats, and a surge of excitement flowed through me. Of course they were all Carrie's feelings. I sighed, a tad annoyed. I didn't appreciate experiencing emotions I didn't want or weren't mine, and it was starting to become a real problem. But Carrie's spirit had a strong willfulness that caught me by surprise when it came to Tree. I didn't like it—not one bit. But I played along and stepped aside. She could take the reins for now. Besides, I had to admit, I was curious about how her boyfriend would react to the beauty spell I cast upon her.

Chapter Eighteen

Carrie

"Carrie?" Tree said in disbelief. I took his hand and pulled him inside, closing the door behind him. His eyes slowly drank in my entire body, from the knee-high brown boots I wore to the skinny black jeans and my low-cut dark purple blouse. "Or is it Isadora?" He pointed to my neck. "I see you're not wearing the crystal Grams told you to wear." He frowned in disapproval.

I slipped my hands inside my back pockets and stuck my hip out. "I'm Carrie, silly. And for your information, I forgot to put the necklace back on. I'm fine, though."

He tilted his head to the side and squinted, scrutinizing me, his expression unsure.

"Do you want me to prove to you it's really me?" I asked, rolling my eyes. "I mean seriously, you should know your own girlfriend."

His shoulders relaxed, and he rubbed his black beanie against the side of his head. "I'm sorry. I've had a rough day." His gaze fell to my breasts. "Where did you get your top? I've never seen you wear it before." He took his gray trench coat off and draped it on the back of the recliner.

"I bought it a while ago but never put it on before," I said, dismissively. "Do you like it?"

He looked at me and slowly nodded, a hunger filling his eyes. "A lot."

My skin heated at the way he stared at me, like he wanted to ravish my body right here and now. Stepping closer to him, I silently dared him to do so. He moved forward, closing the short distance between us.

Cradling my face in his strong hands, he said, "There's something about you I find..." He paused, as if he were at a loss for words.

"Erotic?" I said in a breathy voice.

"Yes," he whispered and kissed me.

I parted my lips, deepening our kiss. Our tongues flicked and rolled against each other. When his hand went between my legs, a deep moan sounded from my throat. He reached down and lifted me with ease. I wrapped my arms and legs around him, my lips still on his.

"Your parents," he whispered breathlessly.

"They won't be home until late tonight," I told him. "They're doing inventory."

He carried me to my room, kissing and nibbling on my neck, driving me insane. With his foot, he slammed the door. Lowering me onto the bed, his long, muscular frame hovered above me. A brief thought entered my mind. Would he be acting this way if Isadora hadn't cast the beauty spell? I wasn't sure, but honestly it didn't matter to me right now. The other night he was unwilling to have sex because of his concern about my health. Besides, I was horny as hell and wanted to take advantage of this opportunity as much as I could.

"I want you," he said, his voice deep and throaty.

He moved my arms above my head and held my wrists in one hand. With his other, he pushed my blouse and bra up. Parts of my body were swollen with desire, begging for attention. When he took an erect nipple between his lips and sucked it, I arched my back and moaned. My nails grazed his back. Hooking my fingers inside his shirt, I tugged it upward. He took it off, along with the rest of his clothes. I followed suit, enjoying the way his lustful eyes devoured every inch of my bare skin.

"God, you're beautiful," he murmured, lowering himself on top of me.

Once again, his lips found mine, our tongues reuniting in passion and hunger. Gently, his hand caressed my inner thigh. I parted my legs, inviting him to continue. His fingers found my sweet place, and he easily slipped two in. Curling them, he pressed against my g-spot. My breaths became erratic as he slowly pumped me, adding pressure to the area every time his fingertips went back inside me. When his gesture became more rapid, I arched my back, and my moans grew louder, my breaths quicker. He persisted in driving me over the edge as he nibbled my ears and then kissed a trail down my neck. He then pulled his hand away and entered me. My vaginal muscles clinched around his hardness, welcoming it. He threw his head back and groaned.

A while later, he held me in his arms, my pink and black checkered comforter covering our bodies. My legs were wrapped around his, and my head rested on his sexy chest. The only thing that could make this blissful moment even better was pizza—after sex pizza with the crust stuffed with mozzarella cheese. Now we were talking.

Tree lifted his head and looked at my digital clock on the nightstand. "Grams is dying," he said, lying his head back down. "She's not going to be able to work with you tonight. I think we should go see her, though."

I wasn't aware Abigail was sick. She appeared fine yesterday. Sure, she seemed exhausted after she performed the awakening spell, but it was getting late, and she had to expend a lot of her own energy to cast it. "How do you know?"

"Rex told me about it earlier. He even had me call his mom to tell her."

"Really?" I propped myself on my elbow and looked at him. "What happened?"

Tree filled me in on the details. I was surprised he actually tried to make contact with Rex's mom. Normally, Tree would balk at calling someone he didn't know or wasn't comfortable talking to, let alone convincing the person to do something. He must have a soft spot for Rex, which I thought was cute.

"I think we should get ready in a few, go get something quick to eat, and then head over to Grams' house," Tree said. "What do you think?"

"I think it's a good idea." I rested my head back on his chest and readjusted my body to its former position against him. "But not yet."

Don't forget about our mission! Isadora's words hissed across every fiber of my being. Silently, I told her to not get her panties in a wad. I wouldn't forget. I had to agree with Tree, so he wouldn't get suspicious.

Tree hugged his arms tighter around me. "We'll give it another half hour."

I ran my fingers across his tight abs and drew slow random designs on his smooth skin. "Good. I'm too comfortable to move anyway."

"I'm worried about you," he admitted, lightly kissing my forehead.

"Why? I'm fine."

"You keep saying you are, but I have a sickening feeling in my gut you're not. I'm concerned Isadora is getting to you."

I stopped tracing circles. "What do you mean?"

"I have to admit," he said. "I'm curious and fascinated by the magic and her, but I..."

"But what?"

"But I feel... no, sense. I sense a darkness brewing inside you. I think you need to resist Isadora. Ignore her. Fight her off."

"Um, she's not a problem," I said defensively, moving back so I could look at him. "Do you realize the horrible shit she went through? Not only was her father and friends tortured to death, the person she wholeheartedly trusted and loved betrayed and murdered her. And he stole a life from her... from me." I sat up and glared at him. My faced burned. "She has every right to regain what she lost, and I'll be damned if I'm going to deny those things from her."

The air grew thick with tension, and I could feel Isadora hanging on my every word. Anxiousness sent my pulse racing. I didn't want to argue with Tree or piss him off, but on the other hand, I thought he was clueless about the hell she went through. Yeah, she was friends with Ayperos, but if it weren't for him, more of the people she loved would have suffered. Not only that, he was more than willing to help her bring Niklas and her friends back. Why? Neither she nor I knew, but at this point, we didn't care. Whatever his agenda was, we'd deal with it later. Dark magic may be frowned upon by those higher than us, but I'd be willing to use it to bring back the people Isadora loved. Besides, it was fun using magic and being powerful, instead of plain Carrie Jacobson who was known for being a dingbat.

Tree rose and sat cross legged. Clamping his hands on my shoulders, he said, "I completely understand the circumstances. Believe me, I feel bad for her. But you don't understand the severity of your situation."

"You don't trust me," I said. "You think I'm weak. Maybe you prefer me being the way I used to be."

His eyebrows furrowed. "Like what?"

"A scattered-brained bubble head, who isn't an asset to our team. I don't even know how to throw a knife." I pointed out, referring to the time when Nathan was teaching us combat skills. "Ever since Abigail did the awakening spell on me," I glanced at the clock—5:32, "less than twenty four hours ago, I've felt more in control and confident than I've ever felt in my entire life."

He cupped my face. "Carrie," he breathed, "I love you for you. I love everything about you. You're not insignificant, and you're a huge help to Paige and Nathan. Don't ever short-change yourself."

"Love is blind," I retorted. "Isadora agrees with me, by the way. Although she says lust tends to cloud ones vision and mind. It did with her."

He dropped his hands and jerked his head back. "She talks to you?" His voice rose in shock.

I made a face like *duh*, but then I realized he wasn't aware that she did. For some reason I thought he already knew. I wasn't sure if what I said was a good thing or bad. Isadora didn't say a word, so I guessed she didn't really care.

Tree heaved an unsettling sigh and stepped out of bed. Grabbing his boxers and jeans off the floor, he said, "We need to go to Grams' house now and see if she can fix the mess you're in before she leaves us."

"Why?"

"Because Isadora is a separate entity, Carrie." He picked up my clothes and tossed them on the bed beside me. "Get dressed."

"What's your problem?" I took a sock, rolled it into a ball, and chucked it at his chest. I did the same thing with the other one, except this time I threw it at his shoulder. He lifted his hand and blocked it, causing the black ball of material to nosedive to the floor. "We already talked about another consciousness living inside me. It's old news. Move on."

"Yes, I know we have," he said, shoving his feet into his combat boots and bending to lace them. In a rush of words, he continued, "But Carrie, she's no longer attached to your soul. When Grams performed the spell, the magic severed Isadora's spirit. She might never be able to be a part of your soul. We have to get rid of her as soon as possible."

"What?" I asked, even though I heard him right. "So Isadora is basically a spirit possessing me, then? Is that what you're saying?"

"Yes."

"What you're saying doesn't make sense, because we're connected. We communicate with each other all the time, and we share memories," I told him, my eyes filling with tears from the overwhelming feeling of sadness rippling through me.

"The awakening spell Grams cast is why you can." He pulled his T-shirt over his head, but when he put his black beanie hat on, his face dropped. He slapped his forehead. "Shit!"

"Now what?" I asked, wiping the tears off my face while I told Isadora I was sorry for what Jaegar had done. I assured her that I would still help undo the curse, and we'd figure something out concerning her existence.

I, too, am sorry, Carrie. I apologize for the actions I'm about to take, but I have no choice. I must survive. I promise you that I will have Ayperos help me locate a soulless vessel. Once he finds an adequate one that meets my standards, I'll perform a transmigration spell, and then you can have your body back.

A fierce wave of energy pushed to the forefront of my mind, shifting it, then streaming down like a waterfall over a rock wall. In panic, I told her to wait, there was no need for her to take full possession of my body. I would step aside like I'd been doing, so she could take control. Besides, I wanted to experience casting more spells, and I wanted to know what it felt like to do black magic. Her memories had given me a taste of its power, but it only piqued my curiosity instead of sedating it. Since our spirits were more or less tangled together, I could actually experience it all, like I had today.

Not this time, Carrie. Your girlish emotions are a distraction and vex me.

"I shouldn't have told you that information," Tree said, repeatedly slapping his forehead. "Shit. Shit. Now Isadora knows. God, I'm such a dumbass."

The energy inside me intensified. I knew Isadora's spirit couldn't root itself to my soul; however, it certainly could crowd into my consciousness, and push me aside in a dark corner like a bully would do to her classmate. I suddenly realized what she was doing, because I could no longer hear her thoughts, which meant she couldn't hear mine either. The strength of her life force startled me. Her essence felt like a large snake squirmy inside my body. I pulled the covers to my mouth and buried my face in them, shivering. At first I tried to resist her by pushing against the growing pressure inside my chest and head. But then an idea struck me, and I stopped fighting. Instead, I held onto the last thread of awareness I had, hoping to fool her into thinking she had succeeded. As I attempt this, once again, I could hear her thoughts. Maybe because I stopped resisting. I didn't know, but I shielded mine by keeping quiet and allowing her to take over.

Isadora was now in charge.

"What's wrong, Carrie?" Jack sat on the bed, bouncing me.

I released the blanket from my face and pointed to the door. "You need to leave."

His eyebrows pulled together, the space between them wrinkling. "Why do you want me to go?" He paused and scooted back, his brown eyes widening. "Isadora?"

I smirked. "The one and only. Now get out."

He stood and leaned forward, towering me. "What did you do with Carrie?"

"Don't worry, handsome," I said, unfazed by the sharp edge in his tone. "I made a promise to her that I intend to keep. She'll return to you again."

"What promise?" he demanded.

"My pledge to her is not your concern. Now go." I flicked my hand in the air toward the door. It swung open and banged against the wall, startling Jack.

"Listen, Isadora," he said, talking fast. "Maybe there's something we can do to help you. It doesn't have to be this way."

"Do you take me as a fool?" I asked. He opened his mouth to speak. I made a quick zipper gesture in front of him. His lips smashed together. He tried to part them but failed. "Silence," I commanded, enjoying the shocked look on his face. This moment reminded me of when I'd done the same thing to Lukas. It pleased me to have the ability to force people to shut the hell up. "I will not make the same mistake twice," I said. "I can sense a ploy brewing inside you, and my patience is wearing thin. I'm going to ask you one more time. Leave now, or I'm going to make you leave."

He made a face and pointed to his mouth.

I mimed an unzipping motion in the air, then jerked my head toward the open doorway.

"I will go," he said, his hands clenching into fists. "But you haven't seen the last of me."

"I wouldn't expect anything less from you," I called out as he stormed from the house, slamming the door behind him.

Throwing the covers off me, I hopped out of bed, feeling more alive than I have since the day Jaegar ended my life. I did a little dance to the bathroom while I sang an old German song I used to love. I thought it would be wise to take another bubble bath and meditate to replenish the magical energy I expended this afternoon. Besides, I wanted to get Jack's scent off my skin and every hint of Carrie's lovemaking with him wiped clean from this body.

Tonight would be the best night of my life, I thought with a grin, adding liquid soap to the rushing water, inhaling the lovely lavender smell. Finally, after hundreds of years of being apart, I'd get to reunite with my loved ones.

My coven.

And so it had begun. A new life in a new era with the ones I loved.

Chapter Nineteen

Tree

I drove around, berating myself for opening my damned mouth. "You're such a stupid, stupid fucker!" I yelled, pounding the steering wheel with the heel of my palm. "Now, what the hell are you going to do?"

I needed to calm down and think. My stomach pinched with hunger. I realized I hadn't eaten anything all day. I'd been too focused on getting my job done and worrying about my situation, so food never entered my mind. Maybe if I grabbed a bite to eat, it would help me clear my head and come up with a viable plan to thwart Isadora's. I imagined the reaping was going to take place sometime tonight, so I needed to act fast.

I found myself driving to Max's father's seafood joint. When I arrived and stepped inside, the smell of fried cod and hushpuppies consumed me. A young guy who looked to be in his early twenties handled my takeout order of popcorn shrimp, fries, and a large root beer. He sort of reminded me of Rex with his messy brown hair and hemp necklace with metal bars strung through it. I'd seen skaters around town wearing similar jewelry. "Where's Max?" I asked him at the cash register.

"He's in the back." The dude hitched his thumb over his shoulder. "Do you want me to get him?"

"Yeah."

I paid the guy and waited while he told Max someone was here to see him. The restaurant was buzzing with chatter, and nearly every booth and table were taken. I hoped Max realized what a gold mine his father had. If Max played his cards right, he'd have a bright future ahead of him. I wondered how his father was holding up with his pancreatic cancer. His predicament made me realize we all had our own personal battles to face and overcome. No one was immune to the countless layers of crisis and heartaches beneath our crusty lives. Something could easily rip it open, dipping its dirty fingertips inside, randomly choosing which catastrophe would befall any individual.

"Tree," I heard Max say, jarring me out of my poetic, morbid thoughts.

Max looked like shit. There were dark circles beneath his bloodshot blue eyes. He flashed me a half-hearted smile. The dimples in his cheeks appeared deeper than normal on his haggard face. His coloring wasn't good either. He looked pale. The spell Carrie cast to give him a boost of energy came to mind. Or was it Isadora who performed it? They were probably working together then, since Carrie mentioned they were communicating with one another. I imagined Isadora allowed Carrie to cast the spell on Max and the one in the forest behind Paige's house. With them as a team, Carrie was able to experience Isadora's power. I could feel my perception sharpening when the revelation crossed my mind. Everything suddenly seemed clearer to me, and I knew why. I'd removed myself from the situation, whereas when I was around Carrie or agonizing over our problems, it hampered my ability to be more attuned to the circumstances at hand. "Max," I finally said, giving him an apologetic smile. "Sorry, man. I was spacing out. How are you? How's your dad?"

"I'm beyond exhausted." He sighed. "My dad's doctor is managing his pain, so he could be worse." His gaze darted around. "Is Carrie with you?"

"No. She had other plans. You know," I said, "what Carrie did to you was a silly trick of the mind. The sudden energy you experienced was probably all in your head."

He rubbed the back of his neck and nodded. "More than likely. But then again, I don't know. It was crazy. I could feel the energy flowing from Carrie to me, and then the lights flickered, and something zapped our palms." Max leaned forward, his tired eyes on mine. In a high whisper he said, "I think Carrie is a witch."

I blinked. I was at a loss for words at first. I didn't expect him to say that. I quickly recovered and gave him a skeptical look. "No, I don't think so," I lied. "She was playing around, using tricks she'd learned on the internet and from her TV show."

"Maybe so." Max shrugged. "I still think she's a witch, though. She just might not be aware she is one."

"Do you believe in witches?" I wondered if he did and what he thought about the paranormal world.

The knowing look in his face grew intense. He nodded, sending shivers up my spine. "I do. And I'll tell ya what—"

"Here's your order," the dude who took it said, setting my drink and a white Styrofoam container on the counter beside the register.

"Thanks," I said, taking a drink of my root beer. The ice cold, dark syrupy flavor tasted awesome. I could tell it came out of a fountain, which was the best.

"No, problem," he said and left.

I stepped closer to Max when he moved away from the counter. "What were you saying?"

"There's crazy shit going on in our world, and most people aren't aware of it," he said.

"Yeah, I know, the government is totally—"

Max's right eye was twitching. "I'm not talking about politics."

"Then what?" I asked. "Did you sleep last night?" He looked like he was going to drop right in front of me.

"No, I haven't slept yet," he answered distractedly. "I had too much energy, but I can feel it wearing off now. I'm going to go home and crash in a minute." He reached up and took hold of my shoulders. "Anyway, this is important, Tree. You know the *Buffy the Vampire Slayer* show Carrie loves?"

"Yeah."

"Well, the same shit is happening in our world... in *our* town, just like in Sunnydale on the show."

I gave him a weird look. "Vampires?"

Dropping his hands, he rolled his eyes, and shook his head. "Not vamps. *Demons.*" He glanced toward the front windows. Two elderly couples were walking up the pier, heading our way. They stopped and turned to look at the river, giving us more time to talk.

"It's possible," I said, making my voice sound indifferent.

"Have you ever heard of the Sheol of Glass?"

Something about that name turned my blood to ice. Goose bumps broke across my flesh beneath my clothes. "No, I haven't. What is it?"

"My father is on some hardcore pain medications, and he's been kind of dopey and somewhat delirious since he's been taking them."

"Yeah." *What is he getting at?*

"He keeps talking to me about the Sheol of Glass, and what's weird is I'm the only one he'll mention it to. If someone is in the room with us or walks in, he'll stop what he's saying, right, frickin', there."

"So what is it?" I asked, having a strong gut feeling this was real and to take Max seriously.

"It's a place where good and bad spirits go. My dad described it as a gray, colorless dimension with large pockets of darkness."

"Why do they call it the Sheol of Glass?"

"According to what my dad said, it's because there's a mirror placed in the center of a tree. Each looking glass is different, by the way, and they're hard to find. Most spirits will walk past one, oblivious to it."

"What are the mirrors for?"

"They're connections... gateways to our world. Only a witch can activate them and bring back a spirit trapped there. Once the spirit leaves, the mirror shatters, spraying glass across the dreary landscape."

"Wow," was all I could say.

"Sometimes," he went on, "an entity will come across one and peer into it. That's why you'll hear stories about someone looking in a mirror and seeing a ghostly figure in it."

The door opened. The two couples we saw a few moments ago walked in, heading our way.

"Listen, don't tell anyone what I told you," he said. "Keep it between us."

"I will, but why did you decide to tell me?"

"My dad told me to tell you," he answered, flooring me. "I was going to call you tomorrow, but then you came in tonight instead."

"Why, though? Why would your dad want me to know?"

"Beats me." He rubbed the corner of his eye. The one that was twitching earlier. "I told you he was delirious."

"Are you going to be okay?"

"I will be once I get some sleep, which I'm going to do in about thirty minutes." His gaze skipped past me to the customers who walked in and were claiming a table near the center of the room. "I'm going to go take their orders before I bail."

"Okay," I said. "If you need anything, let me know. Get some sleep."

"I will. Thanks." He grabbed four menus stacked in a slot on the side of the counter. "See ya around."

I told him bye, my mind buzzing with new information. Once I was back on the road, I drove around while stuffing my face with popcorn shrimp and fries, trying to clear my head. I was still clueless about what to do. If Isadora broke the curse, then what? Would all hell break loose? I needed to find a way to subdue her and get Carrie back. Was the Sheol of Glass the answer to my problem?

I pulled into a gas station and filled the tank, paying with my debit card. As I was putting the gas cap back on, I saw Carrie's red Ford Focus drive by. I hopped in the Scout, shoved the key in the ignition, and gunned it. Luck was on my side. There was a red light down the street, and I was able to catch up. I kept my distance as I followed her out of town, wondering where in the hell she was going. She turned onto US 101 South, heading toward the seaside, like she was going to Cannon Beach. My phone rang. I dug it out of my pocket and pushed the talk button. "Hello."

"Stop following me," Isadora said.

"We need to talk," I told her. "I'm not Jaegar. I promise you I will not screw you over."

"Auf Wiedersehen."

"No. Don't say goodbye," I said, but she already ended the call.

Within a blink of an eye, Carrie's car disappeared.

"You got to be fucking kidding me!" I hollered. I turned around and headed to Grams' house. I hated to intrude on her, especially since she was dying, but I had no other options. I thought about calling out to Rex like I had this morning, but I needed to personally see Grams. She was the one who cast the awakening spell, so maybe she could undo it or perhaps have another solution. Time was running out. I needed to get there as quickly as possible. I pushed my foot down on the gas pedal, praying for help and not to get pulled over by a cop.

* * *

Grams was lying in a queen-sized, four-poster bed made out of dark oak. The head and footboard had ornate designs carved into the wood. The room was full of gorgeous antique furniture. I thought about Carrie's mom. She would love to obtain these pieces for her store.

"I'm sorry to bother you," I said when Grams gestured for me to come closer to her bedside. I moved a Queen Anne chair next to her and sat. "But I need your help."

Her hand fluttered to mine, and I held it. Holy hell, it was cold. Her coloring wasn't good either. She had a gray cast to her face, and a faint smell wafted off her reminding me of sauerkraut and roses. Death was coming. Its scent had already claimed her.

"I know why you're here," she said. I could hear the strength behind her tired voice. She was holding on for some reason. "Rex told me."

I glanced at the foot of the bed where Rex sat. The corner of his mouth curled, and he shrugged. "She wanted to know what was going on with Carrie and Isadora," he told me. "Aesop already informed Grams about the witches' council scrambling for a solution to Carrie's problem, since they're the ones who are really to blame for the mess she's in."

I turned my attention back to Grams. "I don't mean for what I'm about to ask sound like I'm pointing an accusing finger at you, but were you ever aware Isadora could take over Carrie's body? When we told you Aosoth had possessed Carrie, and we didn't want her to go through the same ordeal again, you assured us she wouldn't. Right now, as I speak, Isadora has total control of Carrie, and Isadora is planning something for tonight. Something big. The reaping keeps popping in my head, which leads me to believe that's what she's planning with the drenths."

"Dear me," Grams said, releasing my hand. She attempted to raise herself on her elbows, but she couldn't manage it.

"Allow me to help you." I stood and placed my hand on the hump between her shoulders. Gently, I pushed her forward. With my other hand, I situated her pillow against the headboard, then carefully scooted her in a sitting position. "There you go," I said, covering her with a thick quilt having seen better days. "Are you good?"

She smiled, but it was weak, and the guilt was plain in her milky eyes. "I'm fine. Thank you for being so kind." She paused, then continued. "The monkey who rides on his mother's back will eventually untangle himself from her. He will grow and become independent. He might even go to war against another clan or choose peace instead."

I glanced at Rex. He slowly shook his head and moved his finger in a swirling motion next to his ear.

Riddles.

She was talking in riddles! I thought about some of the bizarre things she said when we first met, like when the cat's away the mice will play. I'd heard the saying before, but now as I pondered it, she meant when Carrie was alone, she and Isadora would play.

What else did Grams say?

Oh, yeah, her hour glass was almost empty. She knew she was going to die. She also mentioned something about a lone wolf, but I couldn't recall exactly what she said, but she was probably referring to Driscol or maybe even Jaegar. I moved to the edge of my chair and leaned forward on my knees. "Grams, what do you mean by what you just said?"

She blinked several times, as if she were refocusing her eyes. "Excuse me?"

"What did you mean about the monkey being on his mother's back? Does it have anything to do with Isadora and Carrie?"

"I never thought of that," Rex said, following my train of thought. I got to hand it to him. He was sharp.

"Riddles," I said, keeping my attention on Grams.

"Yes," she confirmed. "Isadora is alive in our world, and she has two choices." Her gaze dropped to her lap, and she sighed. "I'm afraid she's chosen the wrong one." She looked at me, worried. "I fear for her and sweet, sweet Carrie."

My heart dropped at her dismal response. "Why did you perform the awakening spell if you suspected even the slightest chance this might happen? We trusted you."

"I'm sorry," she said. "The council of witches and I never anticipated how clever Jaegar's spell was. They realize now their mistake and are taking full responsibility."

"What are they doing about it?" I asked.

She frowned. "I wish I had an answer for you, but I don't. Aesop informed me this morning the witches appreciated my help, and my insubordination has now been completely absolved. The council has pardoned me for my misuse of magic on Rex. I can now enter Summerland if it is my desire."

"Grams," Rex said, floating closer to her above the bed, then taking a seat next to her. "I never once resented you for keeping me here with you."

"Yes, but nevertheless," she told him, "I performed dark magic on your spirit for selfish reasons. I didn't want you to leave me, like my precious daughter had. You remind me so much of her. I couldn't—"

"So now what?" I asked, interrupting them. I didn't want to be rude, but time wasn't on my side. I needed to figure out what to do and fast.

"You wait and trust the ancestors," Grams simply stated.

I laughed, though nothing was funny. "Um, no. Like that's not going to happen. How can I trust the witches when they're the ones who played Russian roulette and lost? I need to do something. I can't sit and do nothing."

"You've done all you can," Grams said, then narrowed her eyes to give me a stern look. "The council rarely makes a mistake, and when they do, they're hell bent on fixing it and will not stop until they do. Rest assured, they will correct Carrie's problem."

"I failed." I shook my head in disgust, suddenly angry with myself. "I'm an apprentice light walker, who instead of helping his girlfriend take control over Isadora like I was supposed to have done, I opened my big mouth. I told Carrie that Isadora was no longer attached to her soul."

Rex gaped at me. "You didn't."

I nodded. "Yeah... I did."

Rex blew out a slow whistle. "You totally screwed up."

I made a face. "Gee, thanks. I appreciate it, man."

"What's done is done," Grams said.

I dropped my head in my hands, feeling like shit for letting Carrie down. I'd promised I wouldn't allow anything bad happen, but I was unable to deliver on my oath. Instead, I added fuel to the fire. Some boyfriend I was. Now, I was expected to sit idly by and do nothing. I couldn't. I had to do something, and there was no doubt in my mind Ayperos was involved somehow.

The sound of flapping wings caused me to jerk my head up. A large, brown spotted owl was perched on the footboard, facing Grams. "Aesop," I said. "What are you doing here?" Like he would talk to me. So lame.

"He's giving Grams a message," Rex told me.

Grams stared at Aesop. She never once blinked, reminding me of the staring wars Paige and I used to have when we were kids. I waited for what damned near felt like five minutes, when finally her eyes locked onto mine.

Fear assailed me. I felt cold and then hot. A sour taste rose in the back of my throat, and the room spun. My body swayed. The next thing I knew, Rex was holding me up by my shoulders. His voice sounded distant when he said, "Water" and held a plastic cup to my lips. I drank the liquid, its coolness chilling the back of my throat, taking the nasty taste away.

"All better?" he asked, studying me.

I handed him the cup. "Yeah, thank you. My nerves are shot." Taking a couple of deep breaths, I wiped the sweat off my forehead, thinking what a candy ass I was. I certainly wasn't scoring points in the superhero department.

"The fear of the unknown is an enemy dwelling in all of us," Grams said. "Trust and faith is an armor that one can use to repel it. You've made mistakes, Jack, but we all do. It's called growth. As long as we learn from them and use the experience to move forward, we have not failed." She snuggled deeper into her blanket and continued. "Aesop informed me where Isadora and the drenths are. Isadora has succeeded in breaking her curse."

"Drenths? So there are more now?" I thought of the reaping.

She nodded. "All but one. Ayperos is with them."

"I knew he had his dirty paws in this," I said, balling my hands into fists.

"Are you ready to put the armor on and face these powerful witches?"

I could feel the confusion on my face. "I thought the council didn't want me to."

"They need your help, after all," she answered. "So what will it be?"

I hopped to my feet. "I'm in. Tell me where they are, and I'll do whatever I can to end this once and for all."

Chapter Twenty

Isadora

The lights were on inside the small, rustic cabin nestled among Douglas firs and elms in this remote area. I parked next to a black SUV on the south side, thinking they're here. In a rush of excitement, I stepped out of the car, took a few steps, and nearly tripped over my own feet when the toe of my boot caught a large stone, jerking me forward. I was able to recover my balance and sprint around the corner, where there were bamboo tiki lights purposely spread out in front of the cabin. They were already lit. The flames appeared bright against the backdrop of the night and forest. I could hear dogs whining inside and their anxious barks.

They knew I was here.

My chest tightened with emotion.

The front door swung open before I reached it, and three enormous German shorthaired pointers came barreling toward me. Kneeling, I opened my arms, laughing and crying as I hugged and kissed each one of them. They licked my face, their backsides dancing wildly from the force of their wagging tails.

"We're finally together," I said between silent sobs. "I missed you so." I gave the liver colored dog with the small letter D on his side another hug and showered his face with kisses. "Where's Lukas?" I asked, rising to my feet, meeting Ayperos' gaze.

He stood in front of the open door. The golden light behind him illuminated his tall frame and long black hair, which was tied properly at the base of his neck. He reminded me of a dark angel, here to answer my prayers. "He died decades ago," he told me.

My hand fluttered to my chest. "How?"

"He darted in front of a train."

"Suicide?" I wondered out loud, knowing Lukas was the weak link in our coven. He was probably despondent and could no longer bear what had befallen him.

Ayperos closed the door and descended the short stairs leading off the rickety deck. "I believe so."

"May the Gods have mercy on his troubled soul." I sighed. Out the corner of my eye, I thought I saw a familiar figure. I released a small gasp and jerked sideways. I could have sworn it was Jaegar. "Did you see him?" I pointed in the direction where I thought I saw Jaegar.

Ayperos looked where I was indicating. "See who?" He lifted his eyes and nodded at a high branch in the elm. "Oh, him. Yes, we have company."

There was a large, brown spotted owl perched above us. "Aesop," I said. "But I wasn't talking about him."

Ayperos raised his eyebrows, prompting me to divulge my possible madness. I didn't feel like telling him, so I swung my attention to my coven instead. All three of them were sitting next to me, patiently waiting. My brother Niklas in canine form had a white coat and muzzle, while his ears, face, and tail were black. He also had several large, dark patches on his body, and of course there was a small letter N on his side. Jorsten's coat on the other hand, was grayish white in color with speckled marks throughout it. On his side was the letter J. Like Niklas, Jorsten had large patches on his body and rump, but his were brown, matching the color of his tail.

"Do you have the potion?" I asked Ayperos.

He reached inside his duster jacket and produced three glass vials filled with bright blue liquid. "There is no need for theatrics," he said, referring to casting a circle and calling up the guardians of the four corners. "It wasn't necessary when you cast the spell, and it's certainly not needed to break it. Unless of course you feel the need to do so. I'm obviously not a witch, so what do I know?"

I looked up at the night sky, clustered with bright, twinkling stars. Wispy clouds were circling the waning white moon. Closing my eyes, I flared my nostrils, breathing in my surroundings to center myself. The strong scent of dirt and burnt wood enveloped me. A gentle breeze caused the crisp, cool air to nip at the tip of my nose and cheeks. I wondered if Mother Nature was stirring in response to me, once again, going against her by performing dark magic to break the curse on my coven. The memory of me creating the counter-curse in the presence of Ayperos flashed before me. My heart raced as an affluent source of energy rose, buzzing within me. Everything from my past was much clearer now.

I opened my eyes. "I'm ready."

Ayperos handed me the potions. "Only you can give this to them since you're the one who cursed them."

"Yes, I know," I said. "I think being around my fellows has triggered the rest of my memories." I reached down and petted Jorsten's head.

Ayperos stepped away and moved to the deck. "I'm sure it has... by the way, you look ravishing tonight."

"Beauty spell," I said, and then smiled at the three canines sitting in a half circle around me, patiently waiting. "Are you ready to be human again?" I asked them.

Wagging their tails, they sat up and barked several times.

"I'm going to give the elixir to each one of you," I told them, "but first I need to charge it with the moon's energy, since it's the focal point of power upon the earth."

I held the vials tightly in my hand and raised my arms above my head. Chanting in Latin, I drew down the moon's essence, which I knew channeled forces from the lunar realms and solar system. The white globe turned crimson and wept in thin red bands off the bottom, as if crying bloody tears. The hair on the back of my neck rose, and my hands tingled from its power. Now was the time to impregnate the lunar energy with my desires. I visualized my coven being human once again and me finding a vessel similar to mine in the 1600s. The stars shifted, then fell. Hundreds rained down in bright streaks of light above us in the fashion of an umbrella. It was magnificent.

"So mote it be!" I called out thrice. Once in Latin, then in German, and finally in English.

As soon as I finished saying those four words, the heavens went back to their normal state. No more shooting stars or bloody moon. The process happened rather quickly, and I was pleased with the results. I felt like every molecule in my body was infested with dynamic energy; a strong sense of invincibility overtook me. My mind was sharper and more alert. I couldn't help but grin.

"Nice," Ayperos said, nodding in approval. "You're an amazing witch to watch. Imagine if we had Volac's grimoire in our possession. What wondrous things you could do."

"Yes," I agreed, "and I intend to find and claim it." Not waiting for a reply, I turned to the three German shorthaired dogs still in their sitting positions. "Who wants to go first?"

The grayish white canine with speckled marks glanced at the other two. They jerked their heads in my direction and took a step back. Their behavior made me wonder how Driscol and Niklas could react in the same manner, mirroring each other's movements. They had to be communicating in thought pictures, I rationalized.

Jorsten moved forward and looked up at me. I cradled his chin and told him to open his mouth. He complied. With a steady hand, I poured the elixir down his throat, being mindful not to go too fast. I didn't want to choke him or cause him to gag and inadvertently spit it out. He swallowed the liquid with no problem, then turned and ran away.

"Where are you going?" I called after him, watching him vanish between the trees into the night.

"He'll return," Ayperos said. "Carry on."

I glared at him. The arrogance in his tone annoyed me, and I despised being told what to do. Regardless, if it weren't for him, this would have never taken place. Of course, I wasn't an imbecile. He had his own agenda behind it all. What it was, I did not know, nor did I care. Whatever he required of me or my coven afterward, we would repay our debt to him without question.

I bit my tongue to prevent myself from lashing out at him for throwing orders as if I were his slave and turned my attention on Niklas. Without hesitation, he approached me. Eagerness danced in his brown eyes. His faith and trust in me had never wavered. Even as a child he sought my council. To see it still present within him softened my heart. A newfound love for my baby brother was born. I made a silent vow that I would make his happiness a priority, and he would live a fulfilling life.

"Brother," I said, petting his white coat and dark head. "Soon you'll get to walk as the man you are and bed plenty of women if you so desire."

I gave him the potion in the same fashion as with Jorsten. He took it without incident and ran deep into the forest. A sudden fear gripped me. What if something went wrong, and I had no way of knowing? I wasn't comfortable with them being out of my sight. But it was too late. There was nothing I could do for them now but wait. Ayperos said Jorsten would return. I had to trust his word, and that Niklas would find his way back, as well.

Driscol was last. As I walked toward him, the pit of my stomach fluttered when an image of his tall, muscular body wrapped around mine popped in my mind. A distant stirring in my solar plexus invaded my short, delicious reverie.

Carrie?

The sensation left me as quickly as it came. I was well aware Carrie's spirit was still brimming with life and attached to the soul in this body. However, I had bullied it into submission and appreciated the fact that her insecurities and self-depreciation made it easy for me to do so. I found it unlikely what I felt was her. She was weak, a fault I found unbecoming, even though we were connected in an ethereal way. But I blamed Jaegar for Carrie's flaws and both of our predicaments. I harbored no ill will toward Carrie and would keep my promise to her.

"Driscol," I said, hugging him. "Please stay with me while the transformation takes place." He nudged my face with the side of his. I took it as a silent pledge he would.

I stood and followed the same routine with him as I had with the others. He gulped the fluid, his throat muscles moving in rapid motions. He backed away. My heart stopped in fear he would vacate the premises. He didn't. Instead, he hunched his back and rotated his head in slow circles, then tilted it from side to side, as if he were trying to make out a sound coming from all different directions. His legs shook, and soft whimpers issued from him.

I found myself chewing on my fingernails, which was odd. I'd never done such a thing before. I pulled my hand away and crossed my arms over my chest, cringing at the cracking noises coming from Driscol. The fur on his arched spine split the length of his body from head to tail. It peeled downward, revealing shiny, gray tissue. His muzzle and head were shifting in a grotesque manner. One cheekbone would rise while the other rippled beneath his skin. The process reversed in rapid succession. He lifted his chin like he was going to howl out his agony. His bald ears flattened against his skull, melting like wax into it. Loud popping sounds echoed around us, while his legs and vertebra dislocated and reformed. At the same time, layers of skin sprouted across his body in a peaches and cream color. A dusting of dark hair followed on his arms, legs, and head. His stomach contracted, forming a taut abdomen.

I glanced over my shoulder to see if Ayperos was watching. I didn't see him. Strange. My attention swept back on Driscol, and my heart nearly sprang out of my chest. "Driscol?" I whispered, clutching my breast.

He stood naked before me, stretching his arms and legs. His glorious, muscular body was exactly how I remembered it. My eyes dropped to below his waist, and a devilish grin crept across my face. Oh, what a sight to behold. My body warmed at the thought of him entering me. I looked up to him rubbing his face and running his fingers through his brown hair.

"My god," he finally said more to himself than me. "After hundreds of years, I'm human again. I... I don't know what to say."

"Do you remember your life as a beast?" I asked, noticing him looking in every direction except at me, like he was seeing his surroundings for the first time.

"My vision is less sharp," he mumbled. He blinked and shook his head several times. His hazel eyes skipped to me. They appeared clear and focused now. He smiled, and in quick strides, he crossed the short distance between us. "Isadora!" he exclaimed, throwing his arms around me and spinning us, laughing. I clung to him and joined in his laughter. "Yes, I remember everything and learned loads of things through the centuries... about people, the change in vocabulary, and advancements in our world." We stopped twirling, and he set me back on my feet. Placing his hands on my shoulders, he continued. "I've lived with many families and discovered the most important aspect in life."

"And what might that be, Mr. Strauss?" I asked, feeling a swarm of butterflies in the pit of my stomach again.

He tilted my chin up and looked deeply into my face. "If you love someone, you tell her and spend each and every day showing her how much you do."

My breath hitched in my throat. Was he referring to me?

"I'm in love with you, Isadora," he confessed. "I always have been. The idea and belief of being with you once again is what motivated me to continue on throughout the centuries."

"I love you, too," I said, pressing my body against his, feeling his arousal on my groin.

Right when Driscol's lips brushed mine, Ayperos interrupted us. I wanted to throttle him for ruining this perfect moment and caught myself raising my hand to do so. I resisted the urge and shot him an icy look instead.

He had an arm full of clothes. "I brought you some adequate accouterments to wear for this era," he told Driscol, as he handed him a pair of boxer briefs, jeans, long sleeve black T-shirt, and a gray hoodie. "I trust this will meet your satisfaction?"

"Yes, of course," Driscol said while zipping his jeans up. They hung loose on his hip bone, but not enough to justify the trouble of wearing a belt. "I appreciate your generosity."

Ayperos smiled. "My pleasure. Your socks and boots await you inside the cabin."

"How did you know my size?" Driscol asked.

"I have a long memory," Ayperos told him, heading toward the trees where Jorsten and Niklas entered.

"Where are you going?" I wanted to know.

"They're out there," he said over his shoulder. "Don't you hear them?"

Holding my breath, I listened. In the far distance, I could hear laughter along with hooting and hollering. Driscol and I shared a smile. I made a move to follow Ayperos and go to them, but Driscol caught my arm, stopping me. His soft lips touched mine, sending my pulse racing. Throwing my arms around his neck, I darted my tongue in and out of his mouth. He placed his hand on the small of my back and nudged me closer. I obliged and pressed my body to his. When I deepened our kiss, he released a slow, seductive moan, setting parts of my body on fire. His hand slipped up my blouse, causing my breaths to become erratic.

I wanted him.

God, I wanted him.

"Isadora!" Niklas called out.

Driscol and I looked and saw Niklas and Jorsten running toward us. They both were wearing jeans, but Niklas had on a dark blue hoodie, whereas Jorsten wore a black one. My throat thickened and tears clouded my vision. I blinked them away and ran to my brother.

"Sister," Niklas said, laughing and hugging me when I jumped into his arms. "I missed you terribly."

"And I you," I said, pulling back to get a good look at him. I brushed his black bangs out of his dark blue eyes and grinned. "How are you feeling?"

He tilted his head back and shouted, "I feel marvelous!" He took my hand, twirled me in circles and led me into a merry little dance we used to do many moons ago.

"Jorsten. Driscol." I reached my hand out. Jorsten took it, and Driscol took Jorsten's other hand and Niklas'.

All four of us laughed and danced in a circle. Niklas bellowed a song we all knew quite well. We followed suit and sang along with him.

Under the bright moon our coven meets.
We take each other's hands.
Goddess and Gods we humbly greet.
We form a circle and move in a wicked prance.
We stand our ground and do the witches' dance.
Earth, water, air, fire.
We call upon thee to fulfill our desires.
Earth, water, air, fire.
We call upon thee to fulfill our desires.
Moving clockwise we chant at the top of our lungs.
Bathing in magic, our will shall be done.
The powers we seek is surely ours.
We will no longer live behind iron bars.
Our feet keep moving in a wicked prance.
We continue performing the witches' dance.
Earth, water, air, fire.
We call upon thee to fulfill our desires.
Earth, water, air, fire.
We call upon thee to fulfill our desires.

A clap of thunder halted us. The sky burst open as if someone punctured a hole into it, and a torrential downpour engulfed us.

"Come along and get inside before you catch your death," Ayperos said, jogging to the cabin.

Driscol took my hand. We followed, all four of us still laughing. When we made it inside, Ayperos retrieved towels from the bathroom and handed us each one.

Jorsten stood before the stone fireplace. Pointing to it, he said, "Incendio." A small flame jumped between the logs. It flickered, then went out. He looked at me, perplexed. "What's the meaning of this? Do I not possess magic now?"

"Fear not, my dear friend," I said. "Your powers will return soon enough."

He frowned and dried his dark shaggy hair. The mere gesture caused his rugged appearance to be perceived as brooding, but I knew him well. Jorsten wasn't one to fret over matters if presented with a solution. Desirable or not, he would move on to the next thing for a while.

Niklas elbowed Jorsten aside. "Let's see if a real man can create fire."

Jorsten guffawed. "Please, don't embarrass yourself. You're already digging yourself a hole. Besides, your skills aren't in casting spells. Have you even performed one on your own?"

Niklas cracked his knuckles. "No, but there may be a possibility I received the casting gene the same as Isadora." He rubbed his palms together.

"Only the women in our family have it," I reminded him. "Your gift is in herbology and your quick mind obtaining the knowledge of their magical properties."

"Humor me, sister," Niklas said, not affording me a look. Instead he flicked his hand out, palm facing the logs. "Incendio."

Behind him, I mirrored his movement and silently repeated what he said. A whooshing sound came from the fireplace, and a healthy fire ignited inside it. Out the corner of my eye, I could see Driscol smiling at me. He caught what I'd done. Glancing over my shoulder, I saw Ayperos sitting on a wooden chair near a dark green couch, watching us. He gave me a half nod in acknowledgment.

"Ha!" Niklas said to Jorsten, gloating. "Who's the man now?"

Jorsten scratched his head. "Balls." The side of his mouth twisted in confusion. "Luck."

"What?" Niklas asked.

"I gather it was pure luck," Jorsten said.

Niklas made a face and vibrated his lips. "Are you mad? It wasn't luck. I must..."

"Niklas," I said, guilt pinching my insides. I should have known this would be the outcome of my parlor trick. "I was the one who cast the spell... not you."

Jorsten clapped a hand on Niklas' shoulder and shook it. "I stand corrected. It wasn't pure luck but big sister fooling with you." He winked at me.

Niklas pushed Jorsten's hand off him and stared at me in disbelief. "Why would you toy with me in such a wicked manner?"

"Nikki," I said, using the name we called him at home, "I apologize. I only wanted to pull the wool over Jorsten's eyes and have a little fun."

"At my expense," Niklas spat.

"She meant you no harm," Driscol told him.

"Listen," I said to Niklas, trying to quell his anger, "you're a talented herbologist. You may be lacking in the ability to cast spells, but you have a fantastical gift in the ability to discover and contain such knowledge about the magical properties in each plant. I myself could never measure up to you in that department. So accept what the gods and goddesses have bestowed upon you, for it certainly is a rare trait to possess."

"Quit with the sour face," Jorsten told Niklas. "You're an asset to our coven. Maybe with loads of practice and Isadora as your mentor, someday you may be able to perform magic."

"Niklas," Ayperos said, drawing our attention to him now lounging on the couch. "I've lived for over a thousand years, so consider this piece of wisdom I'm going to share with you."

"What clever advice do you have?" Niklas asked.

"Everyone pines for something they lack, whether it's good looks, intelligence, wealth, a loving relationship, and so forth. What they fail to realize is each one of them has a strength they can use to their benefit. Not to mention, others are probably envious of a quality you fail to acknowledge about yourself. So never covet thy neighbor, for by doing such a thing will blind you from the treasures you carry inside your person."

Niklas thought about it for a minute, then finally said, "You're right."

Ayperos smirked. "Of course I am."

"Do you hold any ill will toward me?" I asked Niklas, grateful Ayperos put everything into perspective.

Niklas shook his head and in a sharp tone, he said, "No. I forgive your lack of consideration for your only living relative."

Ouch. My heart sank, and I hung my head. My brother's resentment was something I didn't think I could bear.

"I'm fooling with you." He embraced me. "My heart would never allow me to harbor anger toward you."

"I'm sorry," I told him, tightening my arms around him. "I would never intentionally harm you."

"Nor I you," he said.

"I'm famished," Jorsten piped. "And I want a good pint of ale."

Ayperos rose to his feet. "I know just the place."

"Are there women to entertain us?" Jorsten asked. "I can use some female attention, and I'm sure Niklas feels the same."

"Indeed," Niklas said, grabbing a pair of socks and boots by the front door.

"Yes," Ayperos said. "There are plenty of attractive women at the club who will indulge your every whim."

"You said the very words I want to hear." Jorsten grinned. "I'm overdue for some feminine loving." He put his hands on his head and swayed his hips.

We laughed at his silly, obscene gestures. Jorsten was the free spirit in our group and always a delight to have around.

We stepped into the night and piled into Ayperos' black SUV. It was no longer raining, but the smell of wet soil and bark still hung in the air. I sat by the window behind the driver's seat, thinking tonight was the best night of my life. An owl hooted outside. I was sure it was Aesop, but I paid no mind to him. There was nothing he could do anyway. Besides, my thoughts were preoccupied with holding Driscol's hand and how much I was looking forward to what other wondrous surprises the rest of the night had in store for us.

Chapter Twenty-One

Tree

The club was on the outskirts of town in an old brick building, tucked away between large trees. I almost passed it while driving on the main road but happened to glance at a side street and saw sticking out of the dirt, a black and white sign in the shape of an arrow pointing east. The name on it said Chameleons.

I parked beside a large oak on the west side of the building. The place was hopping. Vehicles of all makes and models surrounded the area. As I headed toward the front entrance, a sweet triple-black 1968 Dodge Charger R/T caught my eyes. The lights outside the club illuminated the glossy paint, displaying its pristine condition. Whomever owned it was one lucky S.O.B.

My temporary moment of classic muscle car glory ended when I went back to focusing on Carrie and the dire situation we all were in, setting my nerves on edge again. On the way here from Grams' house, my mind wheeled with possible solutions to end Carrie's danger, even though the witch's council said they'd handle it. No conclusive answers came to me, except for one—trust my intuition. Rex wanted to tag along, but Grams and I shut down his request. He wouldn't be safe here. Period. The dark spirits would be able to see his presence as plainly as I could, and they wouldn't appreciate him meddling in their affairs. If they were around, that is, but I had a gut feeling they were. I knew Ayperos was most likely involved because of what Aesop told Grams, and my instincts were telling me with a name like Chameleons, the club had to be owned by a dark spirit, and I was about to walk into their den.

Squaring my shoulders, I took a deep breath. Things were going to get real now. I opened the door and ambled through the smell of alcohol and cigarettes and the sounds of disco music from the loud speakers. I was surprised to see Chameleons was a classy club. From the shabby appearance on the outside, I wouldn't have guessed it. Moving to the back, I leaned against the shiny rosewood wall to evaluate the situation and see if I could single out Carrie among the crowd. The dance floor was in the center of the room. People were moving to an old lame ass *Stayin' Alive* song by the Bee Gees. Beyond it were tables and booths. I noticed a dozen or so people playing cards, drinking, and smoking. In the corner of the room was a sizeable bar with several bartenders behind it, mixing drinks and chatting with the customers camped on the stools. A tall guy with dark, shoulder-length shaggy hair stood at the bar with a large glass of beer in his hand. It looked like he was flirting with the cute blonde girl next to him. They were laughing, and he was making wild gestures with his free hand, like he was telling her a crazy story or maybe even a joke. Looking up at the second level circulating the area, I searched faces of the people I could see hanging near the thick mahogany railing. There was no one I recognized.

Damn.

Maybe I should get a beer and blend in. It seemed like a good idea. At least in my head it did. I highly doubted I'd get carded here. In a casual manner, I wandered around the dance floor, shooting glances at the people moving about. When I spotted Carrie in the back, shielded by the other dancers, I stopped dead in my tracks. My stomach clinched as if someone suckered punched me. Her arms were wrapped around another man, and she was kissing him. He was built, much like me, although I noticed his biceps were larger. My first reaction was sizing him up. I was taller by four inches and probably could take him; however, our altercation would end in a bloody fight. Then, a bizarre thought hit me. This dude had to be Driscol. The room shifted out of place when the image of him as the dog who attempted to attack me yesterday materialized.

Holy hell.

He was Driscol. Somehow, I knew it to be true.

Acting on pure adrenaline, I walked to them and tapped Driscol on the shoulder. "May I cut in?"

"Jack," Isadora said, her voice pitched in surprise. "How in the devil did you find us?"

"I have my ways," I told her.

She laughed. "I'm sure the crone told you our whereabouts."

I pushed Driscol aside. He tumbled sideways to the floor. "I know you're in there, Carrie," I said, looking deeply into her eyes, touching her shoulder. "I believe in you. You must fight her off." I touched my lips to hers and threw every passionate feeling I had for Carrie into the kiss.

"Tree," she whispered between my lips, throwing her arms around my neck, her body melting into mine.

The next thing I knew, my shoulder slammed into a wall across the room. My knees buckled, but I managed to stay upright. Through dazed eyes, I could see Driscol's palm facing me and the dancers standing on either side of the room, watching us with eager looks on their faces. It figured the dark spirits would find a fight amusing. The music stopped.

"I suggest you leave," he said, jerking his head toward the door. It flew open with a bang. He placed an arm around Carrie's shoulders.

She smirked and pointed to the entrance, signaling me to go. "I'm not going to ask you twice."

"I can help you," I said. "I want Carrie back, though."

The blonde gal the rugged dude chatted with earlier, piped up, "What... an apprentice light walker?" She rolled her eyes. "*Please*. The likes of you shouldn't even be here. We don't take too kindly to your kind. You're not to be trusted."

"In that case," the dude with his arm around her waist said, "out." He flicked his hand at me.

I catapulted across the room and through the open door into the cool night, landing on my ass in the dirt. The door slammed shut.

"I take it you're not popular here." Ayperos smiled like a gleeful child on Christmas morning.

I rose and knocked the dirt off me. "This is your fault," I told him, my voice low and pissed. "I have no doubt you helped Isadora break the curse."

He touched his chest, feigning astonishment. "Who me? Now why would I do such a thing?"

The thought of Driscol's hands all over Carrie's body and the possibility they had sex crushed my heart. At the same time, the image infuriated me. In one quick move, I shoved Ayperos and pinned him against a tree. I failed to remember that dark spirits—especially ancient ones like Ayperos—were stronger than the average human. He pushed me, and I stumbled backward, windmilling my arms, only to fall hard on my ass again.

"You're Jack?" A guy asked while I was pushing myself off the ground. He looked to be a year younger than me. He offered his hand, and I took it.

"I am," I confirmed, smoothing my trench coat. "But my friends call me Tree."

His dark blue eyes danced with laughter. "What a peculiar

nickname."

I shrugged. "I'm tall and used to have a Mohawk. It's a long story." I glanced at Ayperos. He remained where he was with a shitty smirk on his face. "And you are?" I asked, focusing my attention back on this dude.

"Niklas," he said. "Isadora's brother."

I blinked in surprise. So this was her brother. The anger I had a second ago simmered. I couldn't help but be fascinated by his presence. "Listen," I said, "I mean Isadora no harm, but Carrie is my top priority, and I'll do whatever it takes to get her back."

"Isadora is the only family I have left," he countered. "I appreciate your woes regarding your beloved, but fear not... my dear sister always keeps her promises. Once she finds a suitable vessel to perform the transmigration spell on, you'll have your Carrie back."

I shook my head. "Isadora has already gone against nature. I believe her powers intoxicated Carrie into siding with her before Isadora decided to take full control over Carrie's body. Soon the dark magic will do the same to Isadora, if it hasn't already." I had no idea where what I said came from, but it felt right. My intuition and perception seemed to be on full auto now.

"If you persist in your endeavor to stop Isadora in whatever she wishes to do," he said, his expression turning dark, "you will risk the wrath of several witches and my own. I will not tolerate threats against my sister and neither will they."

A tall, gorgeous brunette with hair down to her waist opened the door and leaned her head against the doorframe. "Niklas, baby." She pouted. "You said you were going to dance with me."

He glanced behind him and clapped a hand on my shoulder. "I believe the woman of my dreams is calling." A mischievous grin crossed his face. "I shall grant her request, but in the meantime, heed my warning."

Without saying another word, he sauntered to her, and they went inside. I stared after him, my mind racing with jumbled thoughts on what possible options were available. The council of witches was supposed to be taking care of this, but so far, I saw no evidence of them doing one damned thing.

What if Aesop was given misinformation?

No, his information was correct; otherwise, I would have a weird, sickening feeling about it, and I didn't. I thought about the female light walker who had spoken to me. She said observation would sharpen my intuition. It definitely was working, because I was starting to distinguish the difference between my feelings and what they meant.

A sudden epiphany knocked me across the head. Fear, doubt, disbelief, and anger were emotional roadblocks serving no purpose. They only obstructed the truth of the current situation and the legitimate reasons for the actions of the person in question.

Holy hell.

So this was how the light walkers were able to see things clearly. It was like my brain was a Rubik's cube, and each one of my thoughts were a different color. I could feel the shifting inside me, clicking everything into place. Now if only I could have the presence of mind to apply this new knowledge when needed, I'd be excelling in my training to become one of them.

"I can tell your pea brain is tilling the surface of wasteful thoughts, which is allowing useful ones to sprout," Ayperos said, snapping my attention back to him. He made a face as if he ate something sour. "Lovely... I get to have the pleasure of witnessing an apprentice light walker ace a test. Just what I always wanted. I guess I can mark your achievement off my bucket list."

"You can't read minds," I said, even though I wasn't sure. "How do you know what I'm thinking?" I crossed the space between us and stood in front of him to keep our conversation more private.

"I don't," he admitted, "but like your new pal Rex, I can see auras. I also have a knack for reading body language."

"You know about Rex?" I asked, dumbfounded he mentioned him.

"I know a lot of things."

"What else do you know?" I didn't think he'd tell me anything else, but I thought it was worth a shot.

"Have you heard of the Sheol of Glass?"

My stomach dropped, and my blood turned to ice, exactly like when Max mentioned it earlier. I rubbed my arms, staving off the chill in my bones. "I heard about it. Yes."

"So then you're well aware only a witch can allow a soul trapped there escape?"

"Isadora," I whispered, gaping at him. "You slick son-of-a-bitch. You've been helping Isadora and her coven, only so they can release whomever you want from that realm."

"I gathered you would think as much, but you're wrong," he said. "I'm much more inventive in obtaining what I desire."

My mind raced. Since it wasn't Isadora, it had to be another living witch. Carrie was out of the question, because Isadora was now a separate entity. She was no longer attached to Carrie's soul; therefore, she couldn't be a part of it, which meant Carrie wouldn't inherit Isadora's magical abilities. So who could it be? Was there another witch I wasn't aware of? Grams? No, the notion didn't feel right.

Wait a minute.

The council! Somebody from there was working an inside job for Ayperos. My gut contracted. But why would a witch who was held in high regard risk her position? Unless, Ayperos had something she wanted in return for her allowing someone from the Sheol of Glass to escape.

"How in the hell did you get a witch from the council to assist you?" I demanded.

"He does have a brain after all," Ayperos sneered. "And to answer your question... I'm not going to."

"Okay, then," I said, cracking my knuckles in an attempt to not be infuriated by his arrogant, self-important demeanor. What was that epiphany I had moments ago? "Who is it you want released from the Sheol of Glass and why?"

He laughed. It was a hollow, mocking sound that wordlessly told me he thought I was an idiot for thinking he would confide in me. "Let's just say it's insurance for Bael and myself if you, Carrie, and Paige continue to defy us." He paused, and his expression turned serious. "I'm telling you this information even though we abhor each other because you are part of the Devil's third. I'm not pleased about it and neither is Bael, but"—he shrugged—"you are."

"Yeah, so what?"

"So what?" he spat like he had a bad taste in his mouth. "You've witnessed what I'm capable of doing, the limitless resources I have at my disposal, and my astounding wit. If the three of you joined forces with us, we could do marvelous things together."

I scrunched up my nose. "Nah, I don't think so. How about this instead... you stop your conniving ways and accept help from a light walker. You can then move on to a different, more peaceful realm. Hell, I'm feeling generous right now. I'll even help you if I can. How about them apples?"

He grimaced. "I would rather have my eyes gouged out by a thousand toothpicks than accept help from you and your kind."

"Don't ever say I didn't offer to help you," I shot back. I glanced over my shoulder at the entrance to the club. I needed to do something. Maybe if I convinced Niklas to do the right thing, he might listen to me. He seemed like a reasonable guy. I couldn't blame him for looking out for his sister, and I didn't take offense to his earlier threats.

Honestly, I would have been the same in his shoes.

"I think it's about time you go inside," Ayperos said. "The show is about to begin, and your presence will be needed."

I narrowed my eyes, scrutinizing him. "What aren't you telling me?"

He nodded toward the door. "Go on."

I spun on my heel and hurried inside. The music was no longer playing, and a wooden table now dominated the dance floor. People were gathered around it and the dark, shaggy haired guy I kept seeing earlier. He was in the middle of an arm wrestling match. His opponent was a round, red-faced dude with bushy brown hair. Both of them were shirtless, and their huge biceps were bulging from the strain of trying to force the other's hand down.

"You can do it, Jorsten," I heard Carrie's voice ring out above the chatter. "Randall has nothing on you."

I looked, following the sound of her voice and spotted her breaking through the crowd toward the edgy looking guy. She was all smiles and holding Driscol's hand. I had to remind myself it was Isadora's affection toward another man, not Carrie's. But nevertheless, it stung.

"Jorsten. Jorsten," she chanted, cheering him on.

Others chimed in. He smiled, and in a cocky gesture, picked up his beer glass with the other hand and took a swig. The blonde chick who was hanging on him earlier stood behind him clapping, chanting his name along with the crowd. In one swift move, Jorsten slammed Randall's hand down harder than he should have. The crowd erupted into a mixture of surprise and laughter, while a few were jeering Randall.

"You cheating bastard!" He pointed an accusing finger at Jorsten. "You used magic to overthrow me."

"I did nothing of the sort," Jorsten said, unfazed my Randall's outburst. "I won fair and square." He took another drink of his ale, draining his glass. Wiping his mouth with the back of his hand, he grinned. "But if you want to have another go, I'm in."

Randall jumped to his feet, knocking his chair backward. The group around them stepped away. Jorsten rose in a slow deliberate manner, flexing his hands. Glancing around, I saw Niklas exiting a door in the far corner of the room with the hot brunette in tow. His hair was messy, and his gray hoodie appeared wrinkled. The blissful expression on his boyish face shifted into confusion when he saw what was happening. He jogged across the room and stood next to Driscol.

"You filthy liar," Randall said between clenched teeth. "Admit it. You used magic, or your bitch of a friend helped you win." He gestured toward Carrie.

Driscol took a couple of steps forward, but halted when Jorsten placed a hand on his chest. He whispered something to Driscol, then returned his attention to Randall.

"We may be witches," he said, "but we're not without honor. I assure you there was no trickery on our part." He placed his hands on the table and leaned forward. "Your insults toward our high priestess are unappreciated. I suggest you be a gentleman and apologize to her."

Randall guffawed. "In your dreams. The way she's been hanging all over that fool"—he nodded to Driscol—"since the lot of you stepped foot in *our* club, I'd say she's also a whore."

I cringed at the idea of Driscol's hands roaming every inch of Carrie's body. I pushed the disturbing thought aside and focused all my attention on the present circumstances, wondering if I should intervene. I decided to keep my mouth shut and let them have it out.

"I'm not going to tell you twice," Jorsten replied, his body tensing. "Apologize to the lady."

"Or what?" Randall scoffed. "You're nothing without your magic, and soon it'll dry up. I'm not an idiot. I know how it works. Besides,

I'm part of Volac's group. Do you really want to start a war with us?"

Oh, shit. Paige and Nathan told me all about Volac. He was an ancient dark spirit who had a lot of followers. A chaotic future played out in my mind: witches battling a clan of dark spirits, creating a division among malevolent beings. Not good.

Jorsten threw the table aside and punched Randall in the nose. Blood splattered across his face. "I don't take kindly to your threats," he said. "And I don't need magic to kick your sorry ass."

The crowd of people hooted and hollered. Lewd remarks were tossed at Jorsten, while others yelled out their support.

Jorsten threw another punch, but Randall blocked it with his arm and kneed Jorsten in the crotch. His lady friend jumped on Randall's back. Wrapping her arms around his thick neck, she attempted to choke him. He pried her hands off and flung her backward. She landed on her tailbone with a yelp. Then Randall kicked a hunched over Jorsten to the floor.

"Stop!" Isadora commanded, flinging her hands out.

Randall looked at her, his face an awful bloody mess. He froze for a few seconds and smiled when he realized she had exhausted all of her magical abilities. "Now what are you going to do, bitch?"

Driscol's jaw muscles flexed, his complexion beet red. He raised his hand, but Isadora grabbed it. Someone called Randall's name when Jorsten rose behind him. Randall tried to elbow Jorsten in the face, but he ducked and kicked Randall's feet out from under him. His head struck the floor. Jorsten raised his arms. I wasn't sure if he said something, because his back was to me, but it seemed like he was trying to cast a spell. Nothing happened. He raised his foot, aiming for Randall's stomach. Before it made contact, a large black guy stepped in and coldcocked Jorsten with a fist to the eye. Several fights broke out from there. The sound of smacking flesh, grunts, and an endless string of curses filled the room. I moved toward Carrie, Niklas, and Driscol to herd them out of here, but they charged forward and disappeared in the mosh pit of people. My first and only thought was Carrie. There was no way she could defend herself. She was only five-foot-five and was still recovering from the head injury she sustained over a month ago.

Fueled with a major dose of adrenaline and the determination to protect my girlfriend, I moved forward. Bodies flew past me. I flinched and ducked, searching for Carrie. My first thought was she regained her magic, and a small sense of relief washed over me. In that moment, I didn't give a shit if she or her coven were using black magic to hurl the dark spirits across the room. All I cared about was Carrie's safety.

But then I saw him.

Blood drained from my face.

He stood in the center of the room. His black knee-breeches and matching jacket and leather boots were dead giveaways.

Jaegar.

I couldn't fathom how he could be the answer to our growing problems. But then, I remembered Grams saying something about a witch who cast a spell was the only one who could break it. Or was it Rex who told me? It didn't matter. I understood now why his spirit was present, why the council of witches sent him. In reality, though, Isadora's antics are what unleashed Jaegar, who from what I saw so far, was a powerful force our world hadn't seen in centuries. I wondered what he'd do to Carrie's body. Rex told me she'd have to die in order to release Isadora's spirit. However, Carrie was part of the Devil's third, so I would think the council wouldn't jeopardize Carrie's life.

"You," Isadora choked out, less than a yard away from Jaegar.

"You bastard!" With his hands balled into fists, Driscol charged him. "You ruined all of our lives!"

"You robbed my sister. How could you?" Niklas yelled, moving to Jaegar's right in quick strides. "We trusted you, you son-of-a-bitch!"

Jorsten picked up a chair behind Jaegar and raised it, poised to smash it on his head. Jaegar made a gesture above his shoulder, as if he were throwing salt over it. The chair flew from Jorsten's hands and crashed against the wall. It shattered, flinging bits of wood across the room. Jorsten collapsed to the floor. Jaegar flung his hands out, moving them in a half circle. Driscol and Niklas fell in the same manner as Jorsten. All three were out cold. I looked around at the bodies slumped against the walls and on each other. All of them were either dead or in a deep sleep. I wasn't sure which.

"Leave them be!" Isadora screamed.

Like an unfeeling, robotic machine, Jaegar moved toward her. She backed against the wall, looking at him with wide, haunted eyes. "Why? Why did you betray me? You stole so much from me." She broke down in tears.

"Hey!" I called out, running to them. "What the hell are you doing?"

He didn't flinch or even acknowledge me. The dude was like the frickin' terminator. His expression was stoic, his bluish, gray eyes focused ahead of him. He wrapped his hand around Carrie's neck and began choking her, chanting words I didn't understand under his breath. Isadora wasn't fighting him. She continued to cry instead, her expression broken.

Fear and anger raged inside me. There was no way I could quell it. If this was a test, I failed, but I didn't give a shit. He was hurting Carrie, and I was pissed. "Get off her!" I pushed his shoulder back and raised my fist. It froze in midair. I couldn't move it. What the fuck?

Jaegar turned his head and locked his eyes on mine. Something flickered in them, like a lightning bolt in a stormy sky. His features softened, and he spoke in German, but my mind automatically translated his words to English. "The ancestors have granted my freedom, if I make this right. I cannot succeed without you." He placed his free hand on top of my fist. My arm went limp and fell to my side.

"Your beloved will be unharmed." He tightened his grip on Carrie's neck and slapped his other hand in mine. He resumed his incantation.

I tried to say Carrie's name, but it wouldn't reach my lips. I was paralyzed. I couldn't move a muscle. In horror, I watched Carrie close her eyes. The color in her face turned shades of red and purple. He was killing her, and there was nothing I could do. Once again, I failed her.

I failed her.

My body shook. Tears marred my vision. In my mind, I screamed no and to please stop. She was my world—my everything. Please don't.

The floor disappeared from underneath me. I was floating inside a misty cloud. Fragments of brilliant colors sparkled around me. The next thing I knew, I was standing in front of a polished cream colored monolithic building with Corinthian-style columns. The architecture reminded me of the buildings in Rome. The white marble steps shined a golden hue from the veins of yellow in the stone. Water trickled down a surface nearby. Looking around, I was stunned by the tall oaks and gardens surrounding me. There were archways draped with luxurious veins over a carpet of plush green grass. Different types of flowers and shrubs thrived beyond the cobblestone path. I marveled at what a peaceful and breathtaking place this was.

"Jack," a soft female voice said behind me.

I turned and came face to face with a beautiful young woman who appeared to be a few years older than me. Her long black hair hung in waves to her waist, and her dark blue eyes held a curious wonderment in them.

"Isadora?" Somehow I knew it was her, maybe because my mind was a lot sharper here. Also, her long green dress that hugged her hourglass figure wasn't from my time.

"Yes," she said with a genuine smile. She extended her hand, and I took it. "Nice to meet you in a proper manner."

I didn't say anything. All I could think about was Carrie. Was she okay?

Isadora released my hand and frowned. "I'm sorry about overpowering Carrie." She shifted her weight and looked away, then turned her attention back on me. "I had to do what was necessary at the time. I bet she's all right."

"I hope so," I said, unsure.

"Isadora?"

We both turned and saw an older version of Isadora in a dark blue cloak moving toward us along the cobblestone path.

"Momma!" Hitching up her dress, Isadora sprinted to the woman.

While they embraced and laughed, I wondered where Jaegar went and if he was the one Ayperos had talked about. Did the witches release Jaegar from the Sheol of Glass? Was he Ayperos' insurance plan against me and my friends? If Jaegar turned out to be who Ayperos referred to earlier, we were in deep shit. However, as I pondered those questions, they didn't feel right. But then again, my feelings were all over the place, so I didn't know what to think.

"My name is Charlotte," Isadora's mother said to me. Isadora looped her arm around Charlotte's and hugged it. Charlotte placed a hand on my shoulder, and a genuine smile crossed her pretty face. "Thank you, Jack, for bringing my daughter here to me."

"You're welcome," I said. "But honestly it wasn't intentional. I think what happened was more like a fluke than anything else."

"A guide or light walker is the only one who can transport another soul or in Isadora's case... a spirit to this realm. I assure you, what took place wasn't accidental." She reached up, tilted my head down and kissed my forehead. My eyes closed and a spinning sensation overwhelmed my senses. "Thank you," she said, her melodic voice fading in the distance. "You have my sincere gratitude, and I will not forget what you have done."

I opened my eyes and was back in the club, just like that. No floating inside a wispy cloud. No falling down a rabbit hole. No—

Carrie!

She was lying in a fetal position on the floor. I raced to her, praying she was still alive and okay.

Chapter Twenty-Two

Isadora

I never expected to see my mother again. Oh, how I'd missed her so. When she was alive, I was her shadow. She taught me everything she knew about nature and magic. She was the star in my dark, oppressing world that gave me hope for a bright future. When she died, so did the fiery embers in my heart. Each day, little by little, the panes around it would frost. All but one, which remained untouched by the biting cold world. I had guarded my heart the best I could but made the foul mistake of allowing Jaegar passage through the glass. It was a poor decision I paid for tenfold.

Now, Mother held my face in her delicate hands. Her intense expression alarmed me. My forehead furrowed. Was it grave news concerning my eternal fate? By the anxiousness in her deep blue eyes, I knew it had to be along those lines. "The council is waiting for you," she told me. "They went to great lengths to bring you here."

"How do you know?" I asked.

She dropped her hands and sighed. "I'm a member."

"How?" Stunned by this revelation, I wanted to know in what manner it could be possible.

A small smile formed on her lips. "When I transitioned from my life on earth to this one, they recruited me. They admired my skills in creating potions and the service I provided for ailing paupers."

"Little good it did you," I said, not hiding the bitterness in my tone. "You couldn't save yourself with your own remedies and magic."

"Fate had already claimed me," she said dismissively. "My body was beyond repair. The virus was too swift."

"You could have used black magic," I pointed out. "In fact, I should have used it on you, regardless of the consequences."

"Don't say such things, child," Mother said, frowning. She glanced over her shoulder at the Pantheon-style structure I was sure we'd be entering soon. She embraced me and whispered in my ear, "A mother will do anything for her offspring, even if the deed is consorting with malicious beings."

Realizing she was concerned others would hear her, I hugged her tighter and whispered, "What have you done?" I was sure Ayperos had his horned tail wrapped around this.

"No need to trouble yourself," she hushed. "I want you to know I love you and Niklas so much. I did what I had to do for you two." She pulled back and gently brushed a piece of hair away from my face. "My dear," she said in her natural tone of voice now, "performing black magic is against the witch's law... unless our ancestors give their approval. We do have free will; however, there are consequences to our actions."

I nodded, knowing I would have to face whatever punishment would be handed to me. But my thoughts were more occupied on the matter which she spoke of than my own fate. If her peers discovered her treachery, there was no telling what sentence they'd condemn her to. I wished she would confide in me what she had done, but I knew she wouldn't. Besides, what could I do? This time tomorrow, I may not even exist, for all I knew. The joy I felt mere moments ago deflated. There would be no happy ending in my tale. "Where are Niklas,

Driscol, and Jorsten?" I asked, when the thought of never seeing them again wrenched my heart.

"Come along, dear," Mother said, leading me to the marble steps. They had a shiny yellowish tint to them that reminded me of gold bricks. "The council is waiting."

"But what about—"

"I'm not permitted to answer your question," she said as we climbed the steps. I noticed our movements were more like gliding than the actual motion of lifting our legs. "I will tell you this." She gave me a sideways glance. "They're connected to you through your blood. You made it so when you cast your spell long ago."

"What happens to me happens to them?" I guessed. "If I die, they die?"

"Yes."

"Then why didn't Jaegar's spell affect them like it did me when he cast it on my spirit?"

"Because he's clever, and if I daresay, he wanted them to suffer the curse you placed upon them as punishment for their loyalty to you."

We paused in front of a large polished bronze door. The white spiral columns holding the porch up were evenly spaced and enormous. I could see the beautiful gardens from where I stood. The flowering trees were a palette of radiant colors: deep purple, electric blue, red, orange, and the like. They seemed to sizzle across the branches. I had a sudden desire to wander through them and sit under the tall oaks with Driscol.

The door opened, releasing a whooshing sound. We walked in and stood in a vast entrance hall. The odoriferous smell of frankincense and myrrh filled the air. Under the pale lavender light filtering through the arched windows, I noticed statues of women, men, children, and animals set in niches along the richly painted walls. They appeared to come to life with my every move. I continued to stare at them, embroiled in what I could only describe as a bizarre fascination. I raised my hand, and when I did, their eyes followed it.

"This way," Mother said.

I trailed her across the room, then down a narrow passageway until we reached a round wooden door with symbols carved into it.

She pointed to them. "These represent truth, existence, life, knowledge, love, and eternity." She grabbed the black handle and tugged.

We entered a dome-shaped room cast in a warm glow from the many lit candles displayed in fancy candelabras. Vibrant oil paintings in gold spiral frames hung in a row on the wall. Each one was a portrait. Mother's was on the end. The artist had done a wonderful job capturing the glint of curiosity in her eyes. The photos were so well created that they gave the illusion of them being real, as if the women in them would rise from their seats and step out of the frame. To my left was a high platform with a long limestone table facing the room. Behind it sat eight women. All of them were wearing dark blue cloaks like the one Mother had on. Mother kissed my cheek before joining them. She took the empty seat at the end. The other council members nodded to her. She returned their gesture and sat. I straightened my back and clasped my hands behind it. Whatever they decided, rather than make a scene, I'd handle it with grace for Mother.

The witch in the center cleared her throat. She had a stern, narrow face with a long, pointy nose. Her black hair was in a high bun with shocks of silver threaded through it. "Isadora. My name is Agatha. I'm head of the council."

I didn't say anything. Instead, I twisted my lips to the side. My mind quickly accessed what type of individual she was: rigid, strict, and someone I shouldn't cross.

"You've broken countless laws," she continued. "You allied yourself with the dark spirits, and at one time used a cloaking spell so we'd be blind to your antics."

She was right. Before the witch hunts in our town erupted, my coven and I practiced controlling the weather with a spell I created. We performed it out of fun, and I wanted to see if it would work. It didn't. We failed. Then, the frost on the fruits and crop happened, which resulted in a huge loss. The misfortune created economic hardships, and a plague followed. I'd told my coven the night I cursed them we were innocent of the charges Dornheim accused poor Margaretha and the rest of our coven of. But now, as I pondered it, I wondered if those catastrophes were Mother Nature's way of punishing us for trying to control her. Were we the catalyst of those horrific times? I swallowed hard. I couldn't bring myself to accept such a notion. However, I knew the council had no jurisdiction when it came to spells going against Mother Nature. She had her own laws and punishments. I thought about my friendship with Ayperos and some of the other dark spirits. Ayperos had showed me an old *Book of Shadows* he held in his possession, along with the grimoire that was bound in human flesh and now lost. With his permission, my coven and I were able to cast some of the spells that were written in the grimoire, as well as create our own. Beforehand, I'd performed a cloaking charm on myself and coven out of my own spitefulness toward the council. The hostility I felt at the time wasn't individual. It was for the group as a whole. The witch's council were too uptight, and it was none of their business if we wanted to indulge ourselves in entertainment, food, drink, and whatever our hearts desired. We knew if we used too much magic, we would temporarily lose our powers due to our excessiveness. I was working on an ingenious spell to end that vexing problem, and I was proud of the fact they didn't have a clue about it. In my mind at the time and even now as I stood before the panel, I thought witches should be free to do what they want. If they fouled something up or got too big for their britches, it was a universal law their actions would come back to them tenfold. The council shouldn't have the authority to dictate the behaviors of other witches and dole out punishments whenever they saw fit.

"Such defiance in your eyes," said a ginger-haired witch who sat next to Mother. Her bright green eyes held a quizzical look, matching the expression on her lovely face. "Please, speak your mind."

"I see no reason for totalitarianism among our kind," I answered. "What right do you have to push your dogmatic ways on us, and then have the authority and power to sentence us for our wrongdoings?"

"Isadora," Mother warned.

I raised a hand. "Mother, please. This very issue has been troubling me for quite some time." I turned my attention back to the panel. "I don't mean to disrespect your mission or you personally. However, I find it ludicrous that we're subjected to such a regime." There—I said it. I was asked my opinion, so I freely gave it. Whatever repercussions I'd have to face for my loose tongue, I'd take. I was damned anyway and felt no need to cower under their critical eyes.

"I can see why you'd have such bothersome feelings toward us," said a pretty dark skinned witch with a gentle smile. "But your perception of the council is misguided. Everything in the universe has a certain order. True, the universe has its own laws, just like nature does, but each layer in the countless mansions of eternity has its own mandate. We are but one of them, appointed by enlightened souls to keep order among our cohorts."

"You may detest having to answer to us for your delinquent and insubordinate actions with the gifts bestowed upon you," said Agatha. "But it is the way of things."

I didn't say anything. I only nodded. Since I now understood why they were in their positions, I resigned myself to accept whatever they decided to do with me, even though my disagreement toward it all still burned bright inside me.

"You've broken countless laws and should be detained in the Sheol of Glass for however long we see fit for your deplorable behavior," Agatha went on. "However, we've never encountered a case like yours before. Therefore, it changes things."

My heart skipped a beat, and my breath caught in my throat. Was it possible they were going to be lenient?

"We understand the witch trials and the love for your coven drove you to take such drastic measures to keep them safe," the ginger witch said. "But there were other ways to have accomplished it without using dark magic and forcing nature to her knees."

I stared at the flagstone floor, my long hair curtaining my face. It was easy for her to say. Her father and friends weren't in the Drudenhaus being relentlessly tortured by sadistic, evil men. She wasn't living in constant fear of being apprehended in the middle of the night while fast asleep—or when merely strolling through the forest, only to have a monster disguised as a friend throw you to the wolves. Besides, our neighboring towns were sharing the same plight as us. It would have done me and my loved ones no good to flee our homeland. The risk was too great for such a feat.

"Isadora has always been an impulsive child," Mother spoke up. "I'm not excusing her behavior on this matter, but when it comes to the ones who are dear to her heart, her actions are always from love and nothing else."

"Duly noted," Agatha said with a slight nod.

I raised my gaze and caught Mother's. Her expression were equal parts understanding and anxiousness. But then something dark flashed in them when a blonde, freckled-face witch who sat toward the opposite end of Mother piped up about how reckless I still was. To back her claim, she pointed out the energy spell I'd performed on Max and the fire behind Paige's house.

"I allowed Carrie to do those things," I told her, unable to bite my tongue. "Actually, we both performed those spells. I was attempting to help her gain confidence and give her a taste of what it was like to be a witch again. That's what you wanted to begin with, for her to regain the power she had as me, is it not?"

The witches nodded and made agreeing sounds, except the blonde. She was quickly becoming a pain in my ass. The sudden desire to shut her mouth with the flick of my wrist sparked through me. I imagined her lips sewn shut with black thread and an X over her pout. Her wide, doll-like brown eyes would freeze in that manner—in a constant state of surprise and panic. Oh, what a glorious thought that was.

"Your poor decisions," she said, "were a result in showboating your powers. You risked Max's health and exposing us to the world. You also came close to burning a forest and Paige's house down. And"—she raised her finger and poked the air—"you performed a beauty spell to manipulate Jack and Rex, which in a sense is black magic because of your intentions behind it."

"Gwendolyn has a valid point," Agatha said.

"I think a stint in the Sheol of Glass would humble her," Gwendolyn announced with a smug look.

Mother slammed her palms on the table and rose. "Now wait a minute. Don't you think Isadora has suffered enough? Because of Jaegar, she has no soul!"

"Her situation is a tragic one," Gwendolyn said without feeling. "But it taught her nothing. In fact, she resumed her friendship with Ayperos and partied with the dark spirits. Her lust for power still remains, and she will use it in any way she sees fit." She stood and faced Mother, silently challenging her on the matter. "My charges are not unfounded. We all know Isadora was planning on executing a transmigration spell, which is black magic, I might add."

"Ladies," Agatha said in a stern voice, "please, sit down. Quarreling among ourselves will get us nowhere. Besides, I've made my decision."

In unison, Mother and Gwendolyn took their seats. Mother looked at me. Anger blazed in her eyes. She blinked, and the resentment in them vanished. She folded her hands on the table and bowed her head as if in prayer. I threw my shoulders back and raised my chin, reminding myself to handle my punishment with grace.

"Isadora," Agatha said in a strong, authoritative tone, "the charges brought against you boils down to this... your defiance against our laws and constant usage of black magic. Your obstinate lack of conformity is a trait I see no sign of waning. I have, however, taken into account the wretched curse Jaegar cast upon you. Because of it, you have no soul, which I had to consider in my decision on your punishment. Your situation is a tricky one. You're not like the soulless humans on earth. They have no spirit, whereas you, my dear, are nothing but one." She paused and stared at me. I remained still, forcing my expression to be blank. "I'm sentencing you to the Sheol of Glass."

"What!" Mother exclaimed, aghast. She grasped the edge of the table and leaned forward to look at Agatha.

Gwendolyn smiled, obviously pleased with Agatha's decision. I didn't have time to process what it all meant because Mother's outburst startled me, and then a sense of pride followed.

"Calm yourself, Charlotte," Agatha told her. "I still have more to say." Agatha shifted her attention back to me. "You will not remain in this realm for eternity," she stressed. "I will release you when I see fit to do so. Afterward, you will be rehabilitated, and if it's possible, rejoin Carrie's soul. However, I'm not quite sure if that's an option. If not, the other one would be for you to dwell in another realm where you'd been given a purpose for your existence. Something that would satisfy you."

"What about Niklas, Driscol, and Jorsten? What will become of them?" I asked, caring more about their fate than my own.

"Niklas is going through the normal process each spirit experiences when its human body expires," she said. "Driscol and Jorsten, on the other hand, share a similar sentence as you."

"They're already in the Sheol of Glass?" I asked, taking comfort in the fact we'd be together in the dreary realm.

"They are," Agatha confirmed. "But don't expect to cross paths with them while you're there."

"Why not?"

"Because of how vast it is." She smacked her hands together, and I plunged into darkness.

Chapter Twenty-Three

Carrie

I woke up with Tree's wide brown eyes staring at me. A smile stretched across his handsome face when I lifted my fingers to touch his cheek. He captured my hand in his and kissed it. For a minute, I had no idea where I was or whose four-poster bed I was lying in. I felt movement beside me and almost jumped out of my skin when my gaze met Abigail's. She sat next to me, propped against two large pillows. Her withered face had a grayish hue, and there was a slight unpleasant smell spilling from her—a sickly-sweet, pungent acetone odor. I moved my other hand to hers and held it, pretending not to notice how cold it was.

"She's awake!" I heard Rex exclaim. He floated to us and hovered beside Tree. "I knew you would wake up," he said with a huge grin.

"How are you feeling?" Tree asked, his voice low.

"I'm fine," I assured him. "Maybe a little groggy."

Tree glanced at Rex. "How does her aura look?"

Rex pinched his fingers and thumb together and placed them on his lips. He made a kissing sound and dramatically flung his hand back. "Superb."

"I told you I was okay," I said, playfully swatting Tree's arm.

"You enter the land of the living, and then get all abusive and stuff," Tree teased, smiling, but it disappeared when he realized his poor choice of words. He looked at Abigail at the same time I did. "I'm sorry. I didn't mean to be insensitive."

"Your apology is not necessary," Abigail said. "Besides, I'm the one who will be entering the land of the living."

"What's going to happen to Rex?" I wanted to know, worried I'd never see him again. I was also sad to see Abigail leave us, but at the same time, I took comfort in knowing she'd no longer be trapped in a failing body that was becoming a disservice to her. She earned her wings, I thought; it was time for her to fly.

"I asked him the same question earlier," Tree told me.

I looked at Rex. He shrugged. "I'm not sure how it works."

I turned to Abigail. "Do you know?"

"Rex will be given a choice," she said, her frail voice sounding hoarse now. "The decision will be his on what he wants to do."

"What was it like having Isadora inside you?" Rex asked me, changing the subject.

I furrowed my brows in thought. "The experience is kind of hard to describe," I answered. "It wasn't like when Aosoth possessed me. I didn't blackout or anything, and I was able to communicate with her."

"Really?" Rex asked in awe. "Wow. Totally wicked."

"I suppose," I said, enjoying his enthusiasm. "I feel bad for her, though."

"Why?" Tree asked.

"Because of what Jaegar did to her, and now she's gone. I have no idea what has become of her and her coven."

"She's with her mom, I know," Tree said.

I gasped. "Omigod. Really?" My mind raced, wondering how Tree would have knowledge of such a thing. I pushed the hair out of my face and stared at him wide-eyed.

Tree was studying me now. "Do you remember Jaegar choking you?"

I rolled my eyes. "Don't answer a question with a question."

"Do you?"

I sighed and rubbed the spot above my brow. "I do... I remember everything. I had to be quiet, though, and pretend Isadora subdued me. The task wasn't an easy one to pull off, but I did."

Rex floated to my side, interest and horror etched on his face. "Weren't you scared? How could you not fight back during your ordeal?"

"I had no choice." I shrugged. "What I did was the only way to get rid of her, and I had to trust I'd be okay."

Rex pointed at me, impressed. "You're Batman... ah, Batgirl. You're totally badass."

I laughed along with Tree and grinned. "Thank you. Isadora did teach me some things besides magic."

Abigail's attempt to squeeze my hand was weak, but it caught my attention. "What lessons did you learn from her?"

"Her brother Niklas had a similar cross to bear as me," I said. "He longed for magical powers and to be like his sister and friends. I have the same problem. I feel like I have nothing to offer our tight-knit group. I mean, Paige and Nathan are immortal and have extraordinary powers. Not to mention Paige is beautiful, and I'm not."

"I think you are," Tree said.

"You're sweet, but I don't think so," I said offhandedly. "Anyway, Isadora pointed out to Niklas how gifted he is in herbology, and we all have our own special gifts. Then, Ayperos, of all people, put it into perspective for Niklas and me."

"Ayperos." Tree groaned. "Seriously?"

I nodded. "I know, right? I can't remember what he said verbatim, but what he basically told Niklas was everyone pines for something they lack"—I ticked a few of them off on my fingers—"good looks, wealth, wit, etcetera. And we fail to realize we all have a strength we can use to benefit us. If we're envious of other people's qualities or what they have, we won't recognize our own."

"He's correct," Abigail said.

"I may not be Victoria Secret material," I went on, "and I may not have supernatural abilities, but I am me. Yeah, I can be a bubblehead and immature at times... so what? I like who I am. I just have to figure out what I'm good at besides hair, fashion, and accessories."

"Do you have any of Isadora's magical abilities?" Rex asked.

I chewed on my lip and thought about it. "I remember the spells and the things she shared with me, but to actually cast them... I don't know." I suddenly realized Tree never answered my question. I shoved his arm. "Hey, you were going to tell me how you know Isadora is with her mom."

"Oh, right." He flashed me his signature goofy grin, then told us all about his experience and why he thought what he went through was his first taste in being a light walker. "The whole thing was cool," he said. "Her mom seemed really nice. I could tell there was a strong bond between them, like they'd do anything for one another."

The thought of Isadora being reunited with her mom warmed my heart. Maybe she could finally be at peace. I wondered what happened to Niklas, Driscol, and Jorsten and hoped they were okay.

"Carrie," Abigail said. When she breathed in, her throat rattled. "I'm sorry. So is the council for what happened to you. We never meant for it to turn out this way."

"It's alright." A sudden rush of sadness poured over me. Abigail was going to die any second now. The signs were all there. I would never see her again. I knew she was going to. I mean, I thought about it earlier, but it still made my heart heavy—even though I knew her passing was for the best.

"Why the tears, child?" Abigail attempted to lift her hand but couldn't.

Gently, I picked up her hand and held it against my cheek. Her boney fingers brushed the tears off. "I'm going to miss you," I told her.

"And I you," Abigail said. "I have something to tell you before I pass on. Something I've given a lot of thought about."

Alarmed, I returned her hand to her lap. She sounded serious. Tree shifted closer to me and placed steady fingers on my arm. I glanced at him. His brows were pulled together in concern.

"Sure. What is it?" I asked.

"When this body dies, so will the enchantments on my house," she told us.

"I figured so," Tree said.

Abigail opened her mouth to continue, but I interrupted her before she could. "Sorry." I raised my palm to her. "I need to ask you real quick before I forget. What kind of funeral do you want and what shall we do with your remains?"

Tree took my hand and interlaced our fingers together. "Good question, Carrie."

Abigail smiled. It was weak, but I could tell by the warmth in her face, it was heartfelt. "This body will disappear along with the magic." She paused to catch her breath. When she breathed in, I heard the rattling in her throat again. "I appreciate you asking and willing to take on a huge responsibility such as my wishes and remains, which confirms to me the decision I made is the right one."

"What is it?" I asked.

She tried to smile again, but this time she failed. "I'm willing my house and its contents to you." Her gaze skipped to Rex. "Can you get the legal papers and the grimoire please?"

Rex nodded and vanished.

I stared at her, my mouth agape. At first, I thought I heard wrong.

I mean, why would she give this awesome house to me? I had to say something to be sure I wasn't misunderstanding her. "I appreciate your generosity, but why would you will me your house? We hardly know each other."

"I'm aware, dear," she said. "But we're kindred spirits, you and me. Despite what happened to Isadora, I believe you are a witch, and I wouldn't want anyone else to own it."

Rex reappeared with the grimoire and a large manila envelope. He handed them to Tree, who placed both in my lap.

"Good decision, Grams," Rex said, giving her a raised thumb.

I was completely overwhelmed. I didn't know what to say, so I hugged her instead. "Thank you," I finally said.

There was a knock at the front door. Startled, I pulled away. My eyes darted to the bedroom door. I wondered who could be here this late at night. What if it was Ayperos? I wouldn't be surprised if he did show. In a way, I kind of wish he would. I had some questions to ask I was curious about. Granted, I couldn't really trust him, but I still wanted to know what he'd say.

"Jack, can you see who it is?" Abigail asked.

Tree stood. "Of course."

"Do you think it's Ayperos?" I asked Abigail when Tree left the room.

"I don't see why he'd pay me a visit," she said. "Although you never know about him or his motives."

"I'll go see," Rex announced and vanished.

I took Abigail's ice cold hand in mine and held it. "How are you feeling?"

"Tired," she answered, "and anxious."

"What are you anxious about?"

"I can feel my spirit wanting to disconnect from this body, and I know once it does, I'll have to face the music."

"What do you mean?"

"All the bad things I've done... I'm going to have to relive them when I review this life."

"I'm sure everything will be okay. You're not a bad person," I told her.

"My mom is here!" Rex said, suddenly appearing at the foot of the bed. "I can't believe it." He looked both nervous and excited at the same time.

Abigail perked up. "Jane?"

Rex bobbed his head, his eyes huge on Abigail's face.

I heard voices approaching the room. I didn't move a muscle and tried to lend my support to Abigail by lightly squeezing her hand.

"They're in here," I heard Tree say before opening the door.

A petite women with brown hair cut in an inverted bob entered the bedroom. She was definitely Rex's mom. The resemblance between the two was remarkable. Rex moved beside me when Jane halted at the foot of the bed.

"Grandmother," she choked out and cupped a hand over her mouth, bursting into tears.

Abigail reached for her. "Jane."

Jane took Abigail's hand, sat on the bed, and hugged her. "I'm so sorry I didn't come see you sooner."

"You're here now," Abigail whispered.

Normally I'd feel awkward sitting in on this intimate family reunion; however, I wanted to make sure Jane wouldn't say something that would be out of line. I mean, she had once accused Abigail of horrible things. I wanted to make sure she wouldn't do it again.

Jane pulled back and wiped her face with the palm of her hand. "I've been doing a lot of thinking since Jack called me."

Abigail shot Tree a surprised look, then her attention fell back on Jane. "He called you?"

"He did," she admitted. "I was upset because he mentioned Rex. After I disconnected my call with him, I did some serious thinking and soul-searching." Her shoulders slumped, and she continued. "I already knew the answer, but during all these years, it was much easier to blame you for Rex's death, when in reality... I blamed myself."

"It wasn't anyone's fault," Abigail said.

"I was also angry with you for practicing magic and claiming Rex is still around."

"What I said about Rex is true," Abigail told her.

Jane shook her head. "Please, Grandmother... not now."

"She's telling you the truth," I said to Jane.

"And you are?" Jane asked in a snotty tone.

"I'm Carrie," I told her, mirroring her attitude toward me.

"Carrie is a good friend," Abigail said to her granddaughter. "I'm willing the house and everything in it to her"—she indicated to the book and large envelope still in my lap—"unless there are things you'd like to have."

Jane made a face. "I don't care about your house or stuff. All I want is the china tea set we used to have tea parties with when I was a little girl."

Abigail moved her index finger in a circle above the bed in front of Jane. A beautiful white tea set with delicate blue flowers appeared.

Jane shot up off the bed, upsetting the dishes. They clinked together but didn't topple over. "My word! How did you do that?"

"She's a witch," Tree said. "But you already knew that, right?"

"I did, but I'd never witnessed anything like this before," she said, sounding confused. "Mother told me stories about Grandmother casting spells, but I thought..." she trailed off.

"You thought I was batty or in partnership with Satan," Abigail said.

Jane frowned. "I did."

"This house is enchanted," I told her. "But once Abigail passes on, the magic goes with her." Jane gave me a weird look. "It's a long story."

"Your time is almost up," Tree said, eyeing Abigail.

"I love you, Jane," Abigail told her.

"Time?" A confused, startled expression marred Jane's face. "What do you mean? How do you know?"

"I just do," Tree said. "She needs to crossover to Summerland. I can see it manifesting in this room."

Jane laughed. It was an empty sound. "Right and Santa Claus really exists. Give me more credit than that."

I groaned. The woman was not only rude but impossible. I looked at Rex, and he smacked his forehead. How could an awesome kid like him have a mother like her? Maybe his father was cool, and Rex took after him.

"Jack, give me your hand and take Rex's in your other one," Abigail told him.

"Rex?" Jane shrieked. "He's here?" She moved her head back and forth, her eyes scanning the room.

Tree did as Abigail instructed, and Jane gasped.

"Hi, Mom." Rex gave her a half-hearted wave. "Can you see me now?"

Jane sobbed in her hands and nodded.

"Grams was right all along," Rex told her. "I've been with her since my body died."

"H-how?" her tearful voice asked.

"A spell," I said.

"I shouldn't have performed it, but out of selfishness, I did," Abigail admitted.

"I miss you so much, Rex," Jane cried. "I should have paid more attention to you. I'm sorry."

"Don't sweat it, Mom," Rex told her.

Jane clutched her chest with one hand and covered her mouth with the other. She nodded.

"Say your goodbyes now," Tree told us. "Make it quick."

Jane was staring at Rex, so I took the opportunity to give Abigail one last hug. "I'll miss you."

"I'm sure we'll see each other again," Abigail said.

I looked into her milky eyes. "I hope so. Thanks again for your house. I'll take good care of it. Promise."

"I know you will, dear."

Rex reached out to his mom, but she flinched and took a step back. I wanted to grab her by the shoulders and shake her when I noticed the hurt look in Rex's eyes. Really, lady. He's your frickin' son for heaven's sake.

"Rex," I said, catching his attention. I put the grimoire and envelope aside and pushed the covers off me. Slipping out of bed, I opened my arms and gave him a big hug, which caused Tree to let go of his hand. I wanted to stick my tongue out at his mom, but refrained from such childish behavior, although I really wanted to. I released my arms and stepped back, taking a mental picture of him. "Will I ever see you again?"

An impish grin crossed his cute freckled face. "Maybe."

"He's gone," Jane said in a dumbfounded, panic voice. "But you're talking to him as if he's still here. What sort of mind tricks are you people playing?"

I looked at her and rolled my eyes.

Tree took Grams' hand and grabbed Rex's, causing Jane to gasp when he appeared to her again. I happened to glance behind me and noticed a small, golden circle on the wall.

"Who are you?" Jane asked Tree. "How come when you hold Grandmother's and Rex's hand, I can see him?"

"He's a light walker, dear," Abigail said. "He's gaining the ability to connect with both the living and the dead. I took a chance to see what would happen if he held my hand and Rex's at the same time, and it worked. Now you can see him."

"What the hell is a light walker?" Jane asked, annoyed.

"I'm not a light walker," Tree told her. "Not yet. I'm still in training."

"An angel," I said at the same time Tree spoke.

Jane crossed her arms tightly against her chest. "And I'm supposed to believe this?"

"Yes, Mom," Rex said, causing her to give him a startled look.

"I don't know what to believe anymore," she said with an irritable sigh. "For all I know, this can be a trick devised by Satan himself to get me on his side."

I half-laughed. "Yeah. Whatever." Jane got on my nerves, and I wished she would leave.

Abigail was staring past me with a giddy expression. I turned and saw the circle now shimmering and growing in size. A sense of love and warmth enveloped me.

"Do you see it?" Abigail asked me.

I nodded. "I do."

"See what?" Jane demanded.

"The portal opening on the wall," Tree told her.

Jane's eyes and mouth tightened. "I don't appreciate these games you're playing." She picked up the tea set. Her quick gesture caused them to clink together.

"Mom," Rex said in a pleading voice. "They're not messing with you. Please, believe it."

For a second, her hard expression faltered, and her brown eyes softened. I thought maybe she would change her mind, and the ice around her heart would melt.

I was wrong.

As soon as Abigail pointed at the round opening on the wall—which reminded me of a hobbit doorway—and gushed about how beautiful the bright green meadow was, Jane's face twisted into disgust.

She held her hand up, palm facing Rex. "I don't know what's true anymore. I don't know if you're my son or a demon in disguise. For all I know, y'all can be devil worshippers."

"Oh, that's inventive," I snapped, fed up with her bullcrap. "You have no idea how lame you sound."

"I think you should leave," Abigail told Jane. "I love you with all my heart, but I will not allow you to ruin this grand moment for Rex and me."

"Fine." Jane turned to leave, then hesitated. She looked at Abigail and released a heavy sigh. "Despite everything, I love you, too, and I no longer blame you for my son's death. I hope my forgiveness will give you some peace." Without another word, she headed for the door, then screeched when a large, brown spotted owl swooped in. The dishes nearly fell out of her hands, but she somehow managed to steady them.

"Aesop," Rex said, watching him fly through the portal and up into the lilac sky. "See ya around," Rex called after him.

"The owl vanished when he reached the wall!" Jane pointed to where Aesop was. "How can that be? And why was there a damn owl in the house?" She raised her hand before we could respond. "Forget it. I don't want to know. I'm out of here." She turned and left.

"Hallelujah," I said when I heard the front door slam, then flashed Rex an apologetic look. "Sorry. I know she's your mom and all, but she's something else."

"No worries. She's always been that way. She drove me nuts when I was alive," he told me, "which is the reason why I never had a problem when she would ditch me for her friends and send me to Grams' house."

Abigail pushed the covers off her and made a move to get out of bed. Tree rushed to her aid and assisted her to the floor. I found it almost impossible to remove my eyes from the rolling emerald green hills, brilliant flowers, and lilac sky awaiting Abigail and Rex. In the distance, I could see shadowy figures standing around. When Abigail reached my side, I gave her one last hug, and Tree did the same.

"Bye, you guys," Rex said, joining Abigail when she shuffled toward the portal. He grinned and waved. "I'll miss you, but who knows? Maybe I'll be able to visit you again."

"I'll miss you, too," I said, swallowing back the tears in my throat. "I hope to see you again."

"Later, dude," Tree said with a bitter-sweet smile. "I'll keep an eye out for your presence. There will always be a place for you here."

"Thanks!" Rex chirped.

I shifted my attention to Abigail. With each hobbled step she took, she became stronger, younger, and the hump on her back disappeared. Her transformation was amazing to watch and one of the coolest things I'd ever seen. She half turned—her back now straight, her light blue eyes clear and sharp, and her face a youthful Joan Crawford look alike—and blew us a kiss. She turned back around, and as soon as she and Rex stepped onto the grass, a bright light flashed, causing me to shield my eyes. I could hear laughter fading in the distance and several dogs excitedly barking.

"Wow, how cool," I said, looking at the wall where the portal had been. The whole experience kind of messed with my brain, though. It was almost like none of the events we witnessed happened, but they did. Weird.

"Very," Tree admitted, sitting on the bed and pulling me onto his lap. "So much has happened in the last couple of days. The trials we went through are almost hard to believe. We've been through a whirlwind of some crazy ass shit."

"Yeah," I said. "I was thinking the same thing. I can't wait to tell

Paige and Nathan all about it when they get back from Europe."

"Wait till Paige finds out you now own this house and all its contents, including a bitchin' greenhouse."

I looked around the room at the beautiful antique furniture. "I know. I'm finding it hard to wrap my head around. She even left me her spell books and herbs." I noticed there were empty picture frames on the bureau and hanging from the walls. I pointed to them. "I wonder why Abigail's photos are gone."

"I'm betting her personal stuff: photos, clothes, and shoes, disappeared when she left our world. Knowing Grams, she didn't want to burden you with her intimate possessions, and she probably cast a spell so you wouldn't have to deal with them."

"Yeah, that sounds like something she would do," I agreed, my mind still reeling over everything.

Tree laughed. "Your mom is going to flip when she sees all these antiques you own."

I started in his arms when I realized how late it was and that I never called my mom to let her know where I was. "Omigod. I forgot to call Mom. She's going to be pissed off."

Tree hugged me tighter. I leaned into him, enjoying his strong arms around me. "I called her when I was driving here from the club."

I relaxed in his embrace. "Thank you. What did you tell her?"

"I told her you fell asleep at my house, and I will bring you home later tonight."

"What did she say?"

"She said it was fine, and she appreciated me calling her to let her know."

I took his hand and kissed it. "Thank you. You saved my ass."

"And it's a nice one, too," he whispered next to my ear, sending chills across my body.

"Yours is better than mine," I said.

He kissed my cheek. "I disagree."

I shifted in his lap, so I was facing him. "I have an idea you might agree with."

"And what might that be?"

I bounced in his lap. "I want you to move in with me. Here. Like... tomorrow." I grinned.

He leaned back; a surprised and delighted look covered his face. "Really?"

I couldn't contain my enthusiasm any longer. "Yes." I nodded. "Will you?"

"Hell, yeah!" He kissed me, his soft, yummy lips on mine, then he pulled away to look at me. "I love you. I've always have and always will."

"I love you, too."

"This is just the beginning. You realize that, right?"

"Yeah," I said, knowing he was referring to the Devil's third: me, him, and Paige. Although, Nathan had a part in this, as well. I wouldn't even be surprised if Brayden somehow got involved in our future quests to obtain the heavenly items Bael was after. "But if we continue to prepare ourselves, I'm sure we'll be okay." At least, I hoped so.

He looked worried for a second, but then it disappeared. The emotion happened so quickly that I wondered if my eyes were playing tricks on me. I was getting tired I realized.

"I agree," he said, a goofy grin forming on his face. He punched the air with his fist. "Evil forces be damned, because we're like The Justice League and will prevail over Bael's diabolical plans to take over our world."

I laughed. "You're such a dork."

He shrugged. "Maybe so, but it's true."

I stood and took his hand. "C'mon. As much as I would love to stay here tonight with you, I need to go home. Tomorrow morning, we'll tell my parents the good news."

Tree snatched the large manila envelope off the bed and waved it in the air. "You're going to need these papers for proof."

"Good idea."

"Your parents might not approve of us shacking up."

"Well, they'll have to get over it. Besides, they love you and are good friends with your parents. I'm not worried."

He pulled my hand down with his, halting us from exiting the bedroom. "Are you ready for our new life?"

I drew myself up and raised my chin. Looking him straight in the eyes I said, "I am."

He gave me a quick kiss on the lips. "Good. Let's start right now."

With his hand still in mine, and our heads held high, we stepped out into the dark, cold world, determined to make it a better and safer place for everyone.

If you want a deeper insight to some of the characters in this book and story, check out the *Beyond the Eyes* trilogy.

Beyond the Eyes:
Amazon US: www.amazon.com/Beyond-Eyes-Rebekkah-Ford-ebook/dp/B0088JF7HQ/
Amazon UK: www.amazon.co.uk/Beyond-Eyes-Rebekkah-Ford-ebook/dp/B0088JF7HQ/

Dark Spirits:
Amazon US: www.amazon.com/Dark-Spirits-Beyond-Eyes-Book-ebook/dp/B00BEKJ9VG/
Amazon UK: www.amazon.co.uk/Dark-Spirits-Beyond-Eyes-Book-ebook/dp/B00BEKJ9VG/

The Devil's Third:
Amazon US: www.amazon.com/Devils-Third-Beyond-Eyes-Book-ebook/dp/B00GMVJ5CK/
Amazon UK: www.amazon.co.uk/Devils-Third-Beyond-Eyes-Book-ebook/dp/B00GMVJ5CK/

If you enjoyed *Tangled Roots*, I'd appreciate it if you took the time to leave a review on Amazon.com and Goodreads. Your review doesn't have to be long. It would also be cool if you tweet about *Tangled Roots* and recommended it to your friends.
Thank you for your support. I appreciate it. ☺
You rock!

ABOUT THE AUTHOR

Rebekkah Ford grew up in a family that dealt with the paranormal. Her parents' Charles and Geri Wilhelm were the directors of the UFO Investigator's League in Fairfield, Ohio. They also investigated ghost hauntings and Bigfoot sightings in addition to UFO's. Growing up in this type of environment and having the passion for writing is what drove Rebekkah at an early age to write stories dealing with the paranormal. Her fascination with the unknown is what led her to write the *Beyond the Eyes* trilogy and *Tangled Roots.*

Rebekkah has an irreverent sense of humor, adores coffee, and yummy food makes her happy. She loves books, history, antiques, animals, connecting with her fans and other authors, and watching her favorite TV shows (The Originals, The Vampire Diaries, and Supernatural). She feels right at home in the woods and would love to someday live in a cabin deep in the forest.

Visit her online at themusingwriter.blogspot.com and at Facebook.com/RebekkahFord2012

www.ingramcontent.com/pod-product-compliance
Lightning Source LLC
Chambersburg PA
CBHW050018180626
46810CB00002B/470